PRAISE FOR

"*Dying for a Daiquiri*, Cindy Sample's newest laugh-laced who-done-it will make you hanker to visit Hawaii and laugh out loud at this single mom's humor and pluck—even when her life's hanging by a thread. I give five stars—or maybe it should it be five cherries—to this cocktail of a vacation adventure, sexy interludes, raucous laughs, and mystery."

–Linda Lovely, Author of the Marley Clark series

"Cindy Sample has created a heroine all gals can identify with and admire as she keeps going with wit and determination, even in the face of a homicide arrest. Sample's *Dying for a Daiquiri* combines humor, romance and mystery, a recipe that yields a great book. Kick back with a tall, cool drink and enjoy this 5 star read!"

–Mary Beth McGee, National Reviewer, Examiner.com

"*Dying for a Date* is packed with zany characters, humorous situations, and laugh-out-loud narrative. Consider reading this book in one setting, because once you start, you will be reluctant to put it aside."

–Midwest Book Review

"Cindy Sample knows how to weave a story that satisfies and excites. Time literally flew by as I turned the pages… simultaneously harrowing, exciting, tender, and uplifting, a true who-done-it combined with a romance that will warm the heart and sheets."

–Long and Short Romance Reviews

"Sharp intelligence and flippant wit, turmoil and anxiety, danger and deception…all blend into one smooth and tasty read. I hope this turns into a long running series."

–Once Upon a Romance Reviews

"Sample's sleuth is an endearing character readers will adore."

–RT Book Reviews

Other Books in the Laurel McKay series

Dying for a Date
Dying for a Dance

DYING FOR A DAIQUIRI

A LAUREL MCKAY MYSTERY

Cindy Sample

CINDY SAMPLE

DEDICATION

This book is dedicated to my mother, Harriet Bergstrand, the best mother a daughter could ask for, and my wonderful children, Dawn and Jeff, who are the most amazing adults.

CHAPTER ONE

"This mango daiquiri is to die for." I popped a juicy red maraschino cherry into my mouth, lifted my tropical drink and toasted the bride.

Liz's hazel eyes sparkled brighter than the diamond-studded wedding band placed on her left hand three hours earlier. She tapped her creamy piña colada, encased in a coconut shell, against my fruity concoction.

"Here's to a marriage made in heaven." I glanced at the fiery sun hovering above the white-tipped waves, ready for its nightly dip into the ocean. "Or in Hawaii, which is practically the same thing."

"You can't top this romantic scenery, Laurel," she replied, "plus there are…"

"No dead bodies," we said in unison.

Liz and I both laughed. I was grateful my British friend's Valentine's Day ceremony had gone off without a hitch, since her original wedding plans found me waltzing with a killer and narrowly escaping a frigid death in the depths of Lake Tahoe.

I breathed a sigh of relief. My best friend was officially Mrs. Brian Daley. All it took was flying 2,468 miles from Sacramento to the Big Island of Hawaii to make it happen.

Liz smoothed the skirt of her strapless white gown and lifted a perfectly waxed blonde eyebrow. "Maybe you and Tom will be the next to tie the knot."

I stared at the horizon wondering how likely it was that Detective Tom Hunter and I would walk down the aisle any time soon. "I don't

1

see any weddings in my future. Tom and I spent more time together when I was a murder suspect than we do now that we're—" I set my glass on the table to make air quotes for emphasis, —"'dating.' At the rate our relationship is progressing, we'll need a church with extra-wide aisles to accommodate our matching set of his-and-her walkers."

"Such a pity he cancelled his trip."

"According to Tom, his latest homicide case takes precedence over a Hawaiian vacation." I shrugged and sipped my drink. "It seems the only way to woo my cop is with a corpse."

"Nice image, Laurel." Liz wrinkled her nose. "So maybe Tom won't turn out to be your Mr. Right. Don't forget I dated over fifty guys before I found the perfect man."

My best friend wasn't kidding. While I'd embarked on a sensible banking career after college, Liz had traveled to exotic locales, seduced by the glamour of foreign countries. Not to mention foreign men, of all shapes, sizes and nationalities. Her dating memoir should be entitled *Fifty Shades of Romance*.

My brief, almost deadly experience with a matchmaking agency would send most women to a nunnery.

Liz shifted her gaze to her groom who'd replaced his tuxedo with a red-flowered shirt and khaki cargo shorts. Brian had almost completed the metamorphosis from El Dorado County Assistant District Attorney to tourist. Someone just needed to tell him to dump the loafers he'd paired with black socks.

Brian's height made the stocky man chatting next to him look even shorter.

"Your brother and Brian seem to be getting along." Liz blew a kiss at her handsome, fashion-challenged husband. Her new husband and my brother stood at the bar taking turns doing shots, both acting a couple of decades younger than their early forties.

"It's nice to see Dave enjoying himself," I said. "He's looked so stressed the last two days. I swear his hairline's receded another inch since we arrived." I watched my bearded, balding older brother toss back another shot of an alcoholic concoction whose color bore a strong resemblance to Ty-D-Bol.

Yuck.

I peeked at my watch, wondering where my sister-in-law was. "Dave better not get drunk. Regan won't be happy."

"I still can't believe Regan missed our wedding ceremony," Liz said. "I've only met her the one time, but considering we held the reception at Daiquiri Dave's, you'd think she would make it a priority."

My gaze scanned the interior of the restaurant my brother and his wife had opened three years ago. They'd purchased a decrepit local Tiki bar, situated on massive lava rock formations twenty feet above the ocean, and transformed it into one of Kailua-Kona's most popular dining spots. Hard work and an oceanfront setting, combined with twenty varieties of colorful fruit-flavored daiquiris, had paid off.

"Dave mentioned Regan's been putting in long hours at her accounting job, but I don't understand why working at a coffee plantation would be so demanding." I folded and unfolded the tiny lilac paper umbrella that came with my tropical drink. "This is Hawaii, after all. Headquarters for hanging loose."

The sound of chattering female voices drew my attention. "Talk about hanging loose. I think the entertainment just arrived."

The eyes of every man in the place veered to the five bronzed beauties moving through the restaurant. Their fluid grace was either hereditary or acquired through years of hula lessons. The women ranged in size from a five-foot tall gal whose dark hair flowed past her knees, to a lithe dancer whose coconut-shell bra struggled to contain her mammary exuberance, to a woman on the far side of middle age and middle girth. A wreath of woven green ti leaves perched on each dancer's head.

The female leading the procession, who seemed to be drawing the majority of male attention, was Keiki, a server at the restaurant. Keiki performed in their Saturday night shows and on special occasions such as tonight's reception. Her facial features were exotic perfection as was her Hawaiian Barbie body.

The last dancer to climb on the stage also wore a matching sarong and coconut bra, although his shells dangled limply above his skinny waist. What was my friend and Hangtown Bank co-worker, Stan Winters, doing among all of these women?

Liz burst out laughing at my surprise in seeing our gay friend's insertion in the troupe. "You know Stan. He's never met a stage he didn't want to perform on. At least he's not wearing his Zorro outfit and dancing the Argentine tango."

3

Brian and Dave joined us at our large table, which overlooked the crashing surf far below. The bride welcomed her groom with a lusty kiss. My brother sat down and directed his gaze to the dancers on the small stage. As the owner of the restaurant, Dave obviously wanted to ensure every part of Liz's reception was perfect, even the entertainment.

My mother appeared behind me, her smile as wide as the Pacific Ocean that normally separated Dave from the rest of the family. Ten years ago, Dave had moved from the foothills east of Sacramento where we all lived, to Hawaii. Our reunions were infrequent and always far too short.

My mother, the former Barbara Bingham had recently wed Robert Bradford, a retired detective. Despite my initial misgivings about my widowed mother getting involved with the man who'd been determined to prove I was killing off my dates, true love won out. I now couldn't be happier they'd found one another. It helped that my teenage daughter, Jenna, and seven-year-old son, Ben, adored their new grandfather. He'd agreed to babysit them while my mother and I attended Liz and Brian's island wedding.

"I've been looking forward to this show," Mother said. "Maybe I can pick up a few tips and perform a private hula for Robert when I return home." She giggled and attempted to roll her hips, proving once again that the two of us are related and that Hawaiian hip rolling is *not* in our DNA.

I loved that my tall, elegant sixty-two-year-old mother wasn't as uptight as she used to be, but remarks like that made me want to stick my fingers in my ears.

Keiki grasped the microphone. Her sultry voice sounded as seductive as her body looked. She introduced the dancers and congratulated the bride and groom. "Tonight we will perform several dances for you. By special request," she turned and winked at Stan, "our first number is the 'Hawaiian Wedding Song.'" Stan bowed and his wreath slipped onto the stage. He plopped it back on his head where it hung over his left ear.

Three musicians in Hawaiian shirts and khakis strummed their guitars and ukuleles as the dancers began to move. The five women moved as one to the sensuous rhythm. The youngest musician couldn't keep his eyes off Keiki. Although all the women were graceful, she shone like the star she clearly was.

Stan moved like no other Polynesian dancer, sort of a cross between Derek Hough from *Dancing with the Stars*, and MC Hammer, the father of hip-hop. Despite Stan's wild gyrations, when the song ended, I teared up all over again. Just like I'd done earlier at the ceremony.

When a huge round of applause erupted, I worried Stan might plan on becoming a permanent fixture with the troupe, but Dave strode on to the stage, thanked him, and gently shoved him in the direction of the stairs. Stan nimbly hopped down and dragged a bamboo-backed chair over to our table, squeezing in between Liz and me.

One of the servers stopped to take our drink order. "Would you like another daiquiri?" she asked. I nodded and she turned to Stan.

"I'm thinking of going with a Tropical Itch," he said.

I stared at him. "Is that a drink or a disease?"

"Ha, ha. Fruit juice, rum, vodka, and a backscratcher. You can't beat that combination," Stan replied. "Although maybe I should hold off in case they want me to perform an encore."

"In that case, drink up."

"Very funny. That was a blast and the dancers were terrific to me. I appreciate Dave giving me Keiki's phone number so we could practice before the reception. She said she would teach me more dances before we head home. Can't you see me throwing flaming swords in the air?"

Yes, I could. Although I visualized the swords bouncing off Stan's head and searing his remaining hair into a crispy fringe. Stan shifted his chair closer to mine and whispered something.

"I can't hear you," I said. "Speak up." The dancers were performing again and the sounds of "A Little Grass Shack" overpowered his low baritone. He moved so close I could practically taste the wasabi on his breath, which made me crave more of the spicy sushi rolls Dave's chef had prepared for the wedding feast.

"Keiki and her sister, Walea, were arguing before the show," Stan said. "I had a question about the routine and didn't mean to eavesdrop, but I overheard Walea accuse Keiki of carrying on with a married man. Keiki seems like a sweet girl so it's hard to believe."

"That's surprising, but it's none of our business how she handles her personal life."

"I'm afraid Keiki's private life is about to become personal for you." Stan's gray eyes communicated his concern.

"Huh?"

"Keiki is having an affair with your brother."

CHAPTER TWO

My gaze zoomed to the stage where Dave and Keiki stood side by side, deep in conversation, her hand resting lightly on his freckled forearm.

How do you say "Oh crap" in Hawaiian?

"You must have misunderstood," I said to Stan. "Dave would never have an affair. He's one of the good guys."

Dave was twelve and I was ten when our father died in an auto accident. My brother had been my rock during that sorrowful period and through my heartbreaking divorce almost three years ago. He'd flown to California to provide solace after my contractor husband, Hank McKay, had left me for one of his female clients. Hank's definition of multitasking apparently meant nailing his client as well as her shingles.

Dave had not only provided a broad shoulder to cry on, he'd also offered to rearrange my ex's body parts. Now that's a terrific brother!

"Keiki didn't admit they were having an affair, but she didn't deny it either." Stan nudged my arm and pointed at the stage. "Look at the two of them."

Keiki and Dave chatted and laughed together, but that didn't necessarily mean anything. My brother possesses a great sense of humor. His entire staff probably adored him as much as his younger sister did.

"Uh, oh," Stan said. "Look who just arrived."

My sister-in-law walked through the restaurant headed in our direction. Her dark almond-shaped eyes proclaimed her Chinese heritage, while her porcelain complexion and auburn hair were inherited from her Blarney Stone-kissing kin. Today she appeared exhausted, her face alabaster pale above her colorful sundress. The bright red blossoms on her dress matched the flowering hibiscus bushes nestled around the building.

Stan jumped up and offered his chair. Regan nodded her thanks and sat next to me, her eyes glued to the stage where my brother and Keiki conversed. I had no idea if Stan's information about Dave and the dancer was correct, but diverting my sister-in-law's attention from the stage seemed like a good idea.

I smiled at her. "Dave told us you had to meet with your boss today. I'm glad you made it back for the reception."

"I'm sorry I couldn't get here earlier," Regan said. "Koffee Land is hosting a reality show in ten days. The owners, Ritz and Pilar Naygrew, had a ton of stuff to go over with me."

"That sounds exciting," I said, as visions of Hollywood stars danced in my head.

My sister-in-law rubbed her palms over her eyes. "It's far more annoying than exciting at this point. But Ritz is my boss. When he says jump, I leap as high as he sets the bar."

A fruity drink magically appeared in front of Regan. I could never keep these tropical concoctions straight, but this one was about the size of a Honda Civic.

Regan thanked the waitress. "*Mahalo*, Walea."

"You're welcome," said the server. "You missed a terrific show tonight."

Regan nodded towards Dave and Keiki. "I think I arrived just in time to see the 'show'." She picked up her glass and inhaled the cocktail as if it were fruit juice *sans* the alcohol.

Walea gnawed on her lower lip. I leaned forward wondering how she would respond to Regan's remark.

"Can I get you anything, Laurel?" Walea evidently decided to keep mum on the subject of my brother and her sister.

When I declined her offer, she sashayed away, making me wonder if island parents taught their toddlers to wiggle their hips as soon as they learned to crawl.

Dave finally noticed Regan's arrival. He broke off his conversation with Keiki, walked across the stage and down the steps, arriving at our table. He sat next to his wife and aimed a kiss at her cheek. He missed as she rebuffed him and turned to face me.

"How was the ceremony, Laurel?" Regan asked. "Was Liz happy with the location?"

"That small stone church you recommended was beautiful," I said. "I can't imagine a more perfect way for them to begin their life together than getting married in paradise." My eyes veered to the happy couple who were having their picture taken against the backdrop of the lava rock setting.

Regan twisted her gold wedding band as her solemn eyes met mine. "Paradise can be rife with pitfalls." She picked up her drink, seemingly intent on chugging the remainder.

Dave dropped his arm around his wife's shoulders, but she shrugged him off.

"Sweetie," he said, "you know you can't handle alcohol." He attempted to remove Regan's glass. Their hands collided and the fruity concoction crashed to the floor. A red puddle oozed down the bamboo planking. It pooled under the slender, bare feet of Keiki, who was helping Walea clear the tables.

Keiki shot a look at Regan that I was unable to decipher, but she remained silent as she picked up the shards of glass. The youngest musician rushed to help her, but Dave brushed him aside and began to assist the dancer himself.

Regan muttered something under her breath, grabbed her straw tote and stood, her slight frame swaying slightly.

"Are you okay?" I asked as I followed her away from the table.

"I think I've had too little to eat and too much to drink." Regan's eyes welled with tears. "It's been a grueling week, and I'd better go home before I say anything foolish to my husband."

"Is there anything I can do?"

She shrugged. "You can try knocking some sense into your brother."

I pointed at a grove of palm trees to the side of the open-air restaurant. "We're a hard-headed family. Could take a coconut, or two, to do the trick."

Her lips curled up in a weak smile. I was pleased my attempt at levity lightened her mood somewhat. I still found it difficult to accept anything was going on between Dave and the gorgeous dancer, but I wasn't averse to stepping in and finding out.

It had been a few decades since this pigtailed tomboy tormented her big brother, but I felt confident I hadn't lost my touch.

CHAPTER THREE

Nothing beats sleeping in and enjoying a leisurely morning in a tropical setting. The bride's interpretation of leisure, however, differed dramatically from mine. My definition does not include embarking on an early morning snorkel sail after a night of dining, drinking and general carousing. My head felt like a troupe of Tahitian dancers and drummers had moved in overnight. The proportion of rum to fruit juice in those mango daiquiris I'd swilled must be higher than I'd realized.

I shoved a pillow over my face as the cloying sound of "Tiny Bubbles" blasted from the radio. I rolled over to turn off the alarm when someone silenced it for me.

"Good morning, dear. Rise and shine."

Ugh. It was bad enough sharing a room with my mother. Listening to her perky greeting was even more annoying than Don Ho's bubbly wake-up call. My stomach roiled as I eased myself against the padded gold brocade headboard. "Why don't you go ahead without me? I don't think I'm up for a boat ride this morning."

"Don't be silly," she said. "Liz will be crushed if you don't join us. I've already ordered breakfast from room service. Nothing like some hearty oatmeal to keep you regular."

I closed my eyes trying to decide at what age my mother would no longer be interested in facilitating my digestive system. I opened them and squinted at the woman in question. She was dressed in a pair of sea-foam capris and a floral shirt that accented her short feathery blonde hair. With silver sandals, a sea-green tote and matching visor, she looked ready to star in an AARP advertisement to vacation in Hawaii.

The odds of winning the lottery were higher than of me getting out of our morning excursion.

I pushed my rumpled but extremely soft sheets aside and stumbled into the capacious marble bathroom. The oversized Jacuzzi tub beckoned but, with only a half hour to spare, I quickly showered, did my make-up and finished the bowl of heart-healthy oatmeal, made slightly less nutritious with heaping tablespoons of brown sugar and golden raisins added to the contents.

By seven-thirty, Mother and I were standing in front of the elevator, along with a family of six, the kids ranging in age from eight to toddler. I wished my children could have joined me on this trip, but my daughter, Jenna, a high school junior who dreamt of becoming an astronaut, hadn't wanted to miss her SAT study classes. Ben, my seven-year-old, couldn't afford to miss his second-grade classes either. Although my son hadn't been officially diagnosed with ADHD, he possessed "attention discovery disorder." Everything outside the classroom seemed far more interesting than what was happening on the pages of his textbooks.

I pictured Ben giggling with his best friend, Kristy, already almost twice his size. The young girl would top my five foot four and a quarter by fourth grade. Kristy took after her six-foot-three father, Detective Tom Hunter, my on-again off-again boyfriend. I sighed as I pictured Tom's broad shoulders and thick chestnut hair, which occasionally grew past regulation length when he was too busy hunting down murderers to squeeze in a haircut.

Unfortunately, in the six weeks that we'd been seeing each other again, our dates were as infrequent as his visits to Super Haircuts. I'd hoped that a week together in a tropical setting would heat up our relationship, but Tom cancelled two days before we were scheduled to leave, ostensibly to hover over his latest crime scene.

Why couldn't I find a boyfriend who preferred to hover over *me?*

Maybe his official duties weren't the real problem. Perhaps he wasn't interested in me. I was beginning to think it was time to move on. The elevator's ping coincided with the plummeting of my heart at the thought of Tom and me breaking up.

We hadn't even had a chance to ping *together*!

Mother's cell rang as we stepped out of the elevator into the enormous open-air lobby of the Regal Kona Resort. It didn't take a detective to detect the call was from her new husband. Her rose-infused cheeks and giggles reinforced my deduction. Liz and Brian strolled toward us, their arms wrapped around each other's waists. They wore matching blue-flowered shirts and smiles.

Liz's wake-up call had obviously been more arousing than mine.

I was surrounded by people talking and thinking about sex. Enough to make a person gag. Speaking of which, Stan approached dressed in fluorescent floral attire, wearing a straw hat large enough to provide shade for a family of four.

"Nice chapeau," I remarked.

He grinned. "Got it on clearance for fifty percent off. Can you believe it?"

Sure could. But if the wind died down, his hat would make an excellent fan. And if the engine quit, we could use the hat to propel the boat.

Brian went to claim his rental car from the valet while the rest of us stopped at a grass-roofed kiosk for four Kona coffees to go. My cell rang just as I finished doctoring my coffee. My heart sang, hoping the call was from Tom.

I dug in my purse and grabbed the phone. Once I identified the caller, I told my heart to dial it back a notch.

"Hey, Dave," I said. "Are you on your way to the boat?" I picked up the steaming cup and sipped.

"No, I can't go with you guys. I have to meet the police."

My cup missed my lips, but not my navy T-shirt. I asked my brother to hold while I blotted a half cup of coffee from my chest.

"Why are you meeting with the police?" I asked, fearful of his answer.

"A body was found on the rocks below the restaurant. They need access inside."

My stomach clenched at the image of someone lying on the lava rocks far below the building. "How awful. Did they give you any details?"

"No. I assume the tide carried the person there, but I can't imagine who would go swimming in that area. The current is far too dangerous." Dave's voice cracked as he said, "I only hope it isn't anyone I know."

CHAPTER FOUR

Dave's news bummed everyone out, but realistically we realized there wasn't anything our group could do to help him. I knew it would be a trying experience whether Dave personally knew the victim or not. I hoped for my brother's sake that the answer was "not."

Thirty minutes later, we arrived at the Kailua pier. Brian easily located the parking lot recommended for seafaring tourists. We grabbed our assorted beach gear and headed for the boat. Foreign-speaking passengers from the enormous cruise ship anchored in the bay wandered around wearing confused expressions. Several companies offered morning boating expeditions, so the pier was awash in aloha-shirted, fanny-pack-wearing tourists.

The strangely pleasant scent of fish and seaweed reminded me of childhood vacations along the California coast. Eventually we located our boat, the *Sea Jinx*. The name of our vessel didn't enthrall me, but I was pleased it appeared to be immaculate and roomy.

A young woman dressed in a royal-blue polo shirt and form-fitting white shorts, and with a mane of blonde curls secured by a scarf, greeted the passengers. "I'm Amanda, your hostess and marine life specialist," the petite woman announced in an annoyingly perky voice. "Welcome to the *Sea Jinx*. Is this your first time sailing with us?"

Everyone replied in the affirmative as we followed her up the gangway.

"You're all going to have a great time. Let me give you the grand tour." She showed us where the "heads," aka potties to us landlubbers, were located. Then she bounced up the stairs, assuming we'd bounce along behind her.

Amanda must have noticed my red-rimmed, hung-over eyes because she pointed me in the direction of the coffee. A variety of juices and pastries were also set on the bar.

"After a successful snorkel expedition," she said, beaming a 100 watt smile at us, "we'll all celebrate with a Mai Tai."

I was afraid to ask her definition of "successful." Did that mean no one on board ended up as shark bait?

We followed Amanda's instructions to store our gear under bench seats that ran down the center of the main deck. Mother and I sat next to each other on the blue-padded cushions. I immediately proceeded to lather myself with a 15 SPF sunscreen.

Liz plopped down on the slick white non-cushioned seat across from us "You're going to need something stronger than that," she said. As the owner of a full-service spa in El Dorado Hills, she was dedicated to protecting her peaches-and-cream English complexion.

Liz pulled a large tube from her red-striped bag and handed it to me.

"A sunscreen with 120 SPF?" I twisted the cap open. "If I put this on, I'll return home paler than when I left."

"You'll thank me in forty years."

I squeezed the tube. The sunscreen had the viscosity and stickiness of Elmer's Glue and an unusual scent. Lavender combined with skunk. The ointment would definitely repel any men from attacking me. I wasn't confident it would have the same effect on marine life.

Despite my teasing Liz, I had no desire for my fair skin to turn lobster red. I tried to pull my T-shirt over my head so I could spread the lotion across my neck and shoulders, but it caught on the strap of my bathing suit. For a brief moment, I worried about a wardrobe malfunction. Good thing only my mother and Liz were in the immediate vicinity.

As I struggled to slide the narrow neck of my tee shirt over my unruly copper curls, my swimsuit strap was prodded back in place.

"Thanks, Mom," I said.

"Any time," responded a voice at least two octaves below my mother's soprano.

In under a millisecond, I ripped the cotton tee over my head. I found myself staring into a pair of cobalt-blue eyes that reflected even bluer than the surrounding ocean. Eyes filled with amusement. The crinkles around the man's eyes indicated laughing came naturally. He was tall, trim and tan, and I had a feeling he was the captain of the *Sea Jinx*.

I had one additional clue. A captain's hat perched on his thick, sun-streaked blond hair.

He proffered his hand. "I'm Steve Bohannon. You must be Dave's sister. You look like him, except for the beard. And you're, um..." His gaze briefly dropped to my chest, which I could feel turning the same shade of red as my cheeks.

"It's nice to meet you," I said. "Dave said you're hot. I mean, you know all the hot spots, that is, the hot spots to snorkel..." I looked around for something to do besides babble like an idiot. I grabbed the pink container of suntan lotion and squeezed hard.

White goop shot out of the tube, splattering across the zipper of his shorts. I reached out to wipe off the mess then realized my hand was barely an inch from Steve's crotch. What would Emily Post do?

Emily wasn't available, but Stan miraculously appeared with a beach towel in hand. I grabbed the towel and handed it to Steve. He wiped off his shorts and grinned. "There's never a lack of adventure on a boat."

Liz introduced herself and asked if he was ready to leave.

"It looks like all the passengers are on board. We'll be underway in a few minutes."

"We know Dave won't make it, but I haven't seen Regan yet," I said.

"Sorry, that's what I came out here to tell you when you got me a little distracted." Steve's smile proved the combination of white teeth against a dark tan could be equally distracting. "Regan texted she's been delayed so we'll have to go ahead without her."

"Did she mention why?"

He shook his head. "Nope. Just said she'd see you later. Trust me. I'll make sure you have a great time. Don't forget I'm the guy who knows all the 'hot' spots."

* * *

An hour later, I discovered there's hot, and there's steaming hot. The sun's morning rays were hot, but with Captain Steve by my side, the sizzle level climbed so high I worried one of us might spontaneously combust.

I never realized how sexy it could be to have a handsome man help me don swim fins. The Hawaiian version of Cinderella. It almost made me forget Detective What's His Name.

Shame on me. Here I had a boyfriend back home, one who was always there for me.

Sort of. The widowed detective not only had a young daughter to rear, but he'd recently been promoted to head of the homicide division for the El Dorado County Sheriff's Department. Between solving crimes and an occasional Snack Dad moment, there seemed to be little time left for me. I could count our dates in the past two months on one hand and still have a couple of digits left over.

The man kneeling at my feet interrupted my musings. "How does that feel?"

Was Steve referring to the gigantic rubber flippers scraping against my oversized bunions, or the touch of his large hand resting gently on my right calf?

"Fine. Thanks for the help." I stood and wobbled in my webbed footwear.

Steve put his arm around my waist and steadied me. "Hey, Dave's my best friend. I promised I'd make you and your mom my priority."

Steve grabbed my hand and we crossed to the starboard side of the vessel where a ladder hung over the side, dipping into the clear blue water of Kealakekua Bay, a popular dive spot. The white twenty-seven-foot obelisk erected on shore to honor Captain Cook glimmered in the distance. This spot was chosen to honor the sea captain because it was where the natives killed him once they realized he wasn't really a god.

Tough crowd!

I watched Liz step carefully on the ladder, her fins jutting out at an angle. Brian patiently treaded water near the bottom rung. His bride clambered down the ladder with such dexterity one would think she'd been a duck in a former life. They kissed briefly, donned their gear and swam away from the boat, hand in hand. How nice to have someone waiting to explore the underwater magic together.

I must have looked worried because Steve hurried to reassure me. "You'll be fine out there. Timmy and Rafe will keep an eye on everyone in your group."

Timmy, a young man with longish dark hair, gave me a curt nod then moved to the back of the boat.

Rafe smiled wide, exhibiting a large gap where both front teeth seem to have disappeared. "Yes, missy, I look out for you. I will not let no big shark make lunch from you."

"Thanks," I muttered. I hoped any sharks hovering near the *Sea Jinx* were on a low-fat no-protein diet.

I eased down the rungs far less gracefully than Liz. My vision is so bad that if I didn't wear my contacts, I wouldn't even recognize an octopus until it had wrapped all eight tentacles around me. I de-fogged the mask before I secured it and hoped no saltwater would intrude.

The ocean looked dark, deep and scary from my masked perspective, but I hated feeling like a wimp. Plus I was surrounded by other snorkelers. What could go wrong? I secured my snorkel and placed my face down in the water where I discovered an incredible new world.

The schools of brilliantly colored fish stunned me. Tiny yellow fish darted here and there, checking out the chubby mermaid who disturbed their play. Larger fish ogled me and I ogled them back.

I continued swimming away from the boat and a huge rock formation floated up on my right. The rocks slowly moved apart and I found myself face to face with a giant turtle. Then something tugged at my left foot. Was a shark about to turn me into an antipasto platter?

I tried swimming away, but the creature refused to let go. I thrashed my legs in a scissor-like movement disturbing the tiny schools of fish. Within seconds, they disappeared from sight.

My foot finally pulled free and I surfaced. My sigh of relief lasted less than a second before a dark shadow hovered next to me. I squinted at the large mammal, which did not possess a long snout and, oddly enough, wore swim trunks more iridescent than the fish I'd admired moments before.

I straightened and treaded water while I removed my mouth guard to scold my visitor. "Stan, why did you grab me?"

With his head above the waves, Stan fumbled with his own equipment before taking out the piece of rubber stuffed between his thin lips. "Sorry. I was afraid if I didn't latch on to your foot, I'd never be able to stop you. You need to come back to the *Sea Jinx*."

"Is it my mother? Is she okay?"

"Your mother is fine. For now."

"What do you mean?" The heart palpitations I'd felt earlier when I thought I was about to turn into shark bait returned in full force.

"Dave was able to identify the body they found on the rocks."

I put my hand over my heart. "Oh no. Who is it?"

"It's Keiki."

"Omigod. Do they know what happened to her?"

"I don't know the details, but it gets even worse."

"How on earth could it get any worse?"

"They've taken your brother in for questioning."

CHAPTER FIVE

The weather mirrored the group's dour mood on our ride back to the Kailua pier. Dark storm clouds shifted ominously in the sky as we shifted nervously on the boat. Amanda did her best to entertain the passengers by sharing the mating secrets of humpback whales. The subject seemed to enthrall the young woman, but I wasn't in the mood to think about dating or mating, on land or at sea.

The fifty-minute ride felt like fifty hours, although Steve had the engines on full throttle. We found out the police had not officially arrested Dave, but after meeting with him at the restaurant, they'd "invited" him down to the station for further questioning.

I had plenty of my own questions for my brother, especially after Regan's inference the previous evening that something was going on between him and the now deceased dancer. I phoned my sister-in-law, but her cell rang and rang. After landing in her voicemail for the third time, I left a message asking Regan to call back. A matter of life and death.

Once we'd arrived at the Kailua Pier, our small group debated our next move. Neither Steve nor Brian thought barging into the Kona police station was an option. For all we knew, Dave might be gone by now. There wasn't much we could do until we heard from my brother, so we said good-bye to Steve and drove down Alii Drive in search of a place to eat lunch.

As we neared Daiquiri Dave's, we encountered bumper-to-bumper traffic. Several official-looking cars with blue lights on their roofs were parked in front of the restaurant. I imagined it would have been filled with police cars earlier this morning. A few tourists wandered along the street, gawking and snapping photographs of a setting one rarely sees in the tropics—yellow and red hibiscus bushes covered with crime scene tape.

A young couple dressed in sweat-stained T-shirts, jogging shorts and running shoes, darted across the street in front of our car. Brian slowed the vehicle to a crawl to avoid adding any more victims to the local casualty list.

I tapped Brian on the shoulder. "Can we stop for a minute? Let's see what we can find out."

"C'mon, honey, pull over," Liz said. "It's the least we can do. Maybe they'll tell us if Dave is still at the police station."

"Okay." Brian maneuvered the sedan into a grassy patch further up the road. "They might respond to an assistant D.A., even one visiting from California."

I threw the passenger door open before he could yank his keys out of the ignition. Brian might have more official status than me, but Dave was my brother, and his welfare was my top priority. My thin-soled flip-flops skidded on the parking lot's gravel surface as I rushed toward the restaurant. I reached the open door of the building and halted. Although no crime scene tape barred my entry, I was uncertain what kind of reception my appearance would garner.

No one stopped me from entering Daiquiri Dave's, so I walked inside. Off to the left, in a casual setting, tables and chairs rested on a sandy floor in front of a low lava rock wall, the only barrier between the cliff-side restaurant and the pounding surf twenty feet below. Two men stood in the more formal dining room located to the right of the stage.

A gray-haired man wearing a tan print shirt and khakis snapped photos from various angles. The younger, uniformed officer examined the thick ropes securing one post to another, which kept patrons from inadvertently falling over the wall. I recalled that the top rope barely reached my hips. I tapped the younger officer on his navy blue shoulder. He jumped to his feet and glared.

"What are you doing here? Did you not see the crime scene tape?" he asked in slightly accented English. "No one is allowed inside this establishment."

"The tape didn't extend to the entrance so I thought it would be okay."

He stretched his arm and pointed to the doorway. "Please. Leave now."

The older man turned toward me. "Do you have a question, ma'am?"

Ma'am? I turned around to see if my mother had sneaked up behind me. I was decades too young to be ma'amed.

"My brother, Dave Bingham, owns this restaurant. My family just heard the news about Keiki's death and I was curious…"

The detective's dark eyes shifted their gaze from my face to the rocks below. I couldn't help but follow his glance. My heart flopped down to my flip-flops when I realized the beautiful dancer must have fallen over the wall on the opposite side of the restaurant, plummeting to her death.

I stared at the massive lava rocks rising out of the ocean churning below. Last night, a full moon had been shining on the huge waves crashing over their dark surface. The scene epitomized the magic of the tropics. Now the lava formations appeared sinister and threatening.

I rested my hand on a column for support. The officer gently removed it and asked me to step away from the wall. "We don't need any more fingerprints in this area. There's already way too many to sort through."

"Of course, fingerprints are everywhere," I replied. "My best friend held her wedding reception here yesterday. Our group partied until well after midnight."

The two men exchanged glances. The older, informally dressed man guided me to a seat at one of the tables. I collapsed into the chair, my mind swirling with questions. He reached into his pants pocket and grabbed one of those dog-eared notepads all police officers seem to carry.

"My name is Detective Lee, with the Criminal Investigation Section of Hawaii P.D. Since you were here last night, you may be able to help with our inquiry. First, what is your name and how do you know the deceased?"

"I'm Laurel McKay." I explained that Keiki performed with the dancers and helped wait on tables the previous evening. He asked me how long she'd worked at Daiquiri Dave's and what time she left the restaurant last night. I didn't know the answer to either question.

He *did not* ask me if she was sleeping with my brother, which was fortunate because I *definitely* did not know the answer to that question. But given Keiki's fate, I sure would like to find out.

A loud male voice interrupted our conversation. At the entrance, Brian, with our entire party in his wake, argued with a female officer attempting to bar their entry. Even though this section of the restaurant wasn't officially roped off, Detective Lee had indicated they didn't want people traipsing around and leaving additional footprints in the smooth white sand.

But could the police accurately cast footprints from the shifting grains of sand?

The right pocket of my jeans shorts shrieked, startling me as well as the officers. I jumped up, dug into my pocket to retrieve my cell and looked at the display.

Regan. Finally. I breathed a sigh of relief as I hit the green answer button.

"Laurel, what's wrong? Why did you—" The rest of her query was lost when an enormous wave crashed below. I moved away from the wall, attempted to increase the volume on my phone and accidentally hit the speaker button

"I'm at the Lounge. Did you hear the news about Keiki?"

The surf chose that moment to recede, leaving behind a silence as deafening as Regan's next statement.

"I don't want to hear another word about that conniving slut. She's history to me!"

CHAPTER SIX

Sometimes technology sucks.

I slammed my thumb on the speaker button before Regan could convey additional uncensored remarks. The curious expression on Detective Lee's face indicated he'd overheard more than enough.

I plastered my cell to my ear. Regan continued to mutter remarks about Keiki, so I finally raised my voice. "Stop and listen a minute. Where are you?"

"I'm at Koffee Land. That girl has always been a troublemaker. I told Dave we never should have hired her, but Walea pleaded with us to give her a job and—"

I finally shouted into the phone, "Keiki's dead."

If I'd expected Regan to be startled by my announcement, I was wrong. Dead wrong. The silence lasted for a few seconds before she finally responded. "What happened?"

"The police haven't shared the details, but I think she fell over the wall and landed on the rocks below your restaurant."

More silence. Was she paying attention to this phone call or multi-tasking at work while we talked?

"Regan, are you still there?"

"Do they know how she fell?" Regan asked.

I shrugged before I realized she couldn't see my movements over the phone. "I don't know anything about it other than the police interviewed Dave at the Kona police station."

My comment finally provoked a reaction from my sister-in-law.

"Why did they question Dave?"

"I presume because he owns the restaurant."

The detective tapped my shoulder and asked if he could speak with Regan. I handed over my cell.

"Mrs. Bingham, this is Detective Lee." He moved away from the table making it impossible for me to eavesdrop.

My mother suddenly appeared at my side with the rest of the gang not far behind. The police must have relented and let everyone in. I wrapped my arm around my mother's waist and pointed toward the rocks below.

"Oh, my!" She gasped as she looked at the steep drop. "That poor young woman. Do you think she stayed late to clean up and got too close to the ropes? Dave will be horrified if this accident had anything to do with poor workmanship."

Dave would be even more horrified if he ended up arrested for murder.

Our group spent the next fifteen minutes sharing everything we knew with the two officers. Our knowledge ranged from zero to zilch. None of us had met Keiki before last night, but she was alive and well when we returned to our hotel. At least I assumed she was alive. Somewhere around my fourth daiquiri, temporary amnesia set in. With my brother and mother as chaperones, I hadn't worried about letting my curly mop down for a change.

When the officers finished with their questions, it was finally my turn. "Where is my brother? Is he under arrest?"

My mother morphed from a tranquil tourist into her normal intimidating real estate broker persona. "Do we need to hire an attorney? You realize my son is a well-known business owner with a restaurant to run. Not only must he find a replacement for Keiki, but yellow crime scene tape strewn all over isn't going to help his business."

I flinched at her less than sympathetic comments, but even at sixty-two, my mother was prepared to defend her forty-something chicks. I glanced in the direction of Alii Drive, trying to assess the financial impact Keiki's death might have on the restaurant. Based on the substantial number of gawkers wandering up and down the street taking photos with their phones, business might increase out of morbid curiosity.

Stan chose that moment to jump into the conversation and insert his sand-covered flip-flop in his mouth. "Yeah, just because Dave and Keiki were making whoopee—" Stan abruptly stopped talking as six pairs of eyes zeroed in on him.

"Making what?" Detective Lee's heavy black brows merged into one dark suspicious furrow.

Stan's cheeks turned redder than his sunburned forehead. "Um, they were making whoopee pies, um, I mean poi."

"What the heck is whoopee poi?" Liz asked.

Stan sank lower in his chair and mumbled, "You know, when they mash the taro roots, they yell out, um, whoopee?"

If I had a poi pounder right now, I'd be using it on Stan's head. His sunburn must have turned his brain into mush.

The officers abruptly stood, walked away and conversed. Stan slumped in his chair looking wilted as Liz and I glared at him. My mother appeared baffled by the "whoopee" conversation, and I saw no point in enlightening her.

The officers returned to our table and announced we were free to leave. They also informed us they'd finished questioning Dave before we arrived. Before we departed, I needed to get one crucial issue resolved. I asked the detective to follow me over to the bar so I could prevent anyone listening in, especially big mouth Stan.

"You still haven't confirmed if Keiki's death was an accident or murder," I said.

"That is correct." Lee's comment as well as his blank expression revealed nothing.

"What do you think?"

I sensed a glimmer of a smile forming on Lee's otherwise stoic façade, but it was probably a reflection of the sun on his Ray Bans.

"I think you and your family should try to enjoy the rest of your vacation. It may be a day or two before the restaurant can reopen. Do you have any upcoming excursions planned?"

Was the officer attempting to be sociable, or did he want our whereabouts in case anything suspicious turned up? Either way, there was no reason to hide the group activities Liz had mapped out.

"We're planning on driving to the volcano tomorrow then visiting Koffee Land. My brother's wife works there so she's going to give us the grand tour."

"That should be very enjoyable although your sister-in-law may not be available tomorrow. When is your group scheduled to fly home?"

"Sunday. Is that a problem?"

He reached into his pocket and handed me a business card. "Just make sure you contact me before you leave. And Miss McKay—," Lee paused to remove his sunglasses then leaned close. A hint of lime aftershave made me crave a piece of key lime pie. His next statement made me crave something more potent.

"Yes?" I asked.

"Don't let our island's beauty and serenity lull you into a false sense of security. Sometimes the emotions seething below a person's calm surface can create far more damage than a volcanic eruption."

CHAPTER SEVEN

Less than five minutes later, our group was seat-belted and motoring down Alii Drive. Every time I thought of Officer Lee's warning, goose bumps shimmied up and down my arms. It made me suspect that they suspected Keiki didn't accidentally fall to her death.

It was almost two in the afternoon, so we continued south, discovering a restaurant next to Magic Sands Beach. In winter, I'd been told, you could lie on the beautiful sandy beach one afternoon then, after a storm-filled night, discover it magically gone the next day.

We had no problem finding a choice table with an ocean view. The lava rock barrier protecting this restaurant from the pounding surf appeared higher and more secure than Daiquiri Dave's exterior wall. Something my brother would undoubtedly regret for the rest of his life.

The server had just taken our lunch orders when my cell rang. I glanced at the name revealed on the screen and hit the accept button. "Dave, are you okay?"

"I'm fine. It's been a long..." his voice broke and I remained silent while he regained his composure. "Sorry about that. What are you guys up to now?"

I shared our current location then paused when Liz waved a half-eaten wedge of pineapple in my face, mouthing something unrecognizable. "Hold on a minute."

"Are he and Regan still coming to the luau tonight?" Liz asked.

I shook my head at my friend. Liz probably thought a pig roast would be the perfect way to cheer up my brother. Although she might be right. Our company could prove a good distraction for him.

Dave said he needed to track down Regan and check on her plans. I was surprised they still hadn't communicated, but perhaps she was unable to connect with Dave while he was with the police.

"Have you talked with Keiki's sister?" I asked.

"Not yet. I wanted to call you first. I'm not sure Walea or any of her family will even speak to me." He sighed so deeply my phone shuddered. "I still can't believe Keiki fell over the wall. And why was she there all alone so late at night?"

"How do you know she was by herself?"

He paused. "She must have been alone or whoever was with her would have called 911 when she fell. Wouldn't they?"

Not if they were the person who pushed her over.

"Do you know who found her?" I said.

"The officer said some guy staying at the hotel next door got up to go to the bathroom around three-thirty in the morning. He decided to sit on the lanai and catch a moonlight view of the waves crashing on the rocks. Instead he saw the surf crashing …" another catch of his breath before Dave finished, "just below Keiki's broken body. Geez, Laurel, what if my negligence led to her death? How am I going to make this right with her family?"

"Did the police say it was definitely an accident?"

"No, in fact it sounded like they thought the opposite. They weren't particularly forthcoming when I asked questions although they sure asked a ton of their own."

"Like what?"

"They questioned me about Keiki's background, how long she'd worked for us. If she had any enemies or anyone who disliked her. Current and previous boyfriends. If I thought she was using drugs. Weird stuff like that."

"Those aren't unusual questions," I said.

"Well, I'm not the crime show buff you are. I'm strictly a *Kitchen Confidential* junkie."

"Do they think Keiki overdosed? Or committed suicide?"

"Oh, man. I can't imagine any of those things." His voice caught. "She, Keiki, had so much going for her."

"Was there evidence of a struggle?" I asked.

"I don't know. All I heard was the cops found bits of broken glass scattered on the rocks way below the restaurant, but that could have happened days ago."

"What did they—"

"Hey, Regan's on the line. Gotta run. I'll see you later."

A loud click. I found myself staring at my phone while four pairs of eyes stared at me.

"Why didn't you let me talk to Dave?" Mother complained. "Is he all right?"

I nodded and slid my phone back into my tote. "He sounded as good as one would expect."

"Did he learn anything from the cops?" Brian asked. "They didn't test his DNA, did they?"

I frowned, trying to remember standard operating procedures on my favorite crime shows. "Dave didn't say anything about DNA testing. Would the cops automatically test everyone they bring in for questioning?"

Brian pondered my question before replying. "It depends whether they found anything indicating the fall wasn't an accident. I don't know what kind of shape she was in after plummeting twenty feet."

Liz and I both grimaced at the unpleasant image of Keiki's crumpled form.

"If there was any evidence indicating a struggle between her and someone else," Brian said, "they would take the DNA of potential suspects."

"Considering the condition of her body, what could they possibly find?" Mother asked Brian.

"Her hands could indicate if she attempted to defend herself, possibly scratched someone, so the police might find DNA underneath her nails. They'll probably test to see if she had sex with any possible suspects."

Why is it whenever a murder occurs, the topic of sex eventually rears its ugly head?

Liz lifted her glass and proposed a toast. "To Keiki, may she rest in peace. And if someone was responsible for her tragic death, may they rot in hell!"

Mother and I shared a glance as we reluctantly raised our glasses. If someone was to blame for Keiki's death, that person deserved punishment.

I just hoped it wasn't anyone in my gene pool.

CHAPTER EIGHT

After a short and somber lunch, we drove back to our hotel. Brian
announced his plans to take a nap. Liz decided if Brian was sleeping
then she should be shopping. Since Stan acted in the capacity of
unpaid personal shopper for both of us, Liz asked him to accompany
her. I felt torn between watching Stan help Liz rack up frequent
spender points on her Visa, and taking a nap myself. Whether it was
the morning snorkel activity or the chilling news of Keiki's death,
the idea of some quiet shut-eye won out.

Mother and I returned to our room, pleased to find the beds
made and fresh orchids placed in the vase on the desk. She sank into
a comfortable chair and put her feet up on the oversized ottoman. I
stripped off my clothes, slipped a clean extra-large T-shirt over my
head and slid under the sheets. My eyelids were seconds away from
closing. Soon I would forget about everything that had occurred
today. I assumed my mother would do the same.

Silly me.

"Laurel, are you asleep?"

Yes. At least I will be if there are no more interruptions.

I breathed in through my nose and out through my mouth,
willing myself to fall into a quick and oblivious slumber.

"Do you think Dave was having an affair with Keiki?"

Bye bye, dreamland.

I rolled over and faced her. "Why would you ask a question like
that?"

She glanced down at her hands, clasped together as if she was in prayer. Perhaps she was praying for the soul of the deceased dancer. And for my brother.

"Last night, I sensed something was wrong between Dave and Regan, but I couldn't put my finger on it. Then Brian and Stan made some comments today about Dave and Keiki when they thought I couldn't hear them. Your brother is such a good man. I can't imagine him having an affair."

My big brother had been my rock during high school and in the three years since my divorce. But despite what my mother thought, he wasn't perfect. No man is.

I still hadn't forgiven Dave for kidnapping my Barbie doll when we were little and forgetting where he'd buried her in the backyard. After Rex, our Golden Retriever, dug her up and discovered the joys of nibbling on a curvy plastic doll, Malibu Barbie became the only Barbie in the neighborhood with an A cup.

I shook my head clear of childhood memories. "Why don't you discuss it with Dave this evening?"

She vehemently shook her head. "Don't be ridiculous. I couldn't ask him a question like that. I'm not one of those prying mothers."

Really? I wasn't anxious to be a prying sister either, but I was concerned about Dave and Regan.

"I'll try to talk to him tonight, although he'll probably be exhausted from today's ordeal. In the meantime, let's try to enjoy ourselves for Liz's sake. She's worked hard to keep everyone entertained. After all, this is technically her honeymoon, even if she chose to spend it with all of us."

I had a feeling the next time Liz planned an event, no one in my family would be invited.

* * *

Two hours later, Stan, Mother and I stood along the side of the *imu* pit oven where the *kalua* pig roasted. For centuries, the Polynesians had used underground ovens to steam whole pigs, sweet potatoes, even fish and bananas. This particular pit was four feet long and three feet wide with deep sloping sides.

The cook addressed the crowd of curious bystanders, describing how the pit was constructed. First, a layer of covering material, usually taro or green ti leaves, went over the hot lava rocks, followed by a hundred or more banana leaves or stalks, then the native pig, which was covered with more layers. Loose dirt formed the top.

"An all day event," said the smiling chef, whose girth indicated he enjoyed his own cooking.

And I thought making sloppy Joes was a lot of work. There would be no kalua piggy roasts in my backyard anytime soon.

After admiring the imu's skilled workmanship, we wandered over to the bar area, where the thirsty patrons had already formed a long line. I planned to limit my consumption of fruity drinks tonight. I needed a clear head to wheedle personal information out of my brother.

Speaking of the devil, Dave strolled in our direction, deep in discussion with a tall, bronzed male who looked as good striding across land as he did on the deck of his vessel.

My hand involuntarily reached up to fluff my hair, which due to the island humidity, had an annoying tendency to shrivel into tiny corkscrew curls. Too bad the humidity didn't cause my butt to shrivel up a size or two. I smoothed the skirt of my dress, pleased that I'd chosen a light blue sundress that matched my eyes, instead of a plain tee and shorts.

Dave gave me a quick peck on my cheek before turning to our mother who smothered him with a hug. Steve flashed me a smile so sexy my insides turned to poi.

My mother inspected her first-born child like an appraiser at an antiques road show. "Honey, are you okay?"

Although Dave nodded with an affirmative, the dark puffy circles under his eyes contradicted him. In the last twenty-four hours, it looked like he'd also lost even more ground in his battle of the bald.

My mother greeted Captain Steve then looked around. "Where's Regan? Isn't she joining us?"

"She called and said she would try to make it later." Dave's voice sounded as bitter as day-old espresso. "As usual, something came up at Koffee Land."

Mother crossed her arms, looking miffed. "Your wife needs to work on her priorities."

I, too, was surprised Regan hadn't appeared and wondered if it was strictly due to her workload. She hadn't seemed particularly upset about the news of Keiki's death, but maybe she was merely relieved the beautiful dancer was no longer around to tempt Dave. I needed to find a way to get my brother alone sometime tonight and find out the truth.

Hoping to distract my mother from interrogating Dave in public, I decided to make Steve the subject of my own gentle grilling. "Have you always lived on this island?"

He shook his head. "Nope. I'm a Wall Street dropout. Seven years ago I tossed dozens of designer suits and ties in the garbage and hopped on a plane."

"That's impressive. People always complain about their jobs and talk about giving up a high-paced career for a more relaxed existence. You actually did it."

"Those ties felt like a noose around my neck. Even though I left behind the opportunity to make millions, I've never regretted my decision." He gestured toward the sun setting over the ocean. "You can't put a price on this beauty."

I nodded in agreement, although I felt more mesmerized by his gorgeous looks than the beautiful sunset in the background. Steve was not only handsome and charming. There was a depth to him.

"I know you and Dave have been friends for awhile, but how did you two meet?"

My brother smiled for the first time tonight. "C'mon, pal. Share the whole sordid story with my little sis."

"Believe it or not, we met when I was on vacation on the island. I was here with a, um, friend."

Dave snorted. "Steve was here with his fiancée."

My eyebrows rose.

Steve colored under his tan. "We were staying at one of the big resorts. This island had such a strong pull over me, I told her I wanted to chuck my career and move here permanently. We were in love so it never occurred to me she wouldn't feel the same way."

"Instead, she dumped the contents of the ice bucket on his head," Dave chimed in. "Told him to choose between her and the palm trees."

Steve chuckled. "I headed out to find solace and the first person I met was my friendly hotel bartender."

Dave smiled broadly. "I served him. Counseled him. After I closed down the bar, I helped him back to his room, worried he'd get an even frostier reception from his fiancée. She had already packed her bags and left for home. We ended up ordering room service and ate and talked all night long. At least until Steve passed out." He shoved Steve's shoulder. "You're kind of a lightweight, pal."

I could see a deep bond existed between the two men. In the next couple of days, Dave would need all the support he could get. In the distance, I spotted someone hurrying in our direction. Someone who should have been the first person to support my brother in his time of need.

But would she?

CHAPTER NINE

Regan's long auburn hair flew in the breeze, the expression on her face blacker than the sleeveless top and slacks she wore. She marched up to Dave and poked her index finger in his chest.

"I warned you about that slut. Do you know how hard I've worked so you could follow your dream of owning a restaurant?" Regan's face matched the setting sun in its intensity. The crack of her hand meeting Dave's cheekbone was more startling than a gunshot.

"Hey!" He jumped back out of reach, the surprise of his wife's attack evident in his expression. The imprint of her palm stood out against his cheek.

Steve pulled Regan aside. She briefly struggled before bursting into tears. He led her away, quietly rubbing her back in an attempt to soothe her.

"Dave, what on earth is going on with the two of you?" Mother asked.

"Just some issues we haven't resolved. It doesn't concern you in any way."

"But—" She stopped as Dave covered her lips with his fingertips.

"Don't worry about it." He glanced toward his wife. Regan seemed to have calmed as she conversed with Steve. "Why don't you and Laurel get us some seats so we can all sit together tonight? Dinner will be served soon and you don't want to miss the show."

I felt torn between interrogating my brother about his marital issues and keeping my mother distracted. I grabbed Mother's arm and dragged her in the direction of the tables and chairs set up for the luau. In the seating area, she assumed typical Barbara Bradford form, scoping out the table with the best view of the performers. That meant our group would sit by the stage. I hoped Regan would keep any further accusations to herself, at least during the performance. Even though she'd indicated concerns about a possible relationship between Keiki and Dave last night, her violent outburst stunned me. Could my sister-in-law have anger management issues, causing my brother to seek other, more serene arms?

Liz, Brian and Stan interrupted my musings, tropical drinks in hand and orchid leis around their necks.

"Isn't this fabulous?" Liz lifted her lei and sniffed in the sweet scent of the delicate purple blossoms. "Hawaii is absolutely heaven. I can't think of a more relaxing place to be."

Considering Keiki's death, and my brother and sister-in-law's domestic issues, on a scale of one to ten, Hawaii so far only qualified for a two when it came to relaxation. But I agreed the scenery was spectacular. The golden foothills outside Sacramento where I live are beautiful, but nothing compares to a brilliant orange ball of fire slowly sinking into frothy white waves. Palm fronds waving in the breeze, framed its descent.

My backyard scenery also didn't include half-naked men dressed solely in loin cloths, running across my lawn lighting tiki torches, although *that* was a heck of an idea. The eerie sound of a blown conch shell broke my reverie. I gazed in the direction of something even more delectable than the bronzed young men.

Food!

The aroma of roasted pig teased my senses as we approached the buffet. Aloha-shirted servers ladled out concoctions that smelled great but looked unfamiliar until I reached the end of the line. My favorite dinner staple—mac'n'cheez. I had a feeling this breadcrumb-topped delight might surpass the blue-and-yellow-boxed recipe I specialized in making.

With my plate piled high with kalua pork, curries, lomi-lomi salmon, sweet potatoes, and a minuscule portion of the purplish poi, I returned to our table, empty with the exception of one person. My sister-in-law.

DYING FOR A DAIQUIRI

Regan slumped in the folding chair, her chin resting on her tapered fingers, her face blotchy. Remnants of mascara clumped in the shape of a tiny spider indicated she'd been crying.

I set my plate on the red-flowered tablecloth and reached into my shoulder bag for a tissue. I gently wiped the black smudge off her cheek. Tears welled in her eyes.

"*Mahalo*, thank you, for your kindness. I don't know what came over me. I've never hit anyone in my life." Tiny rivulets of water rolled down her pale cheeks. "Now I've probably lost my husband forever."

I dug in my purse for another tissue. "It's totally understandable. You've been working hard and now this horrible accident has occurred."

I pondered the wisdom of bringing up any romantic involvement between my brother and the dancer, but it was time to learn why Regan suspected the worst of her husband.

"Forgive me for prying, but do you honestly think Dave and Keiki were having an affair? It's so hard for me to believe he would do something like that."

Her dark eyes drilled into mine. "If you had spent any time with Keiki, you'd know what I was talking about. She used every inch of her perfect body to get what she wanted."

"But why would she want Dave?" I love my brother, but the guy isn't Brad Pitt, either in looks or bank account.

Regan shrugged. "I'm not sure. Supposedly, Keiki had a challenging childhood. Walea is actually her stepsister. I think there were issues with her own father when she was growing up so maybe she was looking for a father figure."

"Dave said the police asked him about previous boyfriends. Were you aware of anyone Keiki dated—someone who might have been upset with her?"

"She dated one young man, also a dancer, on and off, but dumped him a few months ago. But I know he couldn't have had anything to do with it."

"Why not?" Former boyfriends are excellent suspects. Former husbands who leave you for another woman are even better.

Okay, I was getting off track here. I tuned in again to Regan.

"He died shortly after their break-up."

I gasped. "How tragic. Was it an accident?"

39

"Possibly, although there were rumors he committed suicide because he was so devastated by the breakup. He didn't leave a note so no one will ever know." Regan's face darkened as she scowled. "I used to think your brother was devoted to me. But a woman like Keiki can change a man. And not for the better."

"Yes, but—" My reply was interrupted when Liz, Brian, Stan, and Mother joined us. With Steve and Dave not far behind. By the time the two men arrived, the only available seats were at the opposite end of the table. It was probably just as well Regan and Dave would sit apart. He nodded at her then proceeded to ignore her. She finally left to get some food, rejoining us seconds before the trio of musicians began to play.

As eight female dancers edged toward the stage, I recognized Keiki's sister. I elbowed Stan. "Walea is performing tonight. Don't you think it's odd she's dancing and not mourning her sister?"

He cocked his head. "Even in Hawaii they probably follow that old tenet—the show must go on."

"There must be other dancers who could replace her."

"Not necessarily. This resort only holds a luau once a week. Maybe she needs the money and couldn't afford not to show up. Hawaii is an expensive place to live. I understand many people on this island hold multiple jobs just to get by."

I stared at Walea, performing as if she didn't have a care in the world. She shook her curvy hips, sheathed in a white sarong, and tossed her waist-length hair from side to side.

Maybe Walea did need the money. Or maybe she didn't care that her stepsister had died.

Was anyone mourning the loss of the beautiful dancer?

CHAPTER TEN

The luau entertainment was terrific, although every time Walea returned to the stage, my thoughts drifted to her stepsister's tragic death. The emcee, who reminded me of a tan Jay Leno minus the formidable chin, possessed an excellent sense of humor that helped distract me from my ominous ruminations.

He introduced each number with a brief history of the geographic region in the Pacific where it originated. He explained how the performers portrayed the meaning of Polynesian songs through the actions of their bodies, particularly the use of graceful hand movements.

I glanced over at Regan. She glared at her husband who conversed in low tones with Steve. My sister-in-law looked like she was about to produce a graceful hand motion of her own. One utilizing the third finger for emphasis.

The well-built, oiled bodies of the male dancers captivated me with something more— agility. It made me wonder why Keiki would break up with a dancer her own age and go after my slightly balding, slightly pudgy brother.

The troupe performed a Fijian Dance where the men sat on the floor clapping poles together at an amazing speed and with unerring accuracy. A true crowd pleaser came next— the *Siva Afi* —the daring fire knife dance.

"I wonder how long it would take for me to learn that dance," Stan whispered.

"Folsom Lake isn't big enough to put out the inferno you'd start if you took up fire dancing."

"Party pooper," Stan muttered.

The dancers spun their fiery swords under and around their writhing bodies. At the finale, they threw the flaming batons high enough to reach the satellite servicing my smart phone. I started breathing again once they were all successfully caught.

The men bowed and smiled broadly as the audience roared its approval. The Hawaiian Jay Leno indicated there would be one more participatory dance that included members from the audience. As the performers fanned out into the crowd searching for victims, I lowered my head. The worst thing you can do in one of these situations is make eye contact with a performer.

Stan waved at a handsome young man who must have registered on his gaydar. "Yoo hoo, over here."

As the dark-haired dancer approached, Stan shoved me out of my chair and into the man's muscular arms. What the heck!

Everyone at our table hooted, including Regan, who smiled for the first time that evening.

"I'm Kimo." The young dancer introduced himself as he guided me onto the stage. I stared at the crowd in complete paralysis, wishing that *Pele,* the Hawaiian goddess of fire, would pluck me off the stage and use me as a virgin sacrifice. I'd rather be thrown into an erupting volcano than dance before an audience.

Not to mention, I'd been a practicing virgin since my divorce, so I almost qualified for a sacrificial role!

Kimo moved his muscular tush in a mesmerizing circular motion to demonstrate how to shake my booty. While I had more than enough booty to shake, I couldn't figure out how to do it without looking like a total dweeb. I glanced at the audience awash in a sea of video cameras and phones.

OMG. My inept hips were going viral. I would never get laid again, and I wasn't talking about the floral version.

Two capable hands suddenly grabbed my waist and spun me around.

The gods finally smiled down on me as Steve traded places with Kimo. The ship captain's broad shoulders and back blocked the audience's view of my clumsy gyrations. He gently placed his hands on each side of my waist and before you could say "Liliuokalani," my hips swayed as if they were born to hula.

The last note of the song ended before I was ready to quit our Hawaiian foreplay. The amateurs were ushered off the stage to another round of applause and catcalls. Instead of returning to our seats, I asked Steve to wait with me so I could speak with Walea after the show ended.

Keiki's stepsister, the last woman to exit the stage, stopped to talk to a musician. He placed his ukulele inside a soft-sided case and together they strolled away from the stage, headed in our direction. Our shadowed enclave made Steve and me practically invisible and the couple passed by without a glance at us. I tapped Walea on her shoulder. She spun around, her black eyes fearful.

"Sorry to frighten you," I said. "I wanted to offer you and your family my condolences for your loss. It must be such a trying time for everyone."

A flash of anger replaced the fear in her eyes as she recognized me. "It was your brother who caused my sister to die. I curse the day I introduced him to Keiki."

"I'm certain Dave had nothing to do with her death," I said. "But why do you think she was in the restaurant so late? Was Keiki meeting someone?"

The man standing beside Walea shoved his face so close to mine I could count the pockmarks on his cheeks. "Tell your brother we know what he did. Our Hawaiian gods will not let his actions go unpunished."

Steve inserted himself between the man and me. "Now, listen here—"

An angry rumbling from above interrupted his sentence.

The gods had spoken.

CHAPTER ELEVEN

Those Hawaiian gods are one heck of a responsive bunch. Seconds after Walea's enraged friend threatened us, thunder rumbled across the sky, followed by a huge downpour. Steve grabbed my hand and we ran. Our group was already gathering belongings, ready to dash to shelter.

Heaven forbid a sudden tropical shower disturb Mother's perfect coiffure. She whipped a tiny satchel out of her purse and transformed it into a lightweight slicker. With a matching rain hat.

We hustled across the expanse of lawn that felt like it had grown to the size of a football field. By the time we reached the lobby everyone except my mother was soaked. Steve's wet polo shirt molded nicely to his chest, displaying an impressive six-pack. My soggy sundress clung to my derriere, emphasizing my need to enroll in a Polynesian dance class.

"Thanks for the dance lesson," I said to Steve. I grabbed a towel from the stack the hotel staff dispersed to their drenched luau guests. "Do all ship captains have to learn how to hula?"

He threw his head back and laughed. "It's not a requirement for our license, but I was lucky to get lessons with..." He paused and a pensive expression crossed his face.

I ventured a guess. "Did Keiki teach you?"

Steve nodded. "Keiki occasionally substituted for the *Sea Jinx's* principal dancer. I managed to pick up a few moves from her."

My nosy self was curious what "moves" Keiki and Steve had

shared, but I decided to focus on Keiki's movements with my brother instead.

"I guess you could tell from Regan's outburst that she thinks Dave and Keiki were having an affair," I said. "Did Dave ever confide in you about Keiki?"

Steve's eyes flicked toward Dave, who was leaning against a pillar. "Your brother and I are tight, but we don't pry into each other's personal stuff. Don't you think that's a good policy to maintain?"

Not prying into a pal's love life? As far as I was concerned, true friendship means being there to support a friend's decisions. Also being there to tell them when they are about to screw up.

I sighed. Men seem to have different codes about stuff like this. No wonder they're so clueless when it comes to communicating with the opposite sex.

I glanced at Dave. His eyes were fixed on his wife who conversed with our mother. I wondered what the couple's plans were, or if they were even going home together. This might be my only opportunity to get him alone. I said good-bye to Steve and joined my brother.

"Hanging in there, Dave?"

He nodded but remained silent.

"I spoke to Walea after the show."

That got his attention. "What did she say?"

"Um, she kind of cursed you."

"What?" He rolled his eyes. "C'mon, Laurel. Don't tell me you believe that Hawaiian mumbo jumbo."

Not really. Although that mini-monsoon had erupted within seconds of that scary guy yelling at me. Just thinking about his threat made goose bumps or what the locals call "chicken skin," appear on both arms.

"Walea was with a nasty fella. About your height, dark hair, with lots of acne scars on his face. He played the ukulele at the luau tonight."

"That's Henry Gonzalez, Walea's husband," he replied. "Not the most cheerful guy on the island, but he's an excellent musician." Dave rocked back and forth on his heels. "I should stop by their house. See if there's anything I can do to help."

I rested my hand on his freckled forearm. "I'm not sure they're in the mood for company from you or anyone in our family. Walea sounded like she blames you for Keiki's death."

Dave rapidly blinked away the water that had started to pool in his eyes. "What if they're right and the ropes weren't secured properly? Maybe it really is my fault she's gone."

"No point worrying yourself sick until you find out if it was an accident or not. Did the police say when you can open up again?"

"They said they'd be done tomorrow, but I'm not sure I can handle reopening the restaurant after what happened." He rubbed the corner of his right eye. "It won't be the same without her anyway."

Her? I was about to grill Dave further when Mother joined us. Darn. Any revelations would have to wait. Mother's arm wrapped snugly around Regan, who looked prepared to bolt the second her mother-in-law loosened her firm grip.

"Dave, your wife and I were discussing our expedition tomorrow." Mother placed a special emphasis on Regan's marital status. Subtlety was *not* Mom's middle name.

"I heard you're all driving to the volcano in the morning then Regan's taking you on the coffee tour," he said.

Regan shook her head. "We'll have to delay the plantation tour until the next day. I'm meeting with a Detective Lee tomorrow afternoon at the police station."

Dave's eyebrows jumped an inch. "Why are they talking to you?"

It might be time for Dave to stop watching cooking shows and start catching *Law and Order* reruns.

"Regan is co-owner of the restaurant," I said. "They're probably going to interview all your staff. Most likely they've already spoken to Walea and she's..." My voice dropped off as I realized interviewing Walea and her family wouldn't make the authorities more sympathetic to our family.

"It's not like I have anything useful to share." Regan narrowed her eyes at her husband. "I took a sleeping pill last night so a troop of dancers could have paraded through our condo without waking me up. Should I have heard anything?"

Dave's face paled and his left eye twitched, but he shook his head.

"I'm sure you two have much to discuss." Mother released her hold on Regan and gently pushed her toward her husband. "Go home and get a good night's rest. Brian can drive us to the volcano tomorrow. You can take us on the tour of Koffee Land the next day."

Regan appeared hesitant. I didn't envy her position but Mother was right. It was time for Regan and Dave to sit down and discuss Keiki. And their marriage.

Dave placed his hand on the small of his wife's back. As the couple receded into the distance, I noted the gap between them increased.

Liz, Brian and Stan joined my mother and me.

"We can't do the coffee tour until Tuesday," Mother said. "So why don't we visit the black sand beach at Punalu'u and the volcano tomorrow?"

"Great idea," Stan said. "That beach is loaded with *honu*, huge green sea turtles. I'd love to get a photo of them sunning themselves."

"We can also squeeze in a stop at the Punalu'u Bake Shop," Liz added. "I've been dying to sample their *malasadas*."

"What are *malasadas*?" I asked.

"Very sweet, light and airy pastries. Similar to doughnuts but better. Full of custard or fruit. Some are even stuffed with chocolate cream."

Forget the giant turtles and the volcano.

Liz had me at the chocolate cream-filled doughnuts.

CHAPTER TWELVE

By eight o'clock, we'd all gathered in the lobby. Despite Mother's objections, I skipped my heart-and-colon-healthy oatmeal breakfast. My daily calories were reserved for delicious fried carbs. The sugar-filled pastries might sweeten the grumpy mood brought on by two voicemails I'd just played back.

Last night I'd turned my phone to silent for the luau performance and missed a call from Tom. I couldn't decide if I should be pleased or annoyed that he'd finally phoned. His brief message said he hoped we were all having a great time.

No mention that he missed me. Or longed for my return. Or that he wished he could have joined me at this beautiful tropical resort. My fingers hovered over the phone itching to send an equally curt text message, but I decided to wait. Maybe the magic of this island would restore my spirits.

Jenna, my sixteen-year-old, had also left a message. Though her voice mail kept cutting in and out, I heard her mention something that cost "only two hundred dollars." I texted and asked her to elaborate. With my new stepfather, a retired detective babysitting both kids, I wasn't worried about either of them getting into trouble. The request for something that cost *only* two hundred dollars was more troubling.

But I'd worry about that later. Today I was on vacation.

Three hours and three thousand calories later, with my body stretched out on an inadequately sized beach towel, I attempted to keep the broiling black sand from turning the soles of my feet to burnt charcoal.

My towel rested twenty feet away from some sunbathing sea turtles. After practically inhaling three of the cream-filled pastries at the southernmost bakery in the United States, my body felt bloated. I bet the turtles could move faster than I could. Every now and then, one of the placid creatures would poke his or her head out, gaze at the crowd of tourists and withdraw back into its shell.

I wished I had a cool shell to hide my own sweaty body. The palm trees that lined the Punalu'u Black Sand Beach made for a postcard photo op, but the black sand formed from the lava flowing into the sea had created a molten hot playground for beachgoers.

Mother lay next to me on an oversized hot pink beach towel. She'd rearranged it at least ten times until it sat perfectly perpendicular to the ocean. Her thick-soled flip-flops, a lovely shade of raspberry edged in rhinestones, shimmered in the noon sun.

She rolled over to face me. "This vacation probably isn't what you expected, is it?"

What I'd expected was some quality bonding with the brother and sister-in-law I rarely saw. Not intervening in a domestic dispute that may have turned deadly. I'd also anticipated private time alone with Tom.

I swiped at tiny grains of sand on my legs. "It's not exactly the romantic vacation I envisioned when we initially planned this trip."

"You know how I hate to pry..." I stifled a snort, but my mother has excellent hearing. She sniffed, but continued. "Detective Hunter is a fine man, but maybe he has too much responsibility with his new position to be in a relationship with you. Or with any woman."

"You're probably right. It was silly to get my hopes up for this trip. I kept imagining the two of us sharing romantic evenings—walking the beach together and later making—" My face turned the color of my mother's beach towel when I realized I was about to discuss my sex life with her.

Or my hope that I would finally *have* a sex life once Tom and I vacationed together in Hawaii.

She chuckled. "It's okay, honey. You've been single for a few years now, although not nearly as long as I was alone after your father passed away. Try not having a sex life for almost thirty years."

Talk about TMI! That was way too much information.

After my Dad died, I'd never seen my mother with another man until she started dating Detective Bradford the previous fall. I'd always wondered if she'd squeezed any dating into her busy life once my brother and I moved out. No need to wonder any more.

"How could you tell Bradford was the man for you?" The question had nagged at me since their initial meeting, but I'd never had the nerve to ask, even after they married.

She rolled over on her back and rested her hands on her stomach. "Timing had a lot to do with it. Robert and I are both sixty-two. He was contemplating retirement from the sheriff's department. I was wondering if I'd still be selling real estate and showing houses twenty years from now. I've enjoyed my career, but I haven't had much of a life of my own, other than raising you and your brother."

She sat up and smiled. "I doubt any Realtor on their death bed ever said they wished they'd gotten one more listing."

My turn to chuckle. My mother had been a workaholic all of her life. In the beginning, she had no choice because she needed to support her young family. Once she became the top agent in her office, her competitive nature wouldn't allow her to drop back to number two in sales.

It looked like the new Mrs. Barbara Bradford would finally bring some balance into her life.

"Plus Robert is terrific in bed."

Oh ick! That made for more than enough mother/daughter bonding for me. I leaped off my towel and hotfooted it down to the water where Stan was cooling his heels.

Stan glanced at me as I splashed noisily beside him. "Did those big old turtles scare you?"

Nope, but my mother sure did. Our conversation reminded me of my brother and Regan's strained relationship. The couple had married after a brief courtship and I felt like I barely knew my sister-in-law. I'd looked forward to getting to know her better on this trip but bonding over a dead body was not what I'd had in mind.

After a quick dip in the ocean, we decided to head to the volcano. I tried to clean the sand off my calves with a wet wipe. Dark streaks ran up and down my legs leaving me even stickier. As I reached into my straw tote for a clean towel, I noticed a missed call on my cell.

My brother had phoned but left no message. I tried calling him back, but there was no reception. Maybe I'd have more bars once we climbed higher up. I'd feel more relaxed once we learned more about what happened to Keiki.

At the visitor's center inside the Hawaii Volcanoes Park, we wandered around the displays and watched a mesmerizing and scary film. Kilauea is frequently referred to as a drive-in volcano since it's one of the few spots where tourists can drive past steaming beds of lava. According to Hawaiian folk lore, Pele, the volcano goddess is very unpredictable. The current eruption could go on for another one hundred years or stop tomorrow.

After pondering my most recent conversation with my mother, I decided that Pele and Mom had a lot in common.

After our drive around the crater, we tried to check into the Volcano Village. We discovered there was no room at the inn. Who knew the volcano was a hot destination for celebrating Valentine's Day? None of us wanted to drive the three-plus hours back to our resort in Waikaloa. We piled in the car and headed down to Hilo, a thirty-minute drive.

Liz Googled a discount travel website on her smart phone and booked two rooms at a decent hotel. The honeymooners snapped up a room with a king-size bed. The three of us decided to save money and take a double-bedded room. My mother and I could share a bed and Stan could have the other.

Stan had been my confidant for so long, I often thought of him as the sister I'd always wanted.

My cell rang just as we entered our hotel room. Speaking of siblings...

"Dave, finally. How did Regan's meeting with the police go?"

"She spent almost three hours there, and they took a DNA swab, but she didn't seem too concerned." He paused for a few seconds. "Although that's odd since my wife normally worries about everything. Her staff claims she angsts over every unaccounted for coffee bean."

Hmm. I was surprised they'd taken a sample of Regan's DNA, but maybe the Hawaiian police just believed in being thorough. "Did the police mention when you can re-open the restaurant?"

"They're supposed to remove the crime scene tape early tomorrow. Our insurance agent will meet me at the restaurant around noon. I need to know if..." Dave's voice faltered, "if I was responsible in some way for Keiki's fall."

My heart broke for my brother who had to worry if negligence made him inadvertently responsible for a woman's death.

I tried to boost his morale. "C'mon, Dave, think positive. What are you and Regan doing tonight?"

"She's packing right now. She stays in one of Koffee Land's guest cabins when she needs to be in Hilo overnight. For business." His voice dropped and it almost sounded like he muttered "supposedly."

He coughed. "Anyway, Regan said it would be easier to spend the night there to prepare for your tour tomorrow. She's leaving here in a few minutes."

"What about you?"

"Me? I'm going to grab a six-pack, sit on our lanai and contemplate the meaning of life."

CHAPTER THIRTEEN

Torrents of rain pelted our balcony screen door and woke us early the next morning. According to our guidebook, the eastern side of the island could receive as much as 150 inches of rain per year. No wonder everything was so lush and green. I just hoped all 150 inches didn't fall today.

The group vetoed Liz's plan to pay an early morning visit to a botanical garden. The gang opted for a leisurely breakfast of sweet potato rolls, macadamia nut pancakes and a hearty portion of local bacon. Liz reluctantly acquiesced once I promised we'd return on a sunny day and I'd zip-line through the botanical garden with her.

Luckily for me, the odds of the sun shining in Hilo before we flew home were about as high as the odds of me snapping onto a flimsy rope hundreds of feet above terra firma.

Once we escaped Hilo, the rain magically disappeared and the sun popped out, creating an enormous arched rainbow against the blue sky. We stopped at the Punalu'u Bake Shop on our way to the coffee farm. I managed to make a quick pit stop without succumbing to the purchase of any more pastries.

At the rate I was eating my way across Hawaii, I would need to jog around all 266 miles of the Big Island to work the calories off.

Koffee Land occupied five hundred acres near the quaint town of Honaunau, at the southern end of the Kona coffee district. Regan's employer was one of Kona's largest coffee farms. Most of the eight hundred growers on the island cultivated far smaller holdings, anywhere from one to five acres.

A brilliant lime green sign adorned with bright violet letters announced our approach to Koffee Land. Even the lava rock entry bore the KL logo. A long, winding paved road ended at a modern-looking building, the impressive visitors' center. Covered lanais on three sides allowed tourists to sit and enjoy distant ocean views while they sipped their coffee.

As our group ambled up the sidewalk, we admired the brilliant red blossoms of the bougainvillea bushes planted along the walkway. I pushed open the heavy Koa wood door and my nose led the way into the coffee-scented gift shop.

Welcome to Starbucks on steroids.

A young girl dressed in shorts, a lime green polo shirt with KL embroidered on the pocket, and a name badge that read Tiffany, smiled at us.

"Welcome to Koffee Land. Is this your first visit?"

"Yes," said Mother. "My daughter-in-law, Regan Bingham, is supposed to show us around."

"I'll let her know you're here. Would you like to sample some of our award-winning coffee while you wait?" She pointed to a beige granite-topped counter across the room bearing seven large carafes and a variety of condiments.

Silly question. Liz and Brian were already pouring coffee into paper cups before the young woman could finish her sentence. The rest of us followed suit. Labels on the tall silver carafes told which beans had been ground to make the coffee inside. Small bowls in front of each silver cylinder displayed the actual Koffee Land beans: Standard medium and French roast, Gold label premium versions of each roast, and something called Peaberry. Plus toasted coconut and chocolate macadamia nut.

Yum yum. By the time I'd tasted all the versions, I'd have so much energy I probably *could* run all the way back to the hotel. We jostled each other as we sampled small cups of the steaming liquid.

"Aloha, everyone." Regan joined us, her arms spread in welcome, but her smile seemed strained, and she looked exhausted. Her lime-green shirt hung on her petite frame and emphasized her pallor. It wouldn't surprise me if Regan had dropped a few pounds in the last couple of days.

Criminal investigations can do that to people. In fact, being a murder suspect is the only weight loss program that ever worked for *me*.

"There are so many choices," Mother said. "Can you explain the difference between the assorted roasts?"

Regan pointed to the bowls. "See the difference in the color, size and shape of the various beans? The lightest beans are our medium roast, which technically produces the purest tasting Kona coffee. Many people, especially Starbucks regulars, prefer the darker French roast. The higher temperatures required for their roasting removes some of the natural flavor though."

I mulled that over. "So if I prefer a light roast, I'm not a coffee weenie. I'm really a coffee connoisseur?"

"That's correct." Regan reached into one of the bowls, grabbed a small round bean and passed it around. "Now the Peaberry is our most robust bean."

"Peaberry coffee usually costs more, doesn't it?" Stan asked.

Regan nodded. "It occurs when the coffee cherry yields only one bean instead of the usual two. It's very rare." She paused. "Sort of like a good man."

Before she could elaborate, the door opened and six more caffeine-seeking tourists entered. Regan looked at her watch. "Darn. I hoped to take you on a private tour, but we're short-handed today. Victor needs to leave to help his wife and daughter prepare for Keiki's funeral."

"Keiki's funeral?" I asked. "Why would your staff be involved with that?"

"Oh, I guess you didn't know," Regan replied. "Victor is married to Keiki's mother."

"Her father works here too?"

"Victor is, I mean, was Keiki's stepfather. And he doesn't just work here." Regan gnawed on her lower lip. "Victor is my boss."

CHAPTER FOURTEEN

For a brief moment, you could have heard a coffee bean drop. Then the chatter of the other tourists filled the room.

"Victor married Keiki's mother several years ago," Regan clarified. "Technically he's my boss because he runs the coffee operation. Since I'm the controller, I also report to Ritz Nagrow, the owner. He..." she stopped as two men entered the center from the back of the building. "There's Ritz and Victor now."

A short wiry Asian man in his early fifties conversed with a tall dark-haired man with cinematic good looks. Dressed in an off-white linen blazer and dark slacks, the taller man looked like he'd stepped off the movie set of *South Pacific,* ready to sing "Some Enchanted Evening." I took a wild guess this was the owner. Regan gave a half-hearted wave in their direction and they headed toward us.

She introduced the men to our group. "This is Ritz Nagrow, the owner of Koffee Land. And this is Victor Yakamura."

Mother took Victor's calloused hand in both of hers. "We are all so sorry for your loss."

Victor stared at her with red-rimmed eyes, bordered by crow's feet so deep they appeared etched in stone. "*Mahalo.* Thank you," he said, releasing her hand. "I must go home now and assist my daughter and my wife."

"We'll talk about that matter tomorrow," Ritz said to Victor.

Keiki's stepfather nodded then took his leave.

"How do you like Koffee Land?" The dashing coffee plantation owner's brown eyes sparkled as he beamed at our group. This man was either naturally energetic or he'd just drunk a pot full of Peaberry coffee.

"They just arrived," Regan told Ritz. "I was about to give them a tour."

"Of course, of course. They must have the grand tour," he responded, his voice indicating a trace of an accent. "Feel free to tell them about our upcoming event. But, first, I must go over something with you. Perhaps your guests can sample one of our many delectable items while they wait."

"Um, okay." She pointed to a shelf of brightly wrapped boxes. "If you're hungry, check out our selection of donkey balls. They're really tasty."

Liz and I looked at each other. Did Regan say what I thought she said? We zipped over to the aisle Regan had pointed to and discovered an assortment of Donkey Balls, a local brand of sphere-shaped chocolate candies with flavor options ranging from chocolate-covered macadamia nuts to chocolate and fruit-flavored malt balls larger than a super-sized jawbreaker.

What a great place to work. Caffeine in liquid and solid forms. Liz and I each purchased a pack and shared them with the group while we waited.

Regan looked frustrated when she returned. "Ready for the tour?"

I wondered if everything was okay, but with my cheeks stuffed full of chocolate chunks, all I could do was nod.

As we hiked toward an area planted with coffee trees, Regan provided running commentary. "The history of Kona coffee goes back over 180 years. At one point, all Kona coffee trees came from one single tree in the King of France's private greenhouse."

"Talk about a huge family tree," joked Stan.

Regan politely chuckled then explained that elevations for coffee farms on the Big Island ranged from 1,500 to 3,500 feet. Unlike grapes, which are picked in the fall at the precise moment the vintner determines, coffee cherries don't ripen at the same time. They get picked four to six times a year. Labor costs for hand picking are one of the reasons Kona coffee is so expensive, sometimes exceeding fifty dollars a pound.

Fifty dollars a pound? No wonder they call it Kona gold.

"After the cherries arrive at the mill, the beans are washed then sundried on decks called *hoshidanas*." Regan pointed to a large deck in the distance

"What happens if it rains?" I asked.

"We use lots of tiny umbrellas," Regan responded. When my mouth gaped, she smiled. "A little coffee humor. We have mechanical dryers if needed."

As we continued the tour, I marveled at the similarities and differences between grape growing and coffee farming. More than fifty wineries are located in El Dorado County. Several owners are friends of mine, so I knew a tremendous amount of love and labor went into producing the award-winning Gold Country wines.

"Are all beans grown on this island considered to be Kona coffee?" I asked.

Regan shook her head. "True Kona coffee must be grown within the Kona coffee belt, an area twenty miles long and only two miles wide."

"I read something about a scandal where some grower bought less expensive beans then sold them as one hundred percent Kona coffee," Stan said.

"That was a huge scandal and it led to new laws," replied Regan. "Inspections are now required to ensure that all beans labeled as 100% Kona are grown in the district."

"Next up is the roasting room. After that, I'll show you our latest project. Something no other coffee farm has done." She pointed to a tall wooden tower situated on a distant hill.

"Is that a zip-line tower?" Stan asked.

"Our latest addition," confirmed Regan. "Ritz and Pilar are determined to turn Koffee Land into a destination coffee farm. They want to host weddings, special events, even movies. Our first big event is a new reality show called *The Bride and the Bachelor*. They start taping next Monday."

"That sounds like fun," I said. "Aren't you excited?"

"I guess." Regan nibbled her lower lip. "I personally think if a coffee farm produces fabulous coffee that should be enough. But Ritz thinks on a grand scale. We've just completed the addition of six more 'honeymoon' cabins to the two guest houses that were already on the property, plus an event pavilion and the zip-line, of course."

"Are you going to have zip-line weddings?" Liz turned to her husband. "Darn. That would have been something, wouldn't it, honey?"

Brian's eyes cut to mine. It was a good thing Liz was already married. There was no way this matron of honor would have "zipped" down the aisle.

"Can we ride it today?" Liz asked.

"Not today, although it will be operational before you leave for home. Everything was delayed when we had to stop construction for a few weeks. The coffee farms surrounding us are not happy about our new additions. They keep saying these delays are due to bad *juju*. That the gods don't want the Kona coffee belt turned into Disneyland."

"Those Hawaiian gods are an active bunch, aren't they?" Stan said.

Regan's face turned as white as the fluffy clouds up above us as she replied. "I don't know if the gods were involved or not, but it's tragic when a worker is killed."

CHAPTER FIFTEEN

"Omigod," I said. "What happened?"

"He fell off that zip-line platform." Regan pointed to the tower in the distance. "His boss asked him to stay late to finish something. Supposedly he slipped and fell from the platform to the ground."

"Ouch. That's about a forty-foot drop," Stan said.

"His body wasn't discovered until the following morning. It was horrible." She closed her eyes as if remembering the incident. "Henry was beside himself with grief. And now the poor guy has to deal with his sister-in-law's death as well."

"Henry was his boss? Walea's husband?" I asked. "No wonder he's so..." I wanted to say crabby, but that seemed rude considering what the poor man had recently suffered.

"It's been a tough month for all the staff." Regan glanced down at her watch. "We better get on with the tour. By the time we return, Ritz will undoubtedly have another project for me to work on. I just wish we made money as quickly as he spends it."

As Stan and Brian peppered Regan with questions about the zip-line and other Koffee Land improvements, my phone beeped indicating a missed call from Dave. The reception on this side of Mauna Loa must be iffy. I followed the others into the roasting room, but it was so noisy I slipped out to return my brother's call. In the distance, an SUV climbed the long driveway to the visitor's center. Poor Regan. She would barely finish with our group before leading another tour.

My thumb was poised over Dave's number when the squeal of brakes drew my attention. The vehicle I'd noticed skidded around the last curve and slid into a parking space near the front of the building. The car had barely stopped when two men stepped out. One was dressed in a shirt and slacks and the other in a Hawaii police uniform.

Uh oh. What were the odds the officers stopped by for a free cup of coffee and a Donkey Ball snack?

I shoved my phone back into my cluttered purse. Dave could wait a few more minutes while I found out what was going on. I trotted down the sidewalk and managed to catch up with the officers as they entered the visitor's center. The taller red-haired man was kind enough to hold the heavy door open for me.

Tiffany stood frozen behind the reception counter. Her dark eyes were as huge as the chocolate-covered malt balls I'd crunched on earlier.

"Aloha," she squeaked. "Do you want any c..c..coffee?" Her arm shot out in the direction of the large carafes. Then she raced out the door as fast as her flip-flops would allow.

The two men turned and stared at me, the only other occupant in the room.

"Can I assist you?" I asked the man dressed in civilian clothing.

"Do you work here?"

Since I wasn't dressed in a lime-green Koffee Land polo shirt and I was hauling a huge straw tote with me, I gave him a two for his deductive abilities.

"No, I'm visiting from California. My sister-in-law works here. Are you looking for one of the employees? Several of them are off today due to a death in the family."

"We'd like to speak with Regan Bingham. Is she available?"

"Regan is my sister-in-law. She's out escorting a tour."

The detective's eyes narrowed, and I could swear his jaw squared right before my eyes. He whipped out a pad and pen from his pocket. "Okay, lemme get this straight." His Bronx accent seemed out of place in Hawaii. "Are you saying you're related to Dave Bingham, the owner of Daiquiri Dave's restaurant?"

I nodded. "Dave is my brother. Is he okay?"

"For now."

What kind of an answer was that? I opened my mouth to ask my own questions when the door opened and another man entered the center. He looked startled to see me but quickly recovered. "So, Ms. McKay, we meet again. What a strange coincidence." His tone of voice indicated he didn't think much of coincidences.

Neither did I.

"Detective Lee, what brings you to Koffee Land? Does this have anything to do with Keiki's death?"

He pressed his lips together. "Where is Mrs. Bingham?"

The guy with the Bronx accent turned to Lee. "She's supposedly giving some folks a tour. Some little Hawaiian hottie ran out the door the second we arrived. Should I send Yaku after her?"

"Yes, immediately. And, O'Grady, if you would be so kind as to locate this tour group and bring Mrs. Bingham back here. Then we can finish our business."

O'Grady stuffed his notebook back in his pocket, opened the door and let it slam behind him. Yaku headed outside, leaving me alone with the detective. I decided to be hospitable and offer some refreshments. A little sugar might sweeten his mission.

"Would you like a ball or two while you wait?"

Some days I actually *think* before I open my mouth. Today was not one of them.

A hint of a smile appeared on the detective's face. "*Mahalo*, but I will pass on your offer for now. However a cup of coffee would be refreshing."

His gaze roved around the center as he walked toward the coffee samples. The door opened again and I expected to see O'Grady enter along with Regan and the rest of our party. Instead, a throng of white-haired tourists wandered into the center. Through the open door, I watched more passengers disembark from a parked Paradise Tour bus.

I hoped Regan or Tiffany returned soon, because I was having a difficult enough time playing host to one cop. I had no idea how to entertain a busload of caffeine-starved seniors.

Lee plastered his cell to his right ear and used his palm to cover his left ear to muffle noise from the boisterous group. Apparently, he still couldn't hear. He opened the door and, as he walked out, he mouthed, "Don't leave."

Like I could? I felt like an airport controller directing men and women to their respective restrooms and others to the coffee counter. Where was my sister-in-law and why were the police here in force? If an employee didn't show up soon, I might resort to giving away candy samples. If nothing else, chewing on the huge chocolate spheres would stifle the noise level.

Fortunately, I didn't have to resort to a Donkey Ball free-for-all. O'Grady returned with Detective Lee, Regan and the rest of my gang.

Stan bustled over. "You missed the best part of the tour. Where'd you go?"

"Dave phoned and I went outside to return the call. Before I could buzz him back, these officers arrived, followed by this busload of tourists."

"That red-headed guy said we had to follow him to the center. What's going on?"

"Officer Lee," I pointed in the detective's direction, "wants to talk to Regan."

"Oh." Stan looked left and then right. "So where is she?"

"She's..." I spun around in a circle trying to locate my sister-in-law among the crowd of aloha-shirted tourists.

Lee joined us, looking puzzled. "Do you know where your sister-in-law is?"

I shrugged. Lee motioned O'Grady to his side. O'Grady rushed out the door and Lee began circling the room.

My eyes scanned the center for Regan but no luck. Stan went outside to look for Regan and Tiffany while I entered the ladies' room. After peering at the shoes lined up in each stall, I decided none of the pairs was related to me, although I spied a cute set of floral wedges in the handicapped stall. I would try to make their owner's acquaintance later on.

As I headed back into the main room, Regan and my mother appeared in the rear doorway. Each carried two large carafes of coffee, one per hand. I eased my way around two senior citizens, who debated whether their dentures could handle the jawbreaker-sized chocolate- covered macadamia nuts. As I approached my mother, I reached out to grab one of the containers from her.

"Thanks, honey. Those pots are heavy when they're full."

Lee appeared by my side and offered to carry one of Regan's containers. It was reassuring to see the police in Hawaii were as kind and helpful as everyone else I'd encountered on the island. Whether it was due to the tranquil atmosphere, or lack of crime, it was a refreshing change from the overly suspicious cops I was more accustomed to in California.

We set our carafes on the coffee counter. Regan lined them up in the proper order to match the beans on display. "I better get to the register and attend to all of these customers."

"I'm afraid that won't be possible." Detective Lee's face remained impassive as he reached under the back of his aloha shirt and pulled out something round and silver.

"Regan Bingham, you're under arrest for the murder of Keiki—"

CHAPTER SIXTEEN

Just when you think you can trust a cop, they go and arrest one of your relatives.

The next few minutes were more chaotic than Times Square on New Year's Eve. One would think the presence of a police officer reading Miranda rights to a Koffee Land employee would send the tourists streaking back to their bus, but a pressing need for a Donkey Ball snack seemed to outweigh good manners. A few of the senior citizens refused to leave until someone rang up their orders.

I was ready to grab their walkers and thump them on their fluffy white heads, but help finally arrived. Yaku discovered Tiffany hiding behind a large burlap sack of coffee beans in the back room. She'd worried the police had come to grill her about one of her brothers, known for his expert *pakalolo* farming skills. When she discovered the authorities were more concerned with murder than marijuana, she ventured out to assist the customers.

Detective Lee led Regan out the door and down the sidewalk. I followed them, still in disbelief.

"Let me get Regan's boss," I said. "Maybe he can intervene."

Lee held up his palm, the tips of his fingers almost touching my nose. "Please, let us do our job."

"But—" The roar of a car engine caught my attention. I watched a white Mercedes convertible peel away.

Regan grew even paler. She attempted to lift her arm, but the handcuffs restricted any movement.

"Do you know who was in that car?" I asked her.

Regan's reply was barely audible. "Ritz."

Hmm. You'd think the owner would be concerned about the arrest of an employee. Didn't he see his controller being led away in handcuffs?

Brian grumbled and attempted to throw his legal weight around, but an El Dorado County Assistant District Attorney was weightless in this state. Lee said Regan could contact her husband once they'd completed her processing at the Kona station.

The officers were gentle, but firm, as they led Regan to their car. Tears poured down her cheeks as she bent over and eased into the backseat of the SUV. Liz and I waved at her, sympathetic tears streaming down our faces. My mother was as white as the pearl earrings dangling from her ear lobes, and I worried she might collapse from the strain.

I put my arm around her waist. "Are you okay?"

She nodded. "I'm fine. But that poor child. Why would they take Regan away?"

I turned to Brian. "Did Lee say anything about their reason for arresting her?"

"He said they had new evidence, but they weren't willing to share it with me. Have you talked to your brother? He needs to hire a criminal defense attorney for her."

I dug into my purse, grabbed my phone and speed-dialed Dave. He picked it up on the second ring. "Laurel, finally. Did you get my message?"

"Sorry, I saw you called, but—" I stopped as Dave interrupted me.

"I have good news," he said, "well, news that made me feel better."

Huh? What was Dave talking about? I was beginning to think that after so many years of living on the island, the *Vog*, Hawaii's volcanic version of smog, had destroyed some of his brain cells.

"Remember I was supposed to meet with the insurance inspector today? One of the detectives came by around eleven to remove the crime scene tape so the place would be accessible. I've been tearing myself up thinking it was my fault Keiki fell over the wall. The detective said the autopsy report showed it definitely wasn't an accident."

"Yeah, about that—" I tried to interrupt Dave, but he kept talking, his voice sounding happier than I'd heard in a long time.

"I know it's horrible that Keiki was murdered, but you can't imagine my relief that negligence wasn't the cause of her death. I called Regan with the good news, but she didn't pick up. Maybe we can make a fresh start now that..." His voice trailed off for a minute. "Anyway, with the crime scene tape down, the place is ours again. How about we have a celebration tonight? I'll cook a special Hawaiian dinner for just our family and your friends. What do you say?"

There was really only one thing I could say.

"You may want to put that celebration on hold. Regan was just arrested for Keiki's murder."

CHAPTER SEVENTEEN

A loud thud echoed over the phone line. Either the phone dropped out of my brother's hand, or he was knocking it against his hard head.

"I must have misunderstood you," Dave replied. "I thought you said Regan was arrested."

"That's exactly what I said. Three police officers just took her away. One of them was the detective we met the day they found Keiki."

"Why would they arrest Regan? What did they say?"

"Not much. Brian attempted to question them, but they didn't share anything. The officers are bringing her to the Kona station, and she can call you once she's been processed. Do you know a good criminal attorney?"

"Of course not. What kind of question is that?"

"A practical one. Regan will need a defense lawyer to represent her."

"Damn it. There are probably plenty of people who wanted to kill Keiki."

My blood started to boil hotter than the coffee I'd drunk earlier. "Why did you withhold that kind of information from us?"

The phone went silent. Then Dave said, "Keiki was a complicated person. That's all I'm going to say. Please come to the restaurant, and we'll talk when you all get here. In the meantime, I need to take care of my wife."

The line went dead.

"What can we do to help, luv?" Liz's lower lip trembled, a sure sign she was upset, but trying to keep it together.

My mother slid her arm around my best friend's waist. "Liz, our family has created more grief for you than any bride should have to contend with. Maybe you and Brian should take off on your own and spend some well-deserved time alone. You don't need to be involved in any more of our family crises."

"Thanks, but this is a group honeymoon, and Brian and I are here for you. Right, honey?"

Brian smiled and clasped her hand. "Of course, we are. Now let's drive back to Kona and come up with a plan."

We spent the drive debating the best way to proceed. Mother wanted to stop at the police station to see how Regan was doing, but Brian doubted we'd be allowed to see her. Stan insisted he should infiltrate the dance troupe to snoop and find out who might have wanted Keiki dead.

"I doubt if Walea will let you dance with them again," I said to Stan. "I'm sure she hates Dave, Regan, and anyone affiliated with our family."

He stroked his chin. "Yeah, but we had such a good time practicing that routine together. What if I called her and asked for a private lesson or two?"

"Her family is busy preparing for Keiki's funeral," I said. "Now that the autopsy has been completed, won't they release the body fairly soon?"

"I would imagine within a day or two," Brian responded from the driver's seat. "That's standard procedure in California and it's probably the same over here."

By the time we reached town, the sun had gone to sleep. The parking lot in front of the restaurant remained empty, but the crime scene tape was gone. A sign at the entrance informed potential customers that Daiquiri Dave's Lounge was temporarily closed due to renovation. The only remodeling I could think of was fortifying the lava rock wall Keiki had tumbled over.

Now that they'd arrested Regan, the police must be certain she pushed Keiki over the wall. Even though my sister-in-law disliked the dancer, she wouldn't have resorted to killing her. Would she? That unsettling thought sent shivers from my neck to my tailbone, but I immediately shoved it aside.

The restaurant appeared closed, but the door opened when Brian turned the knob. Inside, the sound of men's voices drew us toward the bar area where Dave perched on one of the bamboo bar stools. A bottle of vodka and a glass filled to the brim sat in front of him. Steve, who occupied the adjacent stool, sipped his own glass of colorless liquid.

I didn't want to seem like a control freak, but surely the two guys had a better plan than getting drunk tonight. Someone needed to spring Regan from the joint.

Dave gulped his drink in two seconds then reached for the half-empty bottle of vodka. I grabbed it first and raised it over my head.

"What is the matter with the two of you?" I glared at both men, equally annoyed with my brother and his best friend. "Drowning your sorrows isn't going to solve anything."

Steve slid off the bar stool with athletic grace and gestured for me to take his place. "Your brother is having a tough time dealing with this situation. You'll be happy to know I'm only drinking Sprite."

My brother spun around on his stool. "Laurel, stop being such a pill. Steve and me—" Dave burped. "We have a plan."

I narrowed my eyes. "What kind of plan? I hope it doesn't involve breaking Regan out of jail."

He shook his head from side to side and frowned. "You are always so negative. Steve and I have it covered. All we gotta do is find the killer ourselves."

He snatched the bottle out of my grasp. "Now how hard can that be?"

CHAPTER EIGHTEEN

We spent the next half hour trying to sober up my brother who continued to insist the local police were only interested in getting the murder off their books.

Brian responded to Dave's assertions. "I don't think you realize the importance of working within the system."

"Based on the stories my sister has shared," Dave said, "that method hasn't worked so well for her in the past."

Brian's face colored as Liz and I traded glances. I had no reason to doubt the competency of the Hawaii Police. Except for the fact that they'd arrested my sister-in-law, which led me to sincerely doubt their investigative prowess.

I also doubted that given my brother's current condition, that he should be cooking in a kitchen full of sharp pointed objects. We locked up the lounge and trooped down the street to the Kona Inn Restaurant, a terrific dining spot located at the Kona Inn Shopping Center. The young hostess showed the six of us to a corner table overlooking a velvety green lawn that marched up to the ocean.

We decided brainstorming would be better without booze so we skipped the tropical drinks and ordered dinner. My nostrils flared as the scent of batter-fried Maui onion rings wafted over from the table next to us. Three succulent orders of onion rings later, we were deep into discussing what we knew so far.

"Someone needs to ask the obvious question," said Brian. "What kind of evidence do the police have implicating Regan?"

Dave drooped in his chair. His initial alcohol-enhanced excitement about helping his wife seemed to have dissipated. "Yesterday, when I was waiting for Regan to finish with the cops, I overhead two officers discuss a bandage Regan wore above her wrist."

My mother looked puzzled. "Since when is a bandage proof someone is a murderer?"

"A scratch or other injury could indicate the suspect fought with the victim," Brian replied. "Regan mentioned they tested her DNA yesterday so they must have noticed something suspicious."

Brian twisted in his seat to address Dave. "Did you see or hear Regan go out that evening?"

Dave's right eye twitched as he replied. "Nope, didn't hear a thing."

Aha! I knew that twitch. My poker-playing teenage daughter had taught me how to read facial expressions and body language. That twitch was a sure "tell" whenever my brother lied. I remembered many a Monopoly game when he claimed to have lost all of his money. Several twitches later, pastel-colored paper bills mysteriously appeared in his shoes and shorts.

So Dave was lying. But about what?

My mother had managed to live in a twitch-free zone for the last forty-two years so she rarely found fault with her eldest child. It was up to me to get to the bottom of this mess.

"Did Regan mention anything about meeting with Keiki after the reception?" I asked Dave.

He shook his head with nary a twitch. Therefore, as far as my brother knew, Regan had not met up with the dancer.

"Will you be able to get her released from jail?" Stan asked.

"According to the attorney Steve found for me, the police can keep Regan under arrest for forty-eight hours before they must decide if there's sufficient evidence to have her arraigned. If the Prosecuting Attorney decides to proceed, the bail could be a million dollars or more. The restaurant and our condo unit are our only collateral. There's no way we have a million dollars in equity."

"Your wife is worth far more than a million dollars." My mother raised her voice as she addressed her only son. "Let me know what you need. I'm sure Robert would agree to help."

I didn't recall my mother offering to provide any collateral when I was almost arrested. All I could remember her telling the detectives was that I was *too* disorganized to commit murder.

Some witness for the defense!

"How did you find an attorney so quickly?" I asked Steve. "You don't hang out with the criminal element, do you?" I snatched another onion ring, expecting him to smile in response.

Steve's gaze drifted out the window and he paused a few seconds before he answered.

"Hawaii may be the Big Island, but it's a relatively small community. You meet people from many walks of life, never knowing if there's a particular reason why you crossed paths with one another."

Steve stretched out his palm and his fingertips grazed mine. His touch startled me, and I inadvertently shoved my chair into the unlucky server standing behind me. Seconds later, waves of molten heat rolled down my body, all the way to the tips of my toes.

My very clammy toes.

Was this what Regan meant by paradise being rife with pitfalls?

CHAPTER NINETEEN

There is nothing less romantic than having a bowl of clam chowder dumped on you. The creamy soup coated every inch of my body. I could feel a couple of clams nestled in the frizzy curls just above my left ear.

On a positive note, Dave smiled for the first time that evening. Steve proved to be a perfect gentleman. He not only refrained from laughing, but he dabbed his napkin in his water glass and slowly, almost sensuously, wiped the creamy chowder off my thighs and calves.

If you've never had a hot guy clean hot soup off your legs, you've really missed out. It was difficult to distinguish whose cheeks burned brighter—mine, or the server who accidentally dumped dinner on me when I bumped into her.

Mother, Liz, and I retired to the ladies' room to determine if there was any permanent damage from my soup shampoo. The two women circled me like hawks assessing their prey.

"I don't know, luv, you're going to need some extra powerful conditioner. Assuming we get it all out." Liz wrinkled her nose. "You may have every feral cat on the island following you down the sidewalk."

My mother scrambled around in her straw tote. She pulled out a pair of scissors and pointed them at me.

My eyes widened. "Where did those come from?"

She shrugged. "I always keep a pair in my purse, along with duct tape. It's my Realtor first-aid kit. I was kind of surprised they missed them at the airport."

I was kind of surprised my mother hadn't been classified as a terrorist.

Between the two of them, they managed to remove most of the chowder without me losing too many strands of hair. I discovered a stray clam and popped it in my mouth. Yummy.

"So where do we go from here?" Liz snipped off a few locks of hair so thick with goop they resembled string cheese.

My mother, head cocked, leaned against a wall papered in a palm tree motif.

"More to the right," she directed my new hair stylist. "What's your plan, honey? We need to prove Regan didn't do it, and we only have three more days on the island."

I whipped my head to the left. Not a good idea. My sudden movement surprised Liz.

"Whoopsie, daisy." She quickly dumped something in the trash that looked like a big chunk of my hair.

"Enough with the trimming. I'd rather have birds pecking at my head than leave myself in your lethal clutches. Mom, do you really expect us to find the killer in your time frame?"

"Robert says the first forty-eight hours are the most important. By tomorrow morning it will be," she peeked at her watch, "seventy-two hours give or take. You have your whole team here to assist you. I'm sure the local police will welcome our input."

Somehow, I doubted that.

"We certainly can't fly home with Regan stuck in jail and a killer still on the loose." Liz handed the scissors back to Mother. "And Brian has a big trial starting on Monday so we can't miss our Sunday flight. C'mon, Laurel, get a move on it."

I rolled my eyes. My team was such a bunch of amateurs. As was I. But I knew just the professional who could help us out. There was nothing like a dead body to get Detective Tom Hunter's attention.

Two hours later, I perched on the rim of the hotel's oversized marble-covered bathtub, cell phone in hand. My mother was already in bed, worn out from the day's activities and the stress of worrying about her son and his wife. It was close to midnight in California so there was a possibility I would wake up Tom, especially if he had his cell sitting close to his bed. Knowing him, he probably slept right next to it.

I would love to switch places with that phone.

The shrill ring of my cell made me jump. "Tom?" I was thrilled the detective was intuitive enough to call me when I needed him most.

"Mom?"

"Jenna, what are you doing up so late. Is everything okay?"

Everything was fine. In fact, it was excellent. One of her classmates invited her to the Winter Ball, which entailed the purchase of not only a new dress, but also shoes, a manicure and a pedicure. She guaranteed she would not let any pre-party planning interfere with her SAT test the same day.

Knowing how goal-oriented my daughter could be, I never worried her social life would interfere with her concentration. Jenna could shop and formulate mathematical theorems simultaneously. She could also calculate every discount combination imaginable long before the register finished totaling her purchases.

My daughter's analytical abilities would have been a huge plus in the Mortgage Underwriting department at Hangtown Bank where I work, but for some odd reason, her current career choice was aeronautical engineering. Not mortgage banking.

Go figure!

By the time Jenna and I hung up, it was close to one in the morning West Coast time. Too late to call Tom. I washed and moisturized my face and covered every inch of my body with the lotion provided by the hotel. The blurb on the bottle guaranteed the silky lotion would caress my skin. I slid under the covers, closed my eyes and let the scent of the fragrant macadamia nut oil lull me to sleep. At this point, I'd take whatever caressing I could get.

The melodic tones of my cell woke me from a rapturous slumber. I could still feel Tom Hunter's arms wrapped around me, his lingering kisses working their way up and down my oiled body, which in my dream was now a svelte size six.

I grabbed my phone before the caller could wake my mother. "Hi, honey," I said in a husky voice.

"Hi, yourself," replied a deep baritone. "You sure know how to make a guy's morning."

Oops. I focused my near-sighted eyes on my phone and noticed the call was from the local area code.

"Who is this?"

"It's Steve. I apologize if I woke you." His tone indicated he was disappointed, not so much that he woke me, but because there was already a "honey" in my life.

"Oh, sorry, I was still in dreamland." I stretched across the bed to see what time it was. Six-thirty? These ship captains are early risers. "I thought you were my daughter calling. Is anything wrong? Is Dave okay?"

"Oh, I'm sure he's as good as he can be in this situation."

"I can't believe they may set Regan's bail at a million dollars. It's not like someone can sneak off this island. You'd need a plane to do that."

"Or a boat," said the *Sea Jinx* captain. "It wouldn't be the first time a suspect used amphibious means for an escape."

Good seafaring point.

"You're probably wondering why I called so early. I'm privy to some information regarding Keiki, but I'm not sure what to do with it. I thought you might be able to give me some advice. Can we meet at your hotel?"

"Sure, when?"

"How about now?"

CHAPTER TWENTY

Men! They have zero concept of how long it takes a woman to make herself presentable. I flung on a pair of khaki shorts and a sleeveless coral top. A swipe of blush, mascara and lipstick, and I was ready. Mother was still asleep so I left the DO NOT DISTURB sign on the door and headed for the elevator.

Even this early, the elevators were crowded with parents, kids, collapsible strollers, and filled-to-the-brim beach bags. When my children were young, Hank and I didn't have the means to take our kids to a five-star hotel like this one. They were lucky to stay at a campground with a flushable potty and running water.

I squeezed into an elevator filled wall-to-wall with toddlers. The lit-up array of numbers indicated the little ones had engaged in their favorite elevator game. After stopping at all twenty-nine floors, the doors opened and I made a dash for it.

Steve talked on his cell next to an ornate stone pedestal table topped by an enormous tropical flower arrangement. He wore his blue *Sea Jinx* polo shirt and khaki shorts that displayed trim, muscular legs.

I sighed. I hate when a man's calves look better than my own. As soon as he noticed me, he finished his conversation and walked over to meet me. Before I could say "Aloha," Steve engulfed me in a welcoming hug that made my nerves tingle all the way down to my pink-tipped toenails. I was still blushing as he led me to the hotel's Island Café where the host seated us at a corner table overlooking a tropical garden. A tiny brook meandered through the lush foliage. Flashes of orange and yellow indicated the koi fish were enjoying a morning swim.

"Thanks for meeting me so early," Steve said. "Our snorkel cruise leaves at nine, and that's followed by an afternoon outing. This was the only time I had available."

"Anything that will help Regan is my first priority. No matter how early."

After our server poured our coffee and scribbled down our breakfast orders, Steve stared at his cup, deep in thought.

I nudged his foot with my sandal.

"Sorry," he said. "I'm struggling with the best way to share this information."

"How about just the facts for now. We can proceed from there."

My goodness, didn't I sound official? I was a regular Nikki Heat!

"Okay. Our brochures advertise that the *Sea Jinx* provides Hawaiian entertainment for the guests on the sunset cruise. The boat isn't big enough for a full troupe, but the guests enjoy the music and dancing along with their drinks and pupus."

I grinned. The thought of those Hawaiian appetizers always brings a smile to my face.

"About a week ago, Noelani, the principal dancer, called in sick. Both Keiki and Walea had covered for Noelani a couple of times in the past. This time Keiki was available and she agreed to perform. As usual, she was amazing. Had the male guests eating right out of her hand. In fact, the tip jar almost wasn't big enough; it overflowed with ten and twenty-dollar bills."

"Sounds like a profitable evening for her," I said.

"Therein lay the problem. The crew and the entertainers normally split the money in the tip jar. You might remember one of my crew, Timmy Soong, from your snorkel cruise. Since Keiki wasn't a regular, he said she didn't deserve as big of a share of the tips. She claimed the jar was full because of her performance. The two of them got into a huge argument. One minute she was yelling at him; the next minute he was shouting at her. From the water."

My eyes widened. "He fell in?"

"She pushed him in. That girl was in great shape." He looked off to the distance and smiled.

Interesting.

The server chose that moment to bring our orders. I was attempting to be good so I'd only ordered the *small* stack of macadamia-nut pancakes. It would be back to boring bran flakes soon enough. Steve dug into his bacon-and-cheese omelet and for a few minutes, we were content eating our excellent entrees.

"So then what happened?" I asked.

"The guys and I pulled Timmy out of the water. Rick, one of the musicians, and Rafe, the other member of my crew, thought it was hilarious. The more they ribbed Timmy, the madder he got. I finally pulled him aside and told him to dry off and cool off. I grabbed some extra cash from my wallet and gave it to Keiki. I figured that was the end of that. As the guys walked away from the boat, their conversation drifted up to us. Timmy yelled a parting remark."

"What did he say?" I asked, stabbing a piece of pancake with my fork.

"You gonna die, bitch."

CHAPTER TWENTY-ONE

My hand shook and my pancake flipped on to the table. "Do you think Timmy killed Keiki? Over something so petty?"

"I didn't even remember the incident until they arrested Regan. But now that the police have definitely declared it was murder, I wonder."

"How did Keiki respond to Timmy's threat?"

"She was real shook up. I didn't want her walking back to her car alone and thought she might like some company. We ended up going over to Hugo's Hula bar and had a couple of drinks. At the bar, she explained that she'd dated Timmy's younger brother for a few years then suddenly ended it two months ago."

"Regan mentioned something about Keiki dumping her former boyfriend and then him tragically dying. Did Keiki say why she broke up with him?"

Steve shrugged. "She didn't elaborate. Said it wasn't meant to be. That it wasn't," he made air quotes, "the direction she intended to go. She had bigger plans."

"Do you think those plans had anything to do with her murder?"

Steve's face paled beneath his tan. "At the time, I didn't give much thought to her comment. Keiki was an attractive woman and she seemed driven. I don't know if she wanted fame, fortune or both. I guess being one of the most gorgeous dancers around wasn't enough for her."

I narrowed my eyes. "Were you interested in Keiki?"

Steve's eyes clouded over, and he appeared distracted for a moment. "Let's say I wasn't completely immune to her charms and leave it at that."

Then he smiled. "Of course, that was before my best friend's little sis stumbled into my life."

I felt my cheeks turning the color of the koi that swam past at that moment. I could swear it winked. Was it just me or did the supersized goldfish also think something fishy was going on?

"Now that the police have confirmed Keiki was murdered, are you going to tell them about Timmy's comment?"

He frowned. "I'm hesitant to talk to them without discussing it with him first. These local kids have a hard enough time making a living. I don't want to do anything that would get him in trouble with the authorities. Timmy's had a tough time this past month dealing with his younger brother's death."

"I understand, but I hate to think of Regan sitting in jail if Timmy had anything to do with Keiki's murder."

"You know, it could have just been talk. Young guys sometimes think they need to put up a macho front when they're around their friends."

"I suppose everyone lets something slip now and then." I recalled some of the maternal comments I'd made over the years. "I might have threatened my children once or twice with a fate worse than death. Like no TV."

"See, it could be nothing." He rubbed his jaw for a minute. "Although that night at the Hula bar, Keiki mentioned a possible stalker. She was positive her car had been tailed a few times."

Now that was interesting. A potential stalker could be a potential suspect.

"Hey, I have a terrific idea." Steve's smile was so infectious the women at the next table seemed to brighten. "Why don't you join us for the sunset sail tonight? You're really good at drawing people out. I'm sure you could find a tactful way to question Timmy. He's not the chattiest guy around, but he would probably respond far better to your questions than to being grilled by his boss."

I wasn't convinced of my ability to draw Timmy out, but, with Regan in jail, I would talk to anyone with information about Keiki's murder. It was the least I could do for my sister-in-law. I pulled out my phone and checked my calendar to see if Liz had made plans for the group that evening.

"Evidently the honeymooners decided to spend a night alone. Should I ask Stan and Mother to join us?"

"We're fully booked so there won't be any extra seats for them." Steve reached out and placed his slightly calloused palm on top of mine. "Besides, once you're done talking to Timmy, you and I can spend some time together. We'll finally have an opportunity to get to know each other better, without being surrounded by your family and friends. What do you say?"

The more important question was what would Tom Hunter say? My inner Laurel warned me to stay far away from bronzed sea captains with bewitching blue eyes.

I told her to mind her own business. I had a date to watch the sun set over the Pacific.

* * *

Four hours later, I sat at a different table in the same restaurant with Mother and Stan, discussing my upcoming boating expedition. The tropical koi swam past our table, their colors so vivid and bright, I almost needed sunglasses to reduce the glare.

"So you and the sea captain are hooking up tonight, huh?" Stan wiggled his brows.

"There will be no hooking up." I scrunched my nose at his comment. "At least for me. I'm only going on board to talk to Timmy from the *Sea Jinx* crew."

My mother dropped today's edition of the local newspaper next to my plate. An unflattering photo of Regan stared back at me from the front page. "I think it's an excellent idea. We need to help free Regan. And soon. This kind of publicity," she scowled and pointed at the paper, "isn't going to help their restaurant one bit. She might even lose her job."

And her freedom, I thought, staring at the black-and-white photo of my sister-in-law.

The article was relatively brief, mentioning only that the Hawaii police had arrested Regan for Keiki's murder, and that she and my brother owned Daiquiri Dave's Lounge, where the victim had also worked.

"I think Steve is right, Laurel. You're easy to talk to, and you never know what you can learn from questioning Timmy," Mother said. "Plus Steve is a nice guy. Handsome, personable, and he owns his own boat."

Stan nodded his agreement. "A man with a boat—the ideal man. Well, he would be if he swam in the other direction."

"So you haven't met any hunky Hawaiian hotties yet?" I asked him.

"The day is young." He looked at his watch. "And in five hours I have a lesson with some Samoan dancers."

"How did you wangle that?"

"Your brother gave me Walea's number, and I called her. She was a little reticent at first, but I overwhelmed her with my charm and she referred me to these guys."

"Will she be there?"

"Nah, she and her husband are performing somewhere tonight. She told me I'm a natural though."

Walea was right on one count. Stan was a natural. But of what, was the question?

"Did she say anything about her sister?" I asked.

He nodded. "She said she was glad the police discovered Keiki's killer so quickly."

"Was she surprised about Regan's arrest?"

He shrugged. "If she was, she didn't mention it to me. She said she was grateful justice had been served, and her family could go on with their lives."

"I can sympathize with Walea, and I feel terrible about her loss," Mother said, "but if we don't find the killer soon, I'm not sure how my son and daughter-in-law will go on with *their* lives."

CHAPTER TWENTY-TWO

When I arrived at the boat that evening, I learned that Walea was substituting for the *Sea Jinx's* principal performer, Noelani, who was sick once again. On a positive note, Noelani was overjoyed to learn her twenty-four-hour flu bug was in reality twenty-four-hour morning sickness.

I was thrilled at the opportunity to see Walea. Keiki's sister might think the killer was behind bars, but I needed to prove otherwise. My empathetic manner would hopefully encourage her to confide in me. Between Walea and Timmy, I could discover some useful facts to help our amateur investigation.

My focus tonight would be 100% on detecting. No distractions whatsoever, not even hunky blue-eyed ones.

Even though I was looking forward to talking with Walea, I should have guessed she wouldn't be happy to see me. Walea and Henry arrived a few minutes after I did, about fifteen minutes before the passengers were to board. She and her husband sent identical glares in my direction. Fortunately, I was standing next to Amanda. The naturalist's bubbly personality could coax a smile out of Jaws.

Amanda threw her arms around Walea as she offered condolences. "Honey, how are you doing? I was so sorry to hear about Keiki."

"*Mahalo*, Amanda. We are still in shock." Walea practically spat at me as she cried out. "What are you doing here? Hasn't your family brought enough pain to mine?"

I took a step back. So maybe Walea *wasn't* in the mood for condolences from me. Amanda took Walea's arm, guiding her to the other side of the *Sea Jinx*. Henry joined Rick in the bow of the boat where the young musician tuned his guitar. I recognized Rick from Liz's reception. The young man's muscular biceps boasted dragon tattoos curling down and around each elbow. As his arm moved up and down so did the dragon's colorful tail.

Walea and Amanda chatted briefly then Amanda left to welcome the passengers. The dancer walked down the stairs leading to the lower deck, her garment bag and flowered tote in her hands.

I followed her down, figuring this might be my only opportunity to speak with Walea in private before she began her performance.

"Can I help you with anything?" I asked.

Her full lips curled in disgust. "What kind of help can you provide?"

She turned away and began pulling assorted items from her oversized bag.

I moved closer. "You can't honestly believe Regan killed your sister."

Walea grabbed a coconut bra out of the enormous tote and flung it at me. I ducked as the hard brown shells narrowly missed my head. The dancer could have doubled as a pitcher for the San Francisco Giants. The bra bounced off a beam then clattered to the floor.

I picked up the apparel-turned-assault weapon, debating if it was safe to return the item to the owner. Since dancing would be somewhat awkward without the upper half of her costume, I reluctantly handed it back to her.

Walea's passionate outburst was short-lived. Her plump body seemed to droop along with her spirit. She muttered a soft *mahalo*. Tears ran down her plain, sorrowful face.

"I apologize," she said. "My family's tragedy is not your problem. I am only mad at myself for talking your brother into hiring Keiki. I thought a steady job and paycheck might keep my little sister out of trouble. But trouble always managed to find her."

"Beautiful women are frequently magnets for trouble," I responded. "And for men."

She nodded in agreement. "Men looked at Keiki like she was their last meal. No matter where we went, they devoured her with their eyes. Once she realized her power over men, especially *haoles*, it turned into a quest for her."

"A quest for money?" I ventured.

She shrugged, the movement fluffing her mahogany mane around her shoulders. "Money, trinkets, power. Whatever she could squeeze out of them. Sometimes I think Keiki did it for the thrill of the chase. Reel in a big fish, gut him, then drop him back in the ocean."

"Someone mentioned she was your stepsister?"

"My father met her mother, Kiana, eight years ago when Keiki was fourteen." Walea gracefully donned her grass skirt then modestly removed her capris. "Kiana worked at the same coffee farm as my father before he moved to Koffee Land. The coconut didn't fall far from the tree when it came to those two women. Kiana went after my father with no holds barred. He left my mother and in less than a year, he and Kiana married. I had a new stepmother and stepsister."

"I can sympathize. My ex-husband left me three years ago for one of his clients. It's tough, especially on the kids."

"It was horrible. My mother fell into a depression so there was no one to watch over my three little brothers but me." A flash of anger surfaced and flared in her eyes. "I hated Kiana for taking my father away from us."

"How did you and Keiki get along?"

"Growing up with three brothers, I always longed for a little sister. All of a sudden, I had one. Whether I wanted her or not." She laughed, but it was a harsh mirthless sound. "Then I discovered if I hung out with Keiki, there were boys surrounding me. For the first time ever. They might have been her cast-offs, but they were good enough for me."

Interesting family dynamic. Was Walea's husband one of Keiki's so-called "cast offs?"

The man in question suddenly ran down the stairs. He frowned when he noticed us together. In an icy voice, his acne-scarred chin almost touching mine, Henry told me to "Stay away from my wife."

I stepped back, relieved when Steve called for me from above deck. I darted up the steps to find a very anxious sea captain holding a tablecloth in his hand. Steve and the crew had waited to cast off because both Timmy and the regular bartender were late. Timmy had finally shown up, but the bartender had called to say his car had been rear-ended.

Before I knew it, I was serving drinks and yummy pupus while maneuvering between passengers who jumped from their seats every time Amanda spotted a whale. At the rate she kept pointing out marine mammals, it looked like the humpbacks were enjoying far more romance on *their* Hawaiian vacation than I was on mine.

Steve had talked me into wearing a makeshift sarong. I wasn't certain the blue-flowered tablecloth that had morphed into a flowing Hawaiian garment was necessary, but it made me feel somewhat exotic.

"All I'm missing is a flower," I complained to Steve as I pointed to the yellow hibiscus clipped over Amanda's ear.

Steve smiled and grabbed a tiny orchid from the bar supply. He tucked it behind my ear, apologized for putting me to work, and told me I was the most beautiful woman on board the boat.

I'm such a sucker for a compliment, especially when an azure-eyed Adonis is the one whispering it in my ear.

My previous boating experiences consisted of me sitting on my butt and watching the shoreline. Balancing a tray of drinks on deck was like roller-skating on a surfboard. I assumed I'd eventually acclimate to the boat's movement, but as the shoreline receded, the choppiness increased. My primary goal was to avoid dumping mai tais or daiquiris on the passengers. So far, I'd limited my spills to my own washable garment.

I'd begun to wonder if I would ever get an opportunity to talk to Timmy when Steve announced the evening's entertainment would begin.

A reprieve at last. After promising one Australian matey I would return with refills once the show ended, I set my tray on the bar and told Amanda I was going below deck to talk to Timmy.

The boat rocked and I teetered on the stairs, grabbing hold of the railing. I finally spied Timmy in the corner, his dark head bent over a small bench. Noise from the ship's engine must have muffled my footsteps. When I tapped him on the shoulder, he spun around faster than a whirling dervish on speed.

One muscular arm wrapped around my neck, squeezing off my windpipe. His hot breath burned the hairs on my nape. Choking, I struggled to push his arm away, but I stopped when I felt the prick of something sharp pressed against my tender skin.

CHAPTER TWENTY-THREE

My body shook with fear and my trembling became so violent, my sarong threatened to slip from R-rated territory into an X-rated tell-all.

"Sorry. You kine spook me." Timmy removed his arm from my neck and slipped the Swiss army knife back into his pocket. "Why you not upstairs?"

I gathered a large breath to calm myself down then let it out. Bad idea. Remind me not to wear a garment secured by only one knot the next time I'm assaulted from behind. I snatched the top of my sarong with both hands and hitched it up to its original PG version.

"I wanted to talk to you," I said. "Is this a bad time?"

Timmy turned his back to me. He shoved a brown paper-wrapped parcel into a canvas knapsack. He threw the bag into a small storage locker, attached a silver padlock to the door and clicked it shut.

He swung around, a tiny crescent-shaped scar on his cheekbone flashing white under his angry gaze.

"Fo' what you want with me?"

I wanted answers. Lots of them. If only I could think of questions that wouldn't upset this intimidating young man. I knew our time alone together was limited so I decided to barge ahead.

"I understand you knew Keiki, the girl found dead near Daiquiri Dave's Lounge."

"Yeah, so. She popular girl." He smirked. "Lotsa guys knew that one."

So I was finding out. I just hoped my brother wasn't a member of Keiki's fan club.

"I'm only interested in one guy. Your brother. I heard Keiki used to date him."

Timmy's face darkened and his hands balled into fists. "Ya, dat bitch, she use him den dump him."

"Used him how?"

"She had dis *"lolo"* crazy idea for making dem both rich. She ask him..." Timmy abruptly stopped.

"Ask him what?"

"Nuttin. At least nuttin to do with her dyin." He raised his voice and shook his fist in the air. "I know she da reason my bruddah kill hisself."

"You don't think it was an accident?"

Timmy stuck his nose so close to mine I could see the two lone hairs he'd missed when he'd shaved his chin. "My bruddah, he good kid. Careful about his work. Maybe it was accident. But maybe Joey kill hisself cause of dat no good *wahine*. It none of your business, so don't go poking your nose where it don't belong."

Footsteps pounded down the stairs. Amanda motioned at us. "It's getting rougher out. We need both of you up here."

I'd been so distracted by our conversation I hadn't even noticed the ship pitching more than ever. I tightened my sarong and followed Timmy as he raced up the stairs. Earlier the clouds had provided a postcard photo opportunity. Now they dumped rain by the boatload.

Amanda shoved a pile of orange life vests at me. "Here. Pass these out to the passengers. Be careful not to scare them. Tell them it's merely a safety measure."

Fine. I had no problem reassuring the passengers. But who was going to reassure *me*?

Amanda and Walea covered one side of the boat and I took the other. Once they finished, the two women urged the passengers to follow them below deck. I handed out my last orange vest then realized I'd been so generous passing life jackets to the passengers that I'd neglected to don one myself.

I looked around and thought I saw Steve running down the stairs to the lower deck but it was difficult to tell with the driving rain. Someone better be piloting this boat. Maybe Rafe had taken over for him. Farther up on the starboard side, I noticed Timmy bending over some type of storage chest. I hustled over and tapped him on his shoulder.

I had to scream above the roaring wind to make myself heard. "Where are the other life jackets located?" He scowled but pointed toward the rear of the boat, so I scurried in that direction.

By now, my sarong felt like a wet shower curtain was plastered to my skin. The straps of my sandals irritated my bunions so I slipped them off and tucked them under a seat. It would be more comfortable moving around the boat without them. A few seconds later, my bare feet slipped on the wet deck. Comfort came at a price. I inched my way across the slippery surface with a death grip on the railing.

How quickly this romantic sunset sail had morphed into a nightmare journey. The lights from the hotels and condominiums lining the shoreline were barely visible through the king-size sheets of rain.

I stumbled on a thick coil of rope and caught myself before I landed on all fours. Whew. That was close. I'd better find those vests and get below to safety.

The remaining orange jackets hung on a couple of hooks. I sidled over and grabbed one for myself. Getting the vest closed over my double D's was a struggle. Someone needed to manufacture a version for the full-figured woman. I finally secured both fasteners and let out a sigh of relief.

I heard a muffled noise behind me just as I grabbed the other two vests. Suddenly I was knocked into the ship's railing. I released my hold on one of the life jackets and tried to grasp onto the slick metal rail.

The boat pitched and I felt another jolt.

Then I was airborne.

CHAPTER TWENTY-FOUR

I hit the ocean with a cannonball splash. Water flew everywhere, including into my nose and mouth.

"Blech." I spewed out a magnum's worth of seawater. I would need a daiquiri the size of a Big Gulp to wash that salty taste away. Good thing I was wearing the life jacket, which kept my tablecloth sarong from slipping off and floating away. Not that it mattered. It was far more likely a shark would turn me into a sushi appetizer than I'd get arrested for indecent exposure.

I stared at the distant lights. Although they were probably only a few miles away, it could have been a few thousand as far as I was concerned. The odds of me successfully paddling to shore were slimmer than of me winning an Olympic gold medal. I yelled until my vocal cords refused to participate, but the *Sea Jinx* continued to recede in the distance. No one would hear me now.

Which made me wonder—did anyone see me go overboard?

My stomach lurched. Not from the churning waves, but from the terrifying question—how did I end up in the ocean? Did a heavy gust knock me over the railing? Or did someone push me?

An important question that needed an answer. But it would have to wait until I resolved the more pressing issue.

How the heck would I get back to shore?

The *Sea Jinx* continued to motor toward the bay and away from me. The only people who might notice my absence were Steve, who was undoubtedly intent on getting his passengers safely back to the pier, and the tipsy Australian whom I'd promised a Mai Tai refill.

My face felt wet from the salt water splashing my chin, combined with the salty tears rolling down my cheeks. I wiped my eyes with my damp fist. This was no time to feel sorry for myself.

If only I had my cell with me. I could have used my iPhone to call for help and the GPS to find my way. And maybe I'd finally have time to finish the e-book I was reading while I waited for help to arrive.

I shook my soggy curls. The salt air must have invaded my brain. I clasped my hands together and prayed to whichever Hawaiian god could turn off this massive spigot of rain.

I wasn't sure if any of the local gods heard my plea, but the rain halted as abruptly as it had begun. The ominous storm clouds shifted apart and a brilliant full moon shone upon the dark water. The man in the moon had never looked so appealing.

A faint noise caught my attention. I squinted and spotted what looked like a small boat heading in my direction. Hallelujah.

I would be rescued in minutes. Unless—

Suddenly I realized the boat aimed directly at me. I waved my arms back and forth and shrieked louder than a stadium full of Justin Bieber fans. Within seconds, the roar of the motor ratcheted down to a purr.

The lights on the twenty-foot vessel blasted me in the face and I screamed again. The boat shuddered and stopped less than six feet away.

I heard someone yell, "Man overboard."

Technically, he was wrong, but this didn't seem the time to go all *women's lib* on him.

"Help," I yelled. I paddled and thrashed my way to safety. No one would ever compare me to Michael Phelps, but I reached the side of the boat without anyone having to dive in and rescue me.

A long hairy arm reached out. I grabbed on to a calloused palm and gratefully let its owner yank me into the boat. Unfortunately, he wasn't completely successful in his mission.

Maybe it was time to lay off those cream-filled *malasadas*.

With my torso stretched across the interior of the boat and my legs dangling over the side, the men decided more assistance was in order. They each grabbed one of my arms and successfully hauled me aboard.

Not a minute too soon. The sound of an enormous fish bouncing its snout against the side of the boat startled us. I stared as the grandson of Jaws displayed a set of teeth that would have scared my dentist into retirement. He flipped his sleek body around, and with one last flick of his fin against our boat, swam away.

I lost it. I stuck my head over the side of the boat and heaved everything I'd consumed that day. Including those macadamia nut pancakes.

One of the men handed me a handkerchief from his shorts pocket. "You are one lucky *wahine*."

I threw him a weak smile as I wiped my face. "I'm luckier than I was a few minutes ago. You saved my life."

"Probably. You were this close to being that fella's dinner." His wizened face cracked into what probably represented a smile for him. He reached into a small cabinet and handed me a thin blanket. "Here. The water temp isn't that cold, but we don't want you going into shock."

I was already shivering so I gratefully wrapped the wool blanket around my sodden body.

My other rescuer started the engine and we headed toward the pier.

"By the way, my name is Glenn Hakanson," said the man sitting next to me. He pointed to the gray-bearded man at the wheel. "And that's Phil. Now who are you and how in the blazes did you end up in the ocean?"

CHAPTER TWENTY-FIVE

I couldn't believe how lucky I was to run into the fishermen before they ran into me. It turned out that Glenn and Phil had been so successful hooking a big fish that they'd stayed out later than usual and then got caught in the sudden storm. I not only bonded with the men but also with their other chunky passenger. The dead tuna glared at me as if he held me personally responsible for Glenn and Phil turning him into someone's ahi dinner.

As we motored toward the pier, I noticed a large boat that looked a lot like the *Sea Jinx* heading in our direction. Someone must have noticed my absence after all. Glenn got on the radio and within a few minutes, he'd connected with Steve. They decided the fishermen would deliver me directly to the pier, which they considered a safer option than handing me off at sea. I was in favor of anything that lessened the odds of me landing in the ocean again.

We arrived at the Kailua Pier shortly after the *Sea Jinx* docked. Several Hawaii fire department vehicles were parked in the loading and unloading area. Although it was reassuring to know they'd noticed my absence, I still questioned if someone intentionally pushed me overboard. If Phil and Glenn hadn't come along when they did, my shark-mangled body parts might not have been discovered until they rolled in with the surf.

Glenn tied up his boat, the aptly named *Survivor*, at the dock. He and Phil helped me climb up onto the pier. The Sea Jinx passengers were disembarking, some of them looking a lot greener than when

95

they'd first boarded. As we drew closer, I spotted Timmy among the departing tourists. I shouted his name. Timmy turned and his eyebrows rose to his hairline when he saw me. He ran off and disappeared behind the ticket building.

At the sound of my voice, Steve looked up, his expression confused. When he recognized the curly-haired woman dressed like a soggy burrito, he dodged around the passengers and ran toward the three of us. Steve scooped me up in a hug and spun me around the dock.

When he finally put me down, he kept my still-trembling hand gripped in his large comforting one. "I was so worried about you. What happened?"

Members of the Search and Rescue team joined us. "Are you okay, Miss? Do you need to go to the hospital? We can get you there in a flash."

I shook my head and droplets of water spewed everywhere, making me feel as attractive as a wet dog. Between my salt-water dunking and over-the-side stomach cleansing, I looked and smelled worse than a sodden Schnauzer.

"I'm fine." No sooner had I uttered those words then I sneezed three times.

"You should get checked out." One of the men eyed me up and down. "Did you hurt yourself when you fell in?"

My eyebrows drew together as I frowned at him. "I didn't *fall* in. I was pushed."

Steve dropped my hand. "Pushed? What makes you say that? I assumed you slipped on the deck and fell overboard."

"Nope, I was definitely pu…" I hesitated and thought back to those moments before I ended up in the ocean. "Well, I think someone pushed me. It's all kind of a blur now."

"You've had quite a scare," said one of the rescue workers. "It might be a few days before you remember what actually happened."

"You're lucky these fishermen found you," his partner added. "It could have taken us hours to locate you. There are some mighty unfriendly creatures in the ocean."

As far as I was concerned, there were *unfriendly* creatures on Steve's boat. Although I'd have to admit I'm not the most graceful person in the world. A big gust could have blown me overboard.

But if that was the case, why did Timmy run away when he spotted me?

The rescue personnel walked away to update the Coast Guard on my safe return. I spun around and scanned the pier. Most of the passengers had dispersed, but the crew and entertainers should still be around.

"Have you seen Walea and Henry?" I asked Steve.

"I think they're packing up their stuff. Do you want to talk to them now?" he asked. "Don't you want to get back to the hotel and get cleaned up?"

Hmmm. Not too subtle. I guess my *eau de ahi* scent wasn't exactly a man magnet. I noticed Walea and Henry walking down the gangway. Her hands moved rapidly as she spoke, although not in the graceful style she used when she performed. It looked like they were arguing.

I broke away from Steve and ran toward the couple, huffing as I drew closer. My few minutes thrashing in the ocean must have depleted my oxygen supply.

"Walea," I yelled, hoping to catch them before they disappeared.

She dropped her garment bag and stared at me as if I was a ghostly apparition.

Did Walea or Henry push me overboard? If so, they'd be better off facing a ghost than the wrath of Laurel McKay.

CHAPTER TWENTY-SIX

"You're alive," Walea cried out.

"You seem surprised." I wrapped the blanket tighter around my shoulders as my eyes shifted from Walea to her husband. Henry set his ukulele case on the dock, pulled out a cigarette and lit it. Despite his calm demeanor, his hand trembled as he shoved the lighter back in his shirt pocket.

"You should go back to your hotel. You could catch cold." Walea picked up her oversized tote and nudged Henry with her elbow. He grabbed his instrument, and the couple headed toward the parking lot conversing in hushed tones. Was it my sashimi scent that sent them away? Or the surprise of seeing me alive again?

It was too bad my son wasn't here. His selective bionic hearing would come in handy since my own ears felt plugged with salt water. Someone screeched my name, and I turned back to the boat.

Amanda raced down the gangway and threw her arms around me. "We were so worried," she trilled. Evidently someone who studies marine life isn't put off by someone who smells like it.

I later learned that Rafe had heard a splash and thought he saw someone in the water, but by then the boat had moved on. He went below to see if any passengers were missing and it dawned on Amanda that I was nowhere around. When they couldn't locate me, Steve realized I must have fallen overboard and called 911. He'd immediately turned the boat around to search for me.

Amanda gave me one more hug then took off. The rescue team again offered to drive me to the hospital but I declined. I've never met a hospital that didn't have a predilection for sticking pointed objects into their patients. After coming within inches of turning into a shark shish-ka-bob, the last thing I needed was to have a gaggle of nurses and doctors poking and prodding at my waterlogged body.

I heard someone calling my name and turned to see Stan scurrying toward us. I smiled at my friend as he rushed across the dock toward Steve and me. I'd forgotten that he'd offered to pick me up since his dance lesson was scheduled to end about the time the *Sea Jinx* docked.

Stan halted a few feet away, his nose twitching as if he'd discovered a bushel of overripe bananas. "You look like something the cat dragged in."

"You're close. But it's more like something the boat dragged in. I fell overboard."

"OMG. Sweetie, you could have drowned."

Yeah, I could have been annihilated in a variety of ways.

"She had a close call," Steve said. "But Laurel's a real trooper." He grabbed my hand as the three of us headed toward the parking lot. Stan discreetly walked ahead. Although it would have been more subtle if he hadn't been humming, "Can You Feel the Love Tonight."

All I could concentrate on was returning to the hotel to a hot bath and a cup of hot tea. And my mommy. No matter how old you are, or how many children you've birthed, there's nothing like having your own mother pamper you after a bad day.

Especially if your day involved someone possibly trying to kill you.

Steve apparently had his own ideas of how to perk up a waterlogged woman. As we reached the ticket building, he pulled me into the shadows. I immediately tensed, but my tension disappeared when he planted a sweet kiss on my lips. My blanket fell to the ground as Steve wrapped muscular arms around me and drew me close. With the blanket no longer draped around me, Steve's hard-as-a-rock body nestled against my wet, covered-with-a thin tablecloth curves.

The *Sea Jinx* captain definitely knew how to make a woman perk up.

* * *

With Steve's heated good-bye kiss coursing through every vibrating nerve in my body, my brain shifted into overdrive on the ride home. I leaned back in the passenger seat and contemplated the surprise kiss as well as my near-death experience.

Since Stan doesn't agree with the philosophy that silence is golden, he interrupted my reverie the minute we reached the highway.

He turned to face me. "Okay, give."

"Hey, watch the road." Why do so many drivers feel the need to make eye contact with their passengers when they converse? Hadn't Stan noticed all the flowers in front of memorials lining both sides of the Queen Kaahumanu Highway?

He pulled his gaze back to the road. "So what exactly happened? I want to know everything. Right up to that smooch Steve planted on you."

Can't put much past my pal.

I relayed the events of the evening beginning with my conversations with both Walea and Timmy and ending with my sudden dunking and subsequent rescue.

Stan shuddered. "Gosh, you are one lucky woman."

"Or one unlucky woman," I muttered.

"Are you certain someone pushed you?"

"I can't be one hundred percent positive." I tried to remember what happened on the boat before I landed in the water, but all I could recall was my harrowing time floundering in the ocean.

"Did anyone act suspicious when you reappeared?" Stan asked, shifting into investigative mode.

I thought about it. "Walea looked startled to see me, but she was below deck with Amanda and the passengers when it happened, so she couldn't have pushed me. Henry seemed nervous when I turned up. I have no idea where he was when I went overboard. And Timmy bolted the second we made eye contact."

Stan's head swiveled ninety degrees as he stared at me.

"Eyes on the road," I said.

He returned his gaze to the highway, which thankfully wasn't as busy as it normally is. "What do you mean Timmy ran away?" he asked.

"After I climbed up on the dock, I noticed Timmy walking away with the passengers. When I called out his name he took off. That's when Steve and the rescue guys spotted me. They raced over and asked a zillion questions. When you showed up, I forgot to mention Timmy's weird behavior to Steve."

"You need to tell the police. First, Timmy threatened Keiki a few days before her death. Then he warned you to back off. Minutes later you were fighting for your life."

"Yeah." I shivered remembering my brief terrifying stint in the ocean. "But Henry could have pushed me in as well. Shoot, one of the tourists might have come upstairs in search of a cocktail refill, accidentally bumped into me and been afraid to admit it."

"Speaking of Henry and Walea, you haven't asked me about my dance lesson," Stan said.

No, I'd been too caught up reminiscing how I'd almost died an hour earlier.

"So how was it? You still have your hair and limbs so I gather sword and fire dancing weren't on the agenda."

"Ha ha. Wait until you see what I can do with a fire baton."

Oh, dear. I could only imagine, but I held my tongue. "I'm glad you had a good time."

"Hey, it wasn't just fun and games. Don't forget I was operating undercover."

I wasn't certain how my slightly-built fair-haired friend could run a covert ops among the huge Samoan dancers, but I went along with his delusional detecting daydreams.

"Learn anything helpful?"

He nodded but kept his eyes front and center. "Just call me Magnum PI. I told the guys what a tough vacation this had been for our group, what with Keiki's death and Regan's arrest. It didn't take long for me to learn that her former boyfriend took it hard when Keiki dumped him."

"I discovered her boyfriend was Timmy's brother," I said. "He seemed really angry toward Keiki. Thinks his brother committed suicide because of her. That his death wasn't an accident."

"According to the troupe, Joey was a terrific dancer. He and Keiki started dating a few years ago. They performed together quite a bit when they were a pair."

"Did she date any of the other guys in the troupe?"

"Not that they mentioned, but she could have. These guys are buff-o! When they get oiled up…" Stan paused. "Oh, well, a guy can dream, can't he?"

"Never stop dreaming," I replied, ever the optimist. Someday Stan would find his Mr. Right. "Did anyone mention any other potential suspects?"

"Supposedly Keiki told Joey she was now seeing an older man. A guy who could provide her with the lifestyle she felt she deserved. Joey was so upset he told his pals he followed Keiki's car a couple of times, wanting to find out who'd replaced him."

"Joey followed Keiki?" Could he have been the possible stalker Keiki had mentioned to Steve? "Did Joey see who she was meeting?"

Stan nodded.

"Wonderful. You did some great investigating. Was it anyone we might know?"

Stan's hands clenched on the steering wheel, but he kept his eyes on the road as he shared the new information.

"Your brother."

CHAPTER TWENTY-SEVEN

Stan delivered my bedraggled body directly to my hotel room, where my mother ministered to my every need. Nothing tops a warm bath and room service, consisting of a cheeseburger, onion rings and chocolate cheesecake, to assist in a near-drowning recovery process. You couldn't ask for more, although even after I devoured the food on all three plates, I still tasted the lingering kiss Steve and I had shared.

When I awoke the next morning, my muscles felt stiff and sore. Black, blue and purple spots speckled my body like a Jackson Pollock painting.

After the previous night's experience, it was nice to receive some positive news for a change. Dave called to tell us the police were releasing Regan. He had no idea if they needed more evidence to pursue a case against her or if the detectives uncovered another suspect. I was thrilled she would be free.

I had almost as many questions bouncing around my overactive brain as I had black-and-blue marks on my body. Questions for both Regan and my brother. Especially after Stan's revelation about Joey spying Dave and Keiki together on several occasions. Did those encounters have anything to do with her murder? Just because Joey spotted Dave and Keiki at locations outside of the restaurant didn't automatically make Dave the mystery man she was dating.

Tonight I would get Dave alone, no matter what it took, and find out the true relationship between him and the dancer. And hopefully find out more about Keiki's stepsister and brother-in-law. Someone was hiding something, and I had the bruises from last night's deep-sea plunge to show for it.

Regan and Dave arrived at the hotel minutes before we departed for the spa. Liz took one look at Regan's wan make-up free face and dispirited demeanor, and insisted she join us. Regan protested at first but I talked her into it. This could be the perfect opportunity to have some alone time with my sister-in-law.

As a spa owner, Liz had negotiated a discount on treatments for all the girls. And Stan.

Liz had signed me up for a seaweed wrap. She claimed the sea kelp that covered me from my forehead to my toes, would remove all the toxins from my body. Considering how much alcohol, chocolate-covered macadamia nuts and onion rings I'd consumed on this trip, my body could officially be classified as a toxic waste site.

Although the dark green mixture didn't smell horrible, the seaweed paste reminded me of last night's involuntary swim. It would have been nice if someone had warned me in advance that the staff member responsible for coating every inch of my curves would *not* be a female.

There I was, practically naked as a pelican, tiny strips of thin paper barely covering my lady parts, when Paoli, the young Hawaiian masseur walked into the room.

He flashed me a grin and told me to relax.

Ninety-nine percent of my body lay exposed and he wanted me to relax?

I gritted my teeth and once Paoli slathered my body with the seaweed mixture and cocooned me in a light wrap, I finally did relax. For a minute. He turned on some New Age music and left me alone with my thoughts.

There is nothing like a dark room, soothing music and no distractions to send my brain zooming in every direction. Even though the police had released Regan, she could still end up spending the rest of her life behind bars. I needed to learn what kind of evidence they had on her, and anything else she knew about Keiki's relationship with my brother.

What better time than now when she couldn't escape my slimy clutches?

I sat up and immediately felt woozy so I waited for my head to clear. Paoli had wrapped me tighter than a taquito. With some difficulty, I finally eased my left arm out first, followed by my right. Then I peeled the sticky wrap off my even stickier body. My pristine white terry cloth spa robe hung from a hook on the wall.

Seconds later, I sneaked out of my room, semi-camouflaged in my seaweed-spotted robe, flip-flops, towel turban, and glasses. The door squeaked but none of the spa staff loitered in the hallway. I sensed they would frown on clients disappearing mid-treatment.

My next dilemma—which closed door led to my sister-in-law?

Poking my head inside each room didn't seem like the best option. The last thing I wanted to do was walk in on a naked stranger. Or worse—a naked Stan. I'd hate to get Liz in hot water with the hotel when she had gone to so much trouble to provide a relaxing afternoon for everyone.

A clear plastic holder outside of each treatment room held a small piece of paper that listed the present occupant's name and schedule of appointments. I crept along the hallway peering inside the holders until I ran across Regan's name. I pushed open the door and slipped inside.

Regan lay on her stomach, her head resting on her hands, her long hair knotted on top of her head. Large black stones decorated her slender back. Liz must have signed Regan up for the hot lava rock massage, thinking it would provide the relaxation she needed after spending two days in the local jail. I imagined it would take more than a massage and some overheated stones to erase the memory of that experience.

I tiptoed inside and bumped my knee into a large tray stand. The magnifying mirror resting on the top tier teetered on the edge, but righted itself without crashing and leaving me with another seven years of bad luck.

At my last calculation, I was at 147 years worth and counting.

I eased around the table and bent over to check on Regan. If she was taking a well-deserved snooze, I'd leave.

Regan lunged at me. Hot rocks flew off the table as her hands closed around my neck.

"Hey, it's me, Laurel," I protested as loudly as someone being strangled can eke out.

Regan released her surprisingly strong grip. She grabbed the folds of the thin towel that covered her and sat up, her legs dangling over the side. With her wild eyes and frizzy auburn hair, she resembled a demented Raggedy Ann.

"Geez, Laurel, you almost gave me a heart attack," she lashed out at me. "What are you doing in my room?"

I grabbed a stool from the corner of the room and plopped down. "I thought this would be a good time to chat." I placed my hand on my chest hoping my heart palpitations would ease up. "Guess my timing could have been better."

"You think?" She tightened her grip on the blanket and glared. "I swear I can't tell if you and your friends are trying to help me or hurt me."

"Help you, of course." Now I was miffed. After all, I'd almost drowned playing detective on her behalf. "Why would you think otherwise?"

She sniffed. "It crossed my mind that one of you turned me in to the police. To protect your brother."

I was almost shocked speechless. Almost.

"We would never do that. Besides, the only thing Dave could be guilty of was negligence, and the police proved Keiki's fall wasn't an accident."

"What about his rendezvous with Keiki the night of the wedding reception?" Regan's dark eyes burned brighter than the hot rocks scattered around the room.

"Dave met with Keiki? At the restaurant?"

She nodded. "The night of the reception I overheard Keiki tell her sister she was meeting her lover later on. When we got to the condo, I told Dave I planned to take a sleeping pill. Instead, I stayed awake to see if he would sneak out to meet her."

These revelations were not relieving my heart palpitations. I breathed deeply as my mind analyzed this new information.

"Did you tell the police?"

"Of course not. I wouldn't do anything to implicate my husband. He may be guilty of adultery, but I can't imagine him as a murderer. Plus I didn't follow him. All I know is that he left the condo—," Her eyes saddened and for a minute she looked like a lost little girl. "I confessed to the police that Keiki and I had words, though."

"When was that?"

"That same night. After I left you, I decided to visit the ladies' room before I drove home. While I was in the stall, I overheard Walea and Keiki discuss her impending rendezvous with the boss that night. I stayed in the stall until they left."

"I'm so sorry." I patted her hand, not knowing how else to comfort her.

"I was devastated by her admission and it took me awhile to get a grip. And to dry off my tears. On my way out of the restroom, I bumped into Keiki. She wore this smug, self-satisfied smile on her face. I totally lost it and accused her of sleeping with Dave. Then I grabbed hold of her arm and shook her."

Regan removed her left arm from the towel and displayed several scabbed-over scratches. "That she-lion clawed me with those dagger-sharp fingernails of hers."

An energy-efficient light bulb flashed in my brain. "So that's why the medical examiner found your DNA under her nails."

Regan nodded. "I don't know if they believed me or not. No one witnessed it."

"What did Keiki say about Dave?"

"She laughed and didn't deny having an affair with him."

"I can't imagine you having the strength to push Keiki over the wall although—," I eyed the hands that attempted to choke me a few minutes earlier.

She held up her arm and flexed a bicep. "The coffee business is great for maintaining muscle tone. Even accountants have to pitch in sometimes and haul huge bags of beans."

Regan slid off the table. "It's just as well you interrupted me. I shouldn't waste time getting spa treatments. I need to get back to Koffee Land. Assuming I still have a job. I haven't spoken to Ritz or Pilar since the police carted me off to jail."

"Don't you think you deserve some R&R before you go back to work? Dave mentioned you've been putting in tons of overtime. He's not too happy about your long hours."

"Maybe not, but it sure didn't take him long to find a replacement for me." Her shoulders slumped and her thin towel slid down her waif-like body. "Dave doesn't get my devotion to my job. Your brother is a wonderful chef and he's terrific with customers. But when it comes to anything financial, the guy is clueless. We couldn't keep the restaurant going if it weren't for my salary."

"Maybe you can find a position that's less onerous, with lower pay, but far less hours."

"I can't leave them in the lurch now. Not with the television crew due on site this weekend. We're hoping once the show is on the air, the publicity will draw attention to Koffee Land and boost coffee sales. Plus Ritz has been very generous to me."

My eyebrows went up at that comment.

Regan put her palm against my back and shoved me in the direction of the door. "I have to get back to work. Trust me. The coffee business can get really complicated sometimes."

I was sure it could, but was anything more complex than murder?

CHAPTER TWENTY-EIGHT

I returned to my treatment room and climbed back on the massage table seconds before Paoli returned. He looked perplexed by the trail of goop spattered across the floor, but he said nothing and merely led me to the Vichy shower room. There I morphed from a Shrek lookalike to a drowned rat.

As far as I was concerned, the benefits of the seaweed wrap were not worth all the bother. Or the expense. From now on, the cheap aloe lotion I purchased at the dollar store would suffice as treatment for my toxic body and scaly skin.

After I showered, shampooed and blow-dried my hair, my next scheduled stop was the manicure station. The last few days had been so stressful, I'd chewed my nails down to their nubs, leaving little left to polish. I hoped the technician could work some mani-magic.

I left the spa and walked into the tranquil beige-on-beige-on-beige hair and nail salon. Liz sat in front of a young nail technician, babbling away. The manicurist filed my friend's nails without once looking up. When I slid into the chair next to Liz, I realized she was chatting on her cell, her ever-present Bluetooth jammed into her ear. My manicurist, who introduced herself as Rose, placed a bowl of warm water in front of me. She instructed me to soak my right hand then she picked up my left hand and began nipping at my torn cuticles.

"Bye, sweetie. Love you." Liz turned to me, her smile wide. "That was Brian."

No, duh.

"He called Tom to discuss that big murder trial your hunky detective has to testify at. The jury selection starts on Monday." She threw a quizzical look at me. "While they were talking, Brian brought up Keiki's murder. And the near drowning of Detective Hunter's girlfriend. Something Tom knew nothing about."

Shoot. I knew I'd forgotten something on my to-do list. Call my boyfriend back home and tell him someone tried to kill me.

"Ouch," I yelped as blood spurted from the cuticle Rose just snipped.

"Sorry. I distracted. You almost drown and don't call boyfriend?" She waved her manicure scissors at me. "Bet he no be happy with you."

Bet she be right. If there was one thing that annoyed Tom Hunter, it was my failure to disclose an almost fatal experience.

"I would have called him this morning if you hadn't insisted on dragging me down here," I accused Liz.

"Nice try," she replied. "How could you forget to call him? Or was it intentional? Maybe you didn't want to tell him about Steve." She tilted her bronze curls in my direction and winked.

"Who Steve?" asked Rose, indicating I should switch hands. "You got you new boyfriend?"

"No, I got no new boyfriend. I mean…" I sat there flummoxed as Rose snipped away at the ragged edges of my cuticles. I really didn't know what my heart or my libido desired. Anger surged through me as I realized none of this would have been an issue if Tom had prioritized me over his career. If we'd been enjoying our time on the island together, there would have been no distractions like the captain of the *Sea Jinx*.

My irritation with Tom disappeared as quickly as it surfaced. Realistically, the detective would always put me behind his career and his daughter. Maybe we were setting ourselves up for failure even before we started anything serious. Was I really attracted to Steve or merely flattered by his attention? Maybe I just felt lonely in paradise. Easily flattered and seduced.

Well, not seduced. Not yet anyway.

But my own situation made me realize how a lack of attention from Regan might have made it easier for Keiki to seduce my brother. What really happened during their rendezvous the night of the reception?

Even more important, what occurred afterward?

"I promise to call Tom," I said to Liz, "but first I need to get Dave alone."

"Another guy? You one busy miss," Rose remarked. Liz giggled while I explained that Dave was my brother and I needed to talk to him that evening.

"So, you have big plans for tonight? What color you like?" Rose pointed to a dazzling and confusing array of polishes.

I glanced at Liz as I pointed to a bottle of *Magnificent Mango Mama* polish. "Do we have plans this evening? What exactly is on the agenda for the rest of the week?"

"Tomorrow I scheduled a ride through the Waipi'o Valley. Doesn't that sound brilliant?"

"It depends what I'm riding. Does it have legs and eat hay?"

Liz shook her head and attempted to look mysterious. "It has wheels and guzzles gasoline."

Rose slapped her palm on the table, "Oh, you take ATV ride. Much fun. Kinda bumpy on trail though. You no mind bumpy ride?"

Are you kidding? That could be my theme song.

CHAPTER TWENTY-NINE

While Mother remained at the spa enjoying a pedicure and reflexology treatment, I returned to the room, delighted for the opportunity to have it to myself. Since the spa required that patrons turn off their cells, I first checked for messages. The second I hit the ON button, a series of text messages beeped on my screen.

"Are you okay?" That was the first text from Tom at eleven a.m.

"Please call me and let me know you're alright." Message two at noon.

"Call me ASAP." Message three at 1:06 p.m.

"What the hell is going on?" Number four at 2:10 p.m.

Not the most amorous of texts. Shakespeare sure didn't have to worry about any poetic competition from my homicide detective. It made me wonder if it was possible to enjoy a romantic relationship with a man who experienced the dark side of life on a daily basis. Was Tom concerned about me or merely annoyed with me?

I hit speed dial to return Tom's call. My heart thumped loudly while the phone rang. I anticipated my call would go straight to voicemail and was startled when his deep baritone came on the line.

"Laurel, it's about time you called."

Grrrr. "Aloha to you, too."

The phone went silent. I visualized him counting to ten before he responded. "Can you imagine what it's like to learn that your girlfriend almost drowned and she didn't bother to call you?"

That was better. He truly was worried about me. And he'd referred to me as his girlfriend. I grinned as I replied, "I know how busy you are. I didn't think you needed anything else on your plate. Two fishermen came to my rescue so everything is fine."

"Brian didn't give me the details so how the blazes did you end up in the ocean? That boat outfit sounds like a shoddy operation. I hope they compensated you for your ordeal."

"Oh, it wasn't Steve's fault someone shoved me overboard."

"Who the hell is Steve? And what do you mean someone 'shoved' you overboard?" The steel in Tom's voice meant he was back in investigator mode.

Here I was apologizing again, a situation that occurred far too frequently in our erratic relationship. I was a grown woman with a career and a family. I didn't need someone telling me what to do. Especially from 2,468 miles away.

"Steve is my brother's best friend and the owner and captain of the *Sea Jinx*," I replied in a voice that dripped stalagmite-sized icicles. "He's been a complete rock for Dave and his wife, and he's been nothing but kind and solicitous of me."

My cheeks flushed as I recalled that extremely solicitous kiss last night.

"If you say so." Tom sounded dubious, but his tone calmed down. "Why do you think someone pushed you overboard?"

I shared the details of Keiki's murder and Regan's subsequent arrest, as well as Timmy's death threat to Keiki and our conversation on board the boat.

By the time I'd finished, the sound of Tom's fingers drumming on the top of his desk was loud enough to provide a backdrop for an entire dance troupe.

"Honestly, I've never met anyone who was such a magnet for murder."

"Hey, it's not like I intentionally go looking for murders to entertain me. That's your job."

"Exactly. My job is to solve homicides. Your job is to drink daiquiris, lie on the beach, and enjoy your vacation." Tom chuckled at what he obviously thought was a cute remark.

I bristled at his laughter. "Excuse me, but remember those last two killers I discovered?"

His laughter abruptly stopped. "What I distinctly remember is how you almost died both times."

Well, yeah. But, technically, I was batting one hundred percent in figuring out whodunit. My timing was just a tad off.

"Promise me you won't interfere in this case. Let the Hawaii police do their job," Tom said.

"I promise I won't get in the way."

"That's the vaguest statement I've ever heard."

"Look, my brother and sister-in-law's welfare is important to me. Besides, the police here don't seem nearly as intelligent as you and your officers." I had no reason to make a statement about the competency of the local police, but a little flattery never hurt.

"Nice try. Now please stay out of trouble."

Yeah, yeah. Heard that refrain before. "It would be a lot easier if …," the phone clicked and I found myself talking to the dial tone, "you were here with me."

CHAPTER THIRTY

Liz had arranged the perfect distraction for our group tonight. One of the largest hotels on the island boasted not only seven restaurants, but guests could travel via electric boat over the resort's extensive waterways. The Grand Canal–Hawaiian style.

Once the five of us arrived at the hotel, I perked up. If Ben were here, my son would have described the resort as ginormous. Four different pools offered swim-up bars, cave-like grottos, waterfalls and meandering streams. Dolphins chased each other around a large pond, every now and then leaping into the air and thrilling the hotel guests.

We strolled down long open-air corridors lined with multi-million-dollar paintings, beautiful vases from various Chinese dynasties and an array of ancient statues. I lagged behind the others, stopping to read the commentary on a bronze statue representing the Hindu goddess Kali, a twenty-four-armed wonder. I eyed my glossy coral-tipped digits and calculated what a manicure would cost the multiple-armed goddess.

My hand was quickly swallowed by a much larger, stronger hand.

I glanced up to see that Steve had joined us. He flashed his body-tingling smile and tilted his head at Kali. "Ever wish you had an extra couple dozen hands and arms?"

My mind raced as I analyzed the benefits of owning so many appendages. The negatives far surpassed the positives so I shook my head. "Two arms and two legs are more than sufficient for someone as uncoordinated as I am."

Steve squeezed my hand. "You don't give yourself enough credit, Laurel. You have a lot going for you—you're attractive, smart and fun. That's why I like hanging out with you."

Responding to compliments is not my forte so I switched directions. "What are you doing here? Don't you have a sunset sail?"

"When they predicted another storm tonight, we cancelled the trip. I didn't want to worry about anyone else falling overboard."

Or anyone else being *pushed*.

"I'm keeping an eye on you tonight. There are too many bodies of water on the hotel grounds for someone with your propensity for falling in." Steve winked, but I sensed an undercurrent of concern. Maybe last night's kiss was more than just relief his best friend's sister hadn't drowned on his watch.

After my irritating phone conversation with Tom, it was nice to have an appreciative male by my side.

"How do you like life on the island?" I asked. "Was it difficult to adapt from your previous career?"

"Not really. I grew up near the Finger Lakes area in upstate New York so I spent my high school summers crewing for some of the locals. Owning a boat seemed natural once I relocated here. Unfortunately, big boats don't come cheap. Plus, I moved here at the peak of the market. Tourism dropped dramatically after 2008, and it still hasn't fully recovered. I love what I'm doing, but it's definitely been a financial struggle."

I smiled sympathetically. My own California residence was still underwater figuratively although not literally. In Hawaii, which was prone to tsunamis, hurricanes and earthquakes, either version was conceivable.

We caught up to the others at the boat stop. Shortly after, our boat glided on its rails down to a Japanese restaurant known for its fabulous sushi creations. We waited ten minutes for Dave and Regan to show up then decided to go ahead without them. The speed and dexterity with which the chef sliced and diced with his perfectly honed blades was impressive, but I wouldn't want to get on his bad side.

Despite the tranquil atmosphere in the restaurant, I sensed the topic of Keiki's murder was never far from anyone's thoughts. Once the chef departed to show off at another table, my mother moved it front and center.

"Steve, my daughter almost drowned after getting pushed off your boat last night. Who do you think did it?"

Mother's questions were even more pointed than the sushi chef's knives.

Steve gazed at me with concern. "I can't believe someone intentionally shoved Laurel off the boat but,—"

"I'm fairly certain I was pushed," I said.

"You don't think the wind combined with the choppy waves could have sent you overboard?"

"No, I don't." Why was it so hard for Steve to believe someone pushed me?

Stan, ever the peacemaker, must have noticed my curt tone. "Let's assume for the purpose of this discussion that someone pushed Laurel over the railing. Who are the potential suspects?"

"Good point," added Brian. "How many crew members were there?"

"My usual crew was on board. You met Rafe and Timmy on our snorkeling expedition. Amanda's our marine expert. We normally have a bartender, but he was sidelined by a car accident, which was why Laurel got drafted to serve drinks. Walea danced and her husband, Henry, and another young guy, Rick, provided the music."

"Okay, that makes six potentials. What about your passengers? Any possibilities?" Brian asked.

Steve shrugged. "Laurel would have a better idea about that. Did you tick anyone off?"

Excuse me? I could feel my eyebrows draw together as I shot Steve a look.

"Sorry." He smiled and rested his hand on mine. "That didn't come out right. Were there any ornery passengers? Anyone drunk enough to accidentally push you off?"

I nibbled my lower lip as I attempted to picture members of the sailing party from the previous evening.

"A guy from Australia got sort of belligerent when I stopped serving drinks."

"You know how those Aussies can be," Steve responded, seeming relieved to point a finger at someone other than his trusted crew.

I wasn't all that familiar with Aussies other than Hugh Jackman. That adorable Hugh could push me into Moby Dick's mouth, and I'd still have a major crush on him.

"Walea and Amanda were below deck with the passengers," I said, "but I have no idea where Rafe and Rick were when I fell overboard. Or Henry. He seemed shaken up when he and Walea saw me at the pier afterward. I suppose the most obvious person is Timmy. He ran away when I called out to him. And when I went below to talk to him earlier that evening, I found him holding some parcels in his hand. He quickly stowed them in a locker."

"Okay, that's a clue with a capital C," Stan said. "He could be smuggling something and was worried you noticed."

Brian cocked his head. "Aren't there a lot of issues with drugs being smuggled in and out of the islands, Steve?"

Steve nodded. "It's a problem, that's for sure. I hate to think one of my crew is involved in something like that though."

"Didn't you say Timmy had a record?" I asked.

"A lot of these kids have something negative in their past. Usually something dumb when they were juveniles. That doesn't elevate him to drug dealer."

"I don't know," Stan said. "I kind of like him for our killer."

"Me too," said Dave, as he and Regan joined our group.

Mother jumped up to hug her eldest and his wife. It was nice to see them together although their body language wouldn't convince Dr. Phil or anyone else that they were a loving couple.

"So who did you all decide was the killer?" Dave asked. He started to put his arm around Regan then hesitated as if gauging her reaction. It was nice to see her lean in rather than push him away. Maybe this horrible situation would bring them closer.

"Yes, what's our next step, Madame Detective?" Stan's grin quickly switched directions into a frown as he stared over my shoulder.

"I think you can leave the next step to us," said a familiar voice.

I twisted in my seat and met the intense gaze of Detective Lee standing next to a smirking O'Grady. "What brings you here, Detective? Would you care to sample some sushi?"

"No, we'll leave the sushi for you. We have an arrest to make."

CHAPTER THIRTY-ONE

"It's about time the police realized Regan didn't murder Keiki," Mother said. "Are you here to apologize?"

Detective Lee looked confused for a second, but that didn't stop him from pulling a pair of handcuffs out of his pocket.

Uh oh. This couldn't be good.

Regan closed her eyes and lifted her arms, prepared for the worst. The detective surprised us and instead asked my brother to stand. The litany began, "Dave Bingham, you have the right to remain silent...."

Lee had barely begun reciting Miranda rights when Mother shrieked in his ear.

"Stop. He didn't do it," she screamed. "I killed Keiki."

Between Mom claiming to be the killer, Regan crying over Dave's arrest and Stan's attempts to secure dozens of takeout boxes for the remains of our dinner, the atmosphere in the Japanese restaurant quickly changed from softly subdued to caterwauling chaos.

Dave remained quiet as Lee cuffed him. He whispered in Steve's ear then attempted to quiet down our mother.

"Mom, it's okay, we'll sort it out at the police station. Settle down."

I'd never seen my mother so agitated. Not even when five of her escrows all contingent upon one another fell apart. And what was the deal with her claim she was the killer?

She began pounding her fist against Lee's chest. He calmly placed his hands on her shoulders and said, "Mrs. Bingham, please settle down or I'll have to arrest you for assault and battery against a police officer."

She held out both arms. "Take me. I'm ready. Just leave my son alone."

Good grief. My mother had been watching too many crime shows. Or drunk too much sake.

I grabbed her arm and dragged her away. "Mom, pull yourself together. Let me find out what's going on." I plopped her down on a cement bench outside the restaurant and went back into the fray. Briefly. The manager of the restaurant shooed our group toward the door. As far as I knew, they hadn't given us a bill for our dinner, so peace and tranquility must be more of a priority than profit.

Brian left us to speak with Detective Lee while Detective O'Grady walked ahead with Dave. Even with his arms cuffed behind him, my brother held his head high.

Brian returned to our group, and Regan questioned him. "What did he tell you?"

He shrugged. "Not much. Some new evidence came up that implicated Dave although I have no idea what it is. You need to contact your attorney and have him meet with Dave at the police station tomorrow."

"What about me?" she asked. "Am I free now?"

Her question surprised me. I would have thought Regan would be more concerned with her husband's situation, but maybe she needed clarification.

"I guess you're free, but I've never seen a situation where one spouse is arrested for murder and then the other spouse is taken in a few days later."

Regan perched on a bench, her contemplative expression looking like she was miles away. Or maybe just wishing she was. Tiki torches burning against the backdrop of a purple, pink and orange sky made the setting a natural for romance. But not for a wife who had just seen her husband hauled off by the police.

Regan finally declared she felt too shook up to drive so Steve offered to take her home. One of us could pick up Dave's car from the hotel the following day.

The occupants of our rental car remained silent as we drove back to our own hotel. My mother's bizarre reaction to Dave's arrest had me worried. I could swear from the minute Lee placed the cuffs on Dave's wrists, her hair had whitened a shade or two. I wished I could beam her husband over from California, not only to provide moral support, but also to give us some professional advice.

Mother and I entered our hotel room. She walked to her bed and flopped down on top of the covers. Directly on the hotel bedspread! Where prior room residents had lain and done who knows what. My mother must be truly upset if she wasn't worried about catching any *hootchy-kootchy cooties.*

"Mom, do you want me to get you an aspirin? Maybe a cup of tea?" She hadn't uttered a word since her restaurant outburst. It was the longest my mother had remained silent since she delivered me into the world.

She continued to lie on the bed, eyes closed, arms crossed over her chest.

"Please talk to me. I'm sure the police have made a dreadful mistake," I said. "It's not like they're used to investigating murders on this island. Why don't you call Robert and see what he recommends?"

She turned her head to the right, undoubtedly to check the time in California. The clock verified it was well after midnight back home.

"It's too late to call him now." She blew out a deep sigh. "I feel like such a failure."

"You? You're one of the most successful women I know."

"Successful in real estate. But I'm beginning to think my parenting skills were lacking. First you were a murder suspect, and now Dave's been arrested. Where did I go wrong?"

I walked over to the bed and kissed her forehead. "This has nothing to do with your parenting. You are a wonderful mother. I still don't know how you managed to do it all. Let's concentrate on the facts and see what we can do to solve Keiki's murder. It's become obvious the police aren't going to do a proper job."

"Your brother has always been kind of bull-headed. But I'm certain he's not capable of murder."

"You admit Dave can be a tad strong-willed?" Her statement was almost as surprising as Dave's arrest.

She smiled. "I know your brother isn't perfect. I may be a mother, but I have two eyes and ears."

Hmmm. How many of Dave's past escapades was my mother aware of? And now that she was sharing, how many of mine? I'd worry about that later. My brother was our top priority for now.

"Why did you tell Detective Lee you killed Keiki?"

She sat up and placed her palms on her cheeks. She looked almost as puzzled as I felt. "I have no idea. Maternal instinct clicking in, I guess."

"I can understand maternal instinct, but what if Dave turns out to be the killer. How far would you go to protect your son?"

CHAPTER THIRTY-TWO

Exhaustion kept us from finishing our discussion. The next morning I did discover how early Mother could wake up to devise a plan to spring her son out of jail.

Said plan included waking me as well. I personally didn't think a sleepy Laurel would be much help, but the clackety-clack of the room service cart, along with the smell of hot coffee, eggs and bacon, was enough to induce me to assist her efforts. My mother must really want my help if she'd ordered this mouth-watering cholesterol-heavy breakfast.

Mother moved the silver-domed plates of food to the small glass-topped table on our lanai. The full circular moon shone bright against the pink streaks beginning to light the morning sky. I poured coffee for both of us and carried the mugs outside, along with cream, sugar and our utensils.

I sipped my coffee and stared at the tips of the distant waves shining iridescent against the black water. The pounding surf reminded me that something hauntingly beautiful could be equally dangerous. The dead dancer was not unlike those waves.

In life and in death, Keiki had impacted the people whose paths had crossed hers. The central question we needed answered was whose path crossed hers last?

Mother put down her cup and picked up her ever-present legal pad and pen.

"I called Robert while you were sleeping, and he offered some excellent suggestions."

I nodded while I crunched on a piece of bacon. A former homicide detective could definitely provide a few helpful tips.

Mother ticked items off as she read them from her list.

"We need to make sure Regan has contacted their attorney, whether Dave wants one or not. If he thinks he's innocent, he might waive his rights which Robert said would be a mistake. I'm sure Regan is as anxious to have Dave released from jail as you and I are." Mother picked up her coffee and eyed me over her cup. "At least, I hope she is. That girl has exhibited some strange behavior."

I crunched and nodded once more. Regan seemed more tightly wrapped than my Saran Wrap. Was there more to their marital issues than she'd already told me?

"Did Robert have any suggestions for our investigation?" I asked.

Her eyebrows drew together as she tapped her pen on the glass-topped table.

"He certainly did," she said in a frosty tone. "He suggested we leave the detecting to the Hawaii police whom he was certain were capable of arresting the guilty party without any help from us. Men!"

"You're never going to convince a homicide detective we're better suited to discover the killer. I don't know if the police are biased against both Dave and Regan or if they think they have sufficient evidence. But we know they're not guilty."

"Exactly." Mother rubbed her pen against her lower lip. "Are you completely positive Regan is innocent?"

"Honestly, I'm not certain of anything except Dave isn't a murderer. I'm also convinced he knows something he isn't sharing. Now that his situation has changed for the worse, maybe he'll come clean with us."

"Do you believe he was having an affair with Keiki?" she asked.

I shrugged. "At this point, I could care less whether Dave had an affair or not. That's for him and Regan to work out. But we need to find out where he went the night Keiki died. Did he have a rendezvous with her or not?"

"If Dave wasn't with his wife at the condo," Mother remarked, "then Regan doesn't have an alibi either."

"What about that mystery man Keiki was dating? It might be Dave but it might not."

"That's true. But how can we find out who she was seeing?"

"We could question Keiki's mother. Girls tell their mothers everything."

She peered at me over her rose-colored reading glasses. "Just like you share everything with me?"

"Point taken." I grinned. "But it's worth a try. Keiki's new older boyfriend could definitely be her killer. And if she didn't confide in her mother or stepsister, maybe one of the other dancers would know his name."

"If it has anything to do with hula, Stan would enjoy investigating," Mother added.

"Yep, the next thing you know he'll be sporting a trench coat and fedora over his coconut shells and grass skirt."

Four hours later, we met up with the gang. By then, I was ready for a nap, and hoped a second breakfast might energize me. I turned the menu over looking for side items and was shocked at the cost.

The hotel's regular blend of coffee was three dollars per cup with refills, but one-hundred-percent Kona coffee was five dollars. The stuff really was liquid gold. When Jay, our waiter, arrived to take our order, I asked if he could distinguish between the two.

"Easily," Jay said, "but I've lived on the island all my life. Of course that doesn't mean I can afford the premium stuff. Not on my wages."

Nice, not too subtle ploy to get a bigger tip.

"But there are plenty of folks who can't tell the difference between Folgers' instant and pure Kona coffee."

"That's Brian." Liz gently punched her husband's arm. "As long as it's hot, he doesn't care if it's fresh ground beans or two-year-old powder."

Brian threw her the look that sent defense lawyers quivering, but Liz just responded by placing a raspberry lip print on his cheek.

"Bring Laurel and me a cup of each, please," Mother asked Jay. "We'll see how refined our coffee palates are."

Jay returned a few minutes later with two large carafes and several empty mugs, which he set in the center of our table. "I thought it would be more fun if you all joined in."

125

Jay poured each of us a small serving from the pots, labeled numbers one and two. We doctored them with cream and sugar to suit our taste. Neither Brian nor Stan could tell one from the other. Mother, Liz and I thought the second, more flavorful pot must be the pure Kona coffee.

"The women won this round." Jay nodded his head in our direction. "It gets harder with the various blends because some coffee makers are more skilled than others."

"Regan told us over three million pounds of green beans are produced annually," Brian said. "If someone could pass off Columbian as pure Kona coffee, they'd have quite the profitable scam."

Leave it to Brian to steer the discussion in a nefarious direction. "The coffee business is truly fascinating." I drained the last drop of my luxury coffee. "I'd love to learn more about it from Regan."

"Has she called?" Brian asked.

I shook my head. "Not yet. I left her a message around seven this morning, but it went directly to voicemail. I assumed she was still asleep. I don't know if she's contacted the attorney or not. For all I know, she's forgotten about Dave, and she's back at Koffee Land lost in the world of debits and credits."

"You can tell she was born to be a CPA for a coffee farm," Stan remarked. When I looked confused, he smirked. "She's a true bean counter!"

I rolled my eyes at Stan's pitiful joke, but it made me wonder if there were other reasons why Regan spent so much time at Koffee Land. She knew her workload frustrated Dave.

Did she have other ulterior reasons for spending her days and occasional nights at Koffee Land? The handsome owner seemed congenial and Regan indicated she liked him. Or did she "like" him? My hormones must be rebelling at my lack of erogenous activity because now I suspected my sister-in-law of having an affair with *her* boss.

Welcome to *As the World Turns – the Hawaii Five-O* version.

Was it possible Regan murdered Keiki so her husband would be jailed, leaving her free to pursue her adulterous ways?

Or did I drink way too much coffee this morning?

"We only have forty-eight hours to find the killer," Mother announced. "We need to split up so we can question everyone on my list. Then we'll—"

Brian interrupted her, using his trial attorney voice to get his point across to us. "Listen, I know you guys think you're Sherlock Holmes, Colombo, and Jessica Fletcher combined, but you need to leave the detecting to the real detectives this time. Lee seems fairly sharp. He also doesn't look like he'd brook the kind of nonsense Hunter lets you get away with, Laurel."

I opened my mouth to protest then decided to stuff it full of scone. Liz could handle Brian.

"Sweetie, we can't just wing our way home without helping Laurel and Barbara." Liz reached out to stroke Brian's back.

"I know this hasn't been an ideal honeymoon," Mother said.

Brian cocked an eyebrow at her.

"The three of us are perfectly capable of handling the detecting without you. Liz, why don't you and Brian go off on one of those expeditions you've booked?"

Liz looked at her watch. "Oh, bollocks, I bloody well forgot about the ATV outing. I wonder if they can reschedule for tomorrow."

I sighed. "I don't think we have time for any more tourist attractions."

"Don't you remember, this was the tour in Waipi'o Valley."

"Oh, yeah," I said. "I was really looking forward to that. The reviews made it sound amazing. A once-in-a-lifetime experience."

"I'll call and see what they can do," Liz said. "What's your first priority on the investigation?"

"My first priority is to get Dave a get-out-of-jail-free card. But I don't even know the name of Regan and Dave's criminal attorney."

Brian waggled his finger in front of my face. "Even if you knew his name, it wouldn't do you any good. An attorney is only going to discuss the case with his client and whoever the client designated as a contact outside the jail."

I swallowed my last bite of scone. "Fine. If we can't get Regan to call us back, and we can't glean any info from Dave's attorney, we'll just have to pay a condolence call to Keiki's family.

"Who knows? Maybe her mother holds the key to solving this murder."

CHAPTER THIRTY-THREE

Shortly after breakfast ended, Regan returned my call. She told me that the attorney would meet Dave at the detention center this afternoon. Just as I'd suspected, Regan was back at Koffee Land. Since she produced the staff W-2's, which included employee addresses, she agreed to give me Keiki's parents' address.

"Don't do anything to embarrass me," she added.

As if being arrested for the murder of an employee, followed by your husband also being held for the same murder wasn't embarrassing.

Regan and I sure had a difference of opinion on many things.

Someday when this whole ordeal was over, I hoped my sister-in-law and I could establish some kind of friendship. Although by then, Regan and Dave might not be married.

Or they might be cohabiting in jail.

Mother and I urged Liz and Brian to enjoy their remaining time on the island alone. We talked them into driving us to the Grand Hotel so we could pick up Dave's car. We didn't think Dave would mind our borrowing it since he wasn't going anywhere in the near future. His red Mustang convertible was a tight fit, but once I put the top down, Stan had more headroom in the rear seat. With my hands on the leather-covered steering wheel, and the wind blowing through my hair, I felt like we were flying.

Oops. I yanked my lead foot off the accelerator. Given their finances, I wondered what Regan thought of Dave's new fire-engine-red sports car. Was my brother suffering such a huge mid-life crisis that the sports car splurge hadn't been enough to make him happy? Did Keiki pursue him or vice versa?

According to my earlier conversation with Regan, Victor should be at home today helping his wife prepare for Keiki's service. I was concerned about intruding on their privacy but at this point, I didn't feel we had a choice. Especially since two of the suspects were relatives of mine. I rationalized our visit by thinking if I were Keiki's mother, my foremost desire would be to see my daughter's killer locked up. And to be one hundred percent certain it was the right person behind bars.

Having resolved my inner turmoil, I mentally rehearsed a few questions for the couple. Once they answered them, we could get out of their hair.

Keiki's mother and stepfather lived a few miles north of Koffee Land. We turned onto their drive, lined with coffee trees. I wondered if Victor ran a small coffee business on the side or if he only sold the coffee cherries to other farms. Several vehicles were parked in a graveled area to the side of the house. They could belong to relatives or friends.

Or even the killer.

Hmmm. What were the odds someone would arrive on their doorstep, casserole dish in hand and admit to the murder?

We walked single file up the wooden stairs to the front deck. I rang the doorbell, which chimed a cheerful melody.

A beautiful woman answered the door. With flowing dark hair and smooth unlined skin the color of café au lait, she looked too young to be Keiki's mother. Victor peered over her shoulder. He looked puzzled then recognition dawned.

I offered my hand and introduced myself. "Hello, Mr. Yakamura. My name is Laurel McKay. Regan is my sister-in law. She introduced us the other day at Koffee Land."

Victor nodded. "Can I assist you with something? Does Regan need anything from me?"

"Oh no, she's fine." Well, as fine as someone whose husband was reclining in a jail cell, for supposedly murdering the stepdaughter of the man I was addressing. "We all feel so bad about Keiki and…"

My voice petered out, and Mother stepped forward. The shiny green foliage of the oversized plant we'd purchased at the supermarket almost hid her face.

"We brought this in memory of Keiki." Mother listed to the left and Victor grabbed the red-flowered anthurium before she or the plant could topple over the deck railing.

"*Mahalo,* for your kindness." He stepped back looking unsure whether to invite us inside or not.

"Hey, there's Walea," Stan piped up. "Yoo hoo, sweetie."

Walea moved forward and whispered in Victor's ear. He hesitated then ushered us into the house.

The Yakamuras' house was decorated in tropical fashion, with dark woods, a flowered sofa and matching chairs grouped around a square mahogany coffee table. An open bar divided the living room from the kitchen, whose countertops overflowed with wall-to-wall casseroles and plates of baked goods. Two women sat at each end of the sofa. Both wore their long dark hair loose and flowing down their backs. I recognized them as dancers from Daiquiri Dave's.

When we walked in, they stood to make room for us.

"Please don't leave on our account," I said to the women.

"No, it is time to go. Walea, we will see you at the restaurant at five." As the dancers sashayed out the door, I marveled again at their sexy walk. It looked so natural that I cocked my hips to the left and right to replicate the swiveling movements they made.

Ouch. I hoped I'd packed some extra Advil.

"Are you performing tonight?" I asked Walea.

She narrowed her eyes. "Yes, money doesn't grow on coconut trees, you know. We are not all rich Californians here on this island."

We are not all rich back in California either, but that wasn't a topic worth quibbling over.

The older woman gracefully pointed to the sofa. We sat down, thigh to thigh, looking as guilty as kids whispering during a church service.

The woman's voice possessed a lilting quality that soothed as she welcomed us. "My name is Kiana. I am Keiki's mother. It is kind of you to come here. You show the true aloha spirit."

I smiled. Demonstrating aloha spirit sounded far better than ferreting out who killed her daughter.

My mother demonstrated her own aloha spirit. "We feel terrible about what happened to Keiki. I wanted to assure you that despite his arrest, my son had nothing to do with your daughter's tragic death."

A flicker of something darkened Kiana's face, but it disappeared, and her countenance regained its former placid demeanor. It made me wonder if she agreed with our assumption that Dave did not kill her daughter. Was there something Keiki's mother was hiding?

Kiana chose to discuss a less confrontational topic than her daughter's murder. "Have you been able to enjoy our beautiful island?"

"We haven't had time for much sightseeing although we're taking the ATV ride at Waipi'o Valley tomorrow," I replied. "Unfortunately, we only have two more days to investigate the murder before we fly home."

"It won't be easy finding Keiki's killer in that amount of time," Stan said.

Kiana placed long elegant fingers against her slender throat. "You are detectives in California?"

I exchanged looks with Mother and Stan.

"We've assisted the El Dorado County Sheriff's Department on several occasions," I mumbled. Fortunately, no sheriff's department representatives were present to debate that fact.

"You are helping the detectives here?" Kiana appeared confused, which was not at all surprising since we were equally confused at this point.

"Yes, we are." The Hawaii police didn't know we were assisting them, but that was a mere technicality. My brother's freedom was at stake here. "We have some excellent leads so far, but we thought it would help to interview Keiki's current boyfriend. Unfortunately we didn't have a contact number for him."

We didn't have a contact name either, but this was no time to split hairs.

Kiana's eyes clouded over. "My daughter used to date a fine young man named Joey. We hoped they would settle down and get married some day. Unfortunately, he died in an accident about a month ago. It was so sad for a young man to have his life cut short that way."

Kiana addressed her husband who'd returned to the living room. "Victor has dealt with so much tragedy lately—at work and at home."

Victor's heavily lined face corroborated her statement. I tried to recall what work-related tragedy she referred to. "There was that horrible accident at Koffee Land when they were building the zip-line. Did you know the young man who died?"

"That was Joey," Walea chimed in, "my sister's former boyfriend."

CHAPTER THIRTY-FOUR

Aha! The plot thickens. In fact, this plot was becoming thicker than poi.

"Oh, I missed the connection." I looked at Victor. "So Keiki's boyfriend worked for you?"

"No, no." He shook his gray head vehemently. "I have nothing to do with the zip-line construction. That is Ritz's crazy—," he paused then started again. "I manage the coffee processing only."

"Walea's husband, Henry, is the contractor for the zip-line." Kiana shifted her gaze to her stepdaughter. Her full lips tightened as she glanced at Walea.

Walea fidgeted as she met Kiana's accusing stare. "It's not Henry's fault that Joey died. I am sure he jumped from the tower because Keiki broke his heart."

"Are you saying your poor dead sister caused Joey's death?" Kiana's voice caught as she wrung her hands together.

"Heh, some sister," Walea muttered.

Victor jumped up and stood in front of Walea. "You must not talk badly about your younger sister."

"Are you kidding?" Walea leapt out of her chair. "That slut of a sister humiliated our entire family." She stormed out of the room and down a hallway that appeared to lead to the rear of the house. Seconds later Walea emerged, purse in hand. Without another word, she left the house, the screen door banging shut behind her.

Victor's hands and voice shook as he stared out the door. "I apologize for my daughter. Keiki's death, following so quickly after Joey's accident, has been a trying experience for our entire family. Henry blames himself for Joey's fall. He feels he should have made the boy wait until the morning to fix the cabling."

"Are you certain it was an accident?" I asked, "Is it possible Joey intentionally jumped?"

The lines around Victor's eyes etched deeper as he shrugged. "At this point does it really matter?"

I thought it might but decided to let that line of questioning die for now. "Do you know who Keiki started dating after she broke up with Joey?"

Kiana, eyes downcast, plucked at the fabric of her dark skirt. When she finally spoke, her voice was barely above a whisper. I didn't want to miss the name of the new boyfriend so I leaned forward.

"My daughter had big dreams. But she didn't always share everything with me."

"Unfortunately," Victor muttered under his breath.

Kiana patted his arm. "Keiki is, was an…an adventurous girl. Sometimes her dreams created trouble. Not too long ago, she mentioned there was a man interested in her. Someone she found intriguing."

"Was it someone she'd met recently?" Mother asked. If the answer was yes, that should eliminate Dave as Keiki's potential lover.

Kiana shook her head. "No, it was someone she had known awhile. Recently he'd taken an interest in her."

My mother's perfect posture wilted and her shoulders slumped. "Someone who might be married?"

Kiana's eyes, darker than French-roasted coffee beans, gazed wistfully at us. "Possibly. I was afraid to ask. All she said was he had money and a nice car."

She lifted her arms in a supplicating manner. "Who he was, I do not know. I'm afraid Keiki has taken his name to the grave with her."

Sadly, whoever it was, may have been the person to send the beautiful dancer to *her* grave.

CHAPTER THIRTY-FIVE

After promising Kiana and Victor we would stop by their house for Keiki's memorial reception on Sunday, we left their home, pondering the implications of Kiana's revelations. The description of Keiki's new boyfriend could fit many men. It also described my brother.

"Should we attend the reception?" Mother asked. "Maybe her parents only invited us to be polite."

I thought it over for a few seconds. "No, I think they were sincere. Our plane doesn't leave until the evening, so we have time."

"Are you kidding?" Stan said. "This is the perfect opportunity to find the killer. Remember all those clues we picked up last time?"

As far as I recalled, my Mother and Liz had each picked up several new clients, but nary a worthwhile clue.

"I bet they'll have a hula tribute to Keiki." Stan's eyes sparkled and he started swaying to the music that must be playing in his head. "I heard they do that in these situations, especially if the deceased was a dancer. Do you think I should offer—?"

"No," Mother and I shouted simultaneously.

Stan looked hurt so I attempted to mollify him "Hey, pal, you wouldn't catch McGarrett dancing when he should be detecting."

He cocked his head. "Good point. Dancing might be a distraction."

Yeah. For everyone else as well.

I glanced at my watch. "Do you want to stop by Koffee Land and check in with Regan? It's almost noon and it's only a ten-minute drive."

"I could use a cup of java." Stan yawned.

"It's probably too soon," Mother said. "But maybe Regan will have an update on Dave's status." The fine lines she tried to conceal with luxury cosmetics were now evident, proclaiming her baby boomer status.

We piled in the car and drove toward Honaunau. Dark clouds crisscrossed the sky, indicating afternoon showers were in the forecast. My ears popped once we reached 2,000 feet in altitude. The higher we climbed, the more exotic the landscaping became. Looking at the large, abundant red blossoms entwined around tall Ohia trees reminded me of a local legend.

Ohia, a Hawaiian chief, supposedly fell in love with Pele's sister, Lehua. Pele, who wanted him for herself, was so furious with Ohia that she turned him into a tree. The other gods tried but were unable to change Ohia back into a man. When Lehua refused to leave his side, they transformed her into a beautiful red flower instead. That way the two could be united forever.

Needless to say, Pele was pissed.

Whether you're a goddess or a mere mortal, true love does not always run smooth. Now if we could only determine who was pissed off enough to kill Keiki.

We drove through the imposing entrance to Koffee Land and followed the long curving drive to the visitor's center. The parking lot seemed more crowded than on our last visit. The center, however, was empty except for Tiffany who stood behind the counter.

"Your parking lot is packed." I said. "What did you do with everyone? Are they all on tour?"

Tiffany shook her head, the ebony strands of her glossy hair flying in every direction. "The television people are here today. They're hosting some kind of reception for the contestants in the gazebo."

Stan's eyes lit up. "Could we take a peek?"

She smiled and shrugged. "I'm not sure. You can ask Regan if it's okay."

"Is she around?" I asked.

"She should be in her office." Tiffany picked up her phone and dialed an extension. While we waited, I perused the goodies in the Donkey Ball aisle. Some folks take Xanax for anxiety. I find that chocolate is cheaper and tastier. With my brother in jail, I could use a pound or two of the over-the-counter medication.

I heard noises and glanced up, expecting to see Regan. Her handsome boss approached, dressed in an off-white suit and Panama hat, looking the picture of a nineteenth-century plantation owner.

Regan followed behind Ritz. I couldn't imagine concentrating on work while my husband languished in jail, but she possessed an amazing loyalty to her employer.

"Ritz, you remember Dave's family." Regan reintroduced all of us to her boss.

He latched on to my mother's hands. "Regan has told me about your son's difficulties. Please let me know if I can do anything to help. The police here are not so experienced in the murder cases. I'm sure it is a big mistake."

Mother gently released her hands from his grasp. "Thank you. I appreciate your offer. This has been a trying vacation. First Regan was in custody and now Dave."

Ritz smiled at my sister-in-law. "I'm most relieved to have Regan back here at Koffee Land. She is the backbone of our enterprise."

Regan's face glowed with the compliment. The owner had definitely mastered the art of positive reinforcement.

"In the brief time that I met her, Keiki seemed like a nice girl," Stan said, "but she's been kind of a vacation wrecker."

I could see Regan mouthing the words "home wrecker" under her breath.

"Ah yes, the young victim. Such a tragedy," Ritz replied.

"Did you know her?" I asked.

He nodded. "She stopped by on occasion to see her stepfather. Keiki seemed to be a source of much frustration to Victor and his wife. A beautiful but confused young woman, I would say. She made Henry crazy, too. Have you met her brother-in-law?"

"Yes, we've met both Walea and Henry. How did Keiki upset him?"

"Henry mentioned she had a drug problem, but I don't know the details. I know he was nervous when she was selected as one of the contestants for the reality show. I think he was afraid she might do something to embarrass the family."

"Keiki was supposed to be on *The Bride and the Bachelor?*" I asked.

"Such a tragedy to have her young life cut short," Ritz said. "This show might have been the impetus to turn her life around. But moving on to happier topics, have you had the opportunity to explore our beautiful island?"

"We're going on an ATV tour in the Waipi'o Valley tomorrow," I said.

"Ah, the Valley of the Kings. Waipi'o is indeed a special place. Make sure you don't miss the view from the rim." Ritz glanced at his watch. "I'm sorry. I have a meeting in Hilo. Again, please let me know if I can be of service." We thanked him and he headed out of the center.

"Have you heard from Dave or his attorney?" I asked Regan.

"Not yet. But it's probably too soon." Regan chewed on her thumbnail. "I need to get back to work. Can I get you anything else?"

Mother looked ready to burst in tears. "This waiting is killing me."

"Could we walk around the grounds?" I asked, hoping that might calm my mother while we waited to hear from the lawyer.

Regan looked relieved to get rid of us. "Sure, just don't disturb the TV crew. They have something going on with the contestants over in the pavilion."

We said goodbye to Regan and Tiffany then walked out of the center. A series of gold arrows pointed to various locations on the property, all of which seemed to lead in the same direction. Even without the arrows, we would have been able to locate the TV crew from the noise.

"Your sister-in-law seems to place far more importance on her career than her husband," Mother confided as we walked side by side down the graded path.

"Maybe it's her method of escape. Burying her head in a spreadsheet could be an accountant's security blanket."

"Humph."

The noise level increased as we drew closer to the pavilion. The structure resembled a gazebo on steroids and could easily provide enough room for several hundred attendees. I didn't see any TV cameras so this must be an informal pre-taping gathering. As we drew closer to the grand pavilion, I noticed a familiar face.

"It's Amanda, the naturalist from the *Sea Jinx*," I said to the others. "I wonder what she's doing here."

The three of us approached the covered structure.

"Hi, Laurel." Amanda beamed a wide smile at us. The red hibiscus over her ear matched the short polka-dot sundress she wore. "Are you involved in the show?"

I shook my head. "My sister-in-law works at Koffee Land so we stopped to see her. What about you? How come you're not out on the *Sea Jinx* today?"

"I'm one of the contestants on *The Bride and the Bachelor*." She bounced up and down in excitement, her long blonde curls and bosom bouncing in tandem. If they judged the contestants on bounciness, she was a shoe-in.

"Congratulations," I said. "So what's the show about?"

Amanda put her hand over her heart. "The girls are all competing for the bachelor, Jacques Andre Cointreau."

Stan whistled. "Isn't he the grandson of Philippe Cointreau?"

She smiled, bubbling over with youthful optimism. "Yes, we have so much in common. I think we're a perfect match."

"That hunk won the *Survivor, the Amazing Race*, and *Dancing with the Stars*," Stan said. "He is a fox-trotting, sea-faring survivalist. You go get him, girl."

She giggled. "I'll give it my best. I just hope I can measure up to the other contestants." She glanced around the pavilion, and I followed her gaze.

Talk about island beauty. Every girl in the room was gorgeous and dressed to kill. But Amanda was equally lovely, and I admired the way she used simple native flowers to accessorize. Some of the women glittered more than the showroom at Tiffany.

"We just learned Keiki was a contestant too," I said. "It's so tragic what happened to her."

Amanda shook her head. "I still can't believe she's gone. We've known each other since high school. It would have been so much fun to be on the show together. I heard the police finally arrested her killer so that's good."

"They did not arrest the right man," Mother shouted, surprising me with her intensity.

Amanda edged away from our group. If the young girl thought my mother was intimidating now, she should try negotiating a contract with the Queen of Centurion Realty.

"The man they arrested is my brother," I explained to the frightened young woman. "We're all upset because we know he didn't do it. We just need to prove it to the police before we leave the island Sunday. That gives us only two more days. Do you have any idea who would want to kill Keiki?"

She shook her curls, her eyes welling with tears. "Poor Keiki. You probably heard what happened to her former boyfriend, Joey?" She looked at us and we all nodded. "Well, his brother, Timmy, hated Keiki. I was on the *Sea Jinx* one night when he threatened her, although I can't imagine him following through with it."

"How about any new boyfriends?" Stan asked. "We heard she started dating an older man."

She pondered our question. "Keiki never mentioned anything to me. Although I did see her with—," Amanda stopped and eyed the ground. "It was probably nothing."

"No clue is unimportant when it comes to my son," Mother said using a gentler tone this time. We didn't want to frighten the young woman away if she possessed some valuable information.

Amanda toed her sandal in a circular motion in the grass, seemingly reluctant to disclose one of her friend's possible suitors. A tall woman with a clipboard and a frown called out Amanda's name, beckoning at her.

"I've gotta go," she said.

"Please tell us what you were going to say," I pleaded with her. She waved back at the other woman indicating she was on her way.

"Okay, I saw Steve and Keiki together a few times. But it was almost a month ago and probably didn't mean anything. "She blasted a Crest-white smile at me. "Besides, I think Steve really likes you, Laurel."

The clipboard-carrying woman called Amanda's name again, angrily tapping her foot as she glared at our group.

"Sorry," Amanda said. "I really must go."

"Good luck, dear." Mother patted the young woman on the arm.

Amanda smiled a thanks and scurried away to join the others. Mother and I chuckled as we left the pavilion.

"Ah, youth, the stars are aligned," I said, "therefore it is my fate—"

"To meet my mate," Stan sang out. "Hey, she's a cute kid. I hope this show works out for her. Everyone deserves to meet their Mr. Right."

My lower lip trembled, and I sensed a lone tear rolling down my cheek. Everyone does deserve to meet Ms. or Mr. Right. But once the initial romance wears off, how do you keep a relationship going strong? The unhealthy relationship of my brother and his wife saddened me, as did the memory of my own broken marriage. How could the joining of two people in love lead to so much disappointment? And tears.

And as I was discovering on this island—betrayal!

CHAPTER THIRTY-SIX

We continued on the path that led uphill away from the pavilion toward the vista point. After a short walk, we reached the crest. Two men conversed at the base of a tall tower.

"What a spectacular view," Mother said.

She wasn't kidding. A lush green valley surrounded us, the undulating hills covered with tall Ohia and Koa trees, abundant ferns and an occasional zip-line tower. In the distance, the ocean sparkled as if diamonds were dancing on the crests of the waves.

We strolled over to check out the view from the tower, which was at least forty feet tall.

"This isn't operational yet," the shorter man announced. He wore a large diamond stud in one ear and sported dragon tattoos on each of his muscular arms. He and his arms looked vaguely familiar, but since many young men on the island had tattoos, I doubted his was the only fire-breathing arm in Hawaii.

"We were just admiring the scenery," I said. "Will the zip-line be running soon?"

"We're testing it today," said the other worker. "It needs to be ready by Monday for the reality show. After that, it will open to the public. You should try it sometime."

I looked at the belts, hooks and pulleys intended to haul a person a thousand-plus feet to the next tower with a mere two-hundred-foot drop over the valley below.

"That small contraption can hold me?" Both men laughed at my skeptical tone.

"Yes, miss," replied the older, heavy-set man. "Trust me. If it can hold us, it can hold you."

Stan moved closer to the tower. "Oh, you can ride tandem on this zip-line. That's a nice feature."

"The TV show needed to have two people go at the same time, and our boss thought that would be an added attraction. Sometimes people feel more comfortable if they're zipping next to a friend."

"Can more than one person ride together on the same line?" I asked.

He nodded. "Sure, you and your mom could ride together as long as your combined weight didn't exceed 270 lbs."

Mother glanced at me then shook her head slowly. Was she implying I'd eaten one *malasada* too many for her to feel comfortable flying through the air with me?

"I've always wanted to try zip-lining," Stan said. "How safe is it? Someone mentioned there was an accident here not long ago."

The men shared a look. The young tattooed fellow was about to speak when the older man laid a hand on his shoulder. "That accident had nothing to do with the safety of these lines. We're about to take a ride to the next tower now. Stick around and watch."

The workers climbed four sets of stairs to reach the platform at the top of the tower where a third man waited. Even from this distance, I recognized Henry, their boss, glowering at us as usual.

We watched as they hooked themselves into the harnesses and tested the clamps from the upper line. Henry gave them a thumbs-up, and they took off. They waved back at us as they flew down the line. The smaller, wiry one leaned backward and spread his colorfully inked arms out wide, displaying the familiar "hang loose" Shaka sign so popular in the islands.

"That looks like fun." Stan's gaze followed the men's swift ride across the canyon.

That depends on your definition of "fun." I'd personally prefer to pull my upper lip over my forehead than go zipping through the air.

"Regan must have an update on Dave by now," said Mother, all business. "If not, then it's high time we drive to the detention center and find out what's going on ourselves."

We strolled past the pavilion, which was filled with more estrogen per foot than most men would want to handle. That Jacques Cointreau must be one hearty dude.

I couldn't imagine competing for a guy on national television. It was hard enough dating someone without having millions of viewers watching your every move.

When we arrived at the center, Tiffany was busy ringing up coffee purchases. Mother and Stan needed to visit the restrooms so they headed in that direction. I knew the offices were located in the back of the building, so I decided to find out if Regan had an update yet.

I walked through the closed back door into a short hallway. The first office, dark and empty, was presumably Victor's. In the next, Regan sat behind a functional modern desk, hands clasped under her chin, peering at rows of tiny numbers on her computer screen. I knocked on her door, and she jumped.

"Laurel, you startled me. What are you doing back here?"

"I wanted to see if you'd heard anything new about Dave."

"The attorney called a little while ago." Regan leaned back in her chair and rubbed both eyes.

I sat in the one extra wooden chair in her tiny office. "This has to be so hard on you."

"It's a nightmare. In my heart I know Dave didn't do it, but then sometimes I wonder…" Her voice trailed off, and her eyes widened. "I wonder if my husband did kill Keiki."

I jumped up, put my hands on her desk and leaned over, our chins practically touching. "You can't be serious. You believe your husband—my brother— could commit murder? You two really do have a screwed-up marriage."

Regan shrank back in her chair. "I don't know what to think about my marriage. I can't remember the last time Dave confided in me about anything." She opened a drawer, grabbed a tissue and blew her nose. "And it's been months since we've made love."

Okay, this was awkward. Why did all of my family members feel obligated to share the details of their sex life, or lack thereof, with me?

Regan cleared her throat. "I better get back to work."

"Will we see you tonight?"

She shrugged. "I don't know how late I'll be working. I've taken over some of Victor's duties during his absence. We've had

144

issues with our crops due to the borer beetle invasion, so we don't have nearly the quantity of beans we thought we'd have for sale. Between Ritz's spending for all the improvements and less coffee revenue than I anticipated, our bottom line isn't looking good. I'll be glad when Victor returns. Maybe he can figure out why there's such a shortage."

"That reminds me, Victor and Kiana invited us to Keiki's memorial service. Are you going?"

Her face paled. "I suppose I have to or Victor will be offended. I'm sure Ritz and Pilar will attend as well. As for Dave…who knows if he'll still be in jail or…?"

My cell rang. I picked up, hoping the caller would have an answer to Regan's question.

"Hey, Steve. Do you have any news?"

"I do, but where are you?"

"We're still at Koffee Land. I'm in Regan's office right now."

He paused for a few seconds. "Call me back when Regan isn't around."

I glanced at my sister-in-law who was listening intently to my end of the conversation.

"Sure, we're leaving soon. Thanks for the call."

Regan interrupted before I clicked to end the conversation. "Does Steve have any news?"

"Not really. He wanted to see how we were doing. I should leave you to your work."

"Okay, I'll keep you posted and please do the same if you hear something first."

I hugged her good-bye then bolted down the hall and out the door leading into the center. Stan and my mother stood by the register chatting with Tiffany. I joined them.

"Do you have any news about Dave?" Mother's voice cracked slightly and she dropped the bottle of passion fruit jelly she'd been holding. Tiffany caught the jar before the sticky substance could crash and explode all over the counter.

"I'll update you in the car." She paid the bill and I scurried out the door, with Stan and Mother on my footsteps. I was anxious to call Steve back and learn why he wanted Regan kept in the dark.

I dialed from the parking lot.

"Is it safe to talk?" Steve asked.

"I'm with Mother and Stan, getting in the car. Why are you acting so mysterious?"

"Try to stay calm and don't let your mother get freaked out."

If Steve thought that comment would calm me, he was wrong, because I was the one starting to freak.

"Dave will be released in an hour or so," he said.

"That's terrific news. But why can't Regan..." I could feel my mother's eyes boring into my head. "Do we need to pick him up?"

"No, I'll get him. Basically, after talking to the police, Dave doesn't want to be with Regan."

Sometimes I'm quick. Sometimes not. "Huh?"

"He's afraid to be with her. Thinks she really could be Keiki's killer."

CHAPTER THIRTY-SEVEN

It was a good thing Stan was at the wheel, because Steve's remark would have sent me off the road with the convertible wrapped around a huge banyan tree.

"Laurel, are you there?" I could hear Steve yelling. My brain felt as frozen as the hand clutching my cell.

"Yeah, just a little shell-shocked," I replied. "What does Dave want to do?"

"I'm going to pick him up as soon as the police finish processing his paperwork. He can spend the night at my place," Steve said. "It's not like Regan has been all that interested in springing him."

Unfortunately, that was too true. Why couldn't my sister-in-law put as much effort into her marriage as she did her job?

Steve continued. "Besides, Dave has some information he wants to share with you. Says his little sister can probably out-detect the cops on this island."

Aw shucks, I thought, blushing at the compliment.

"I'll be busy with our sunset sail tonight, but you and Dave can talk at my condo. Just try to keep it to yourself. He's been worried about the stress and its impact on your mother."

I agreed and hung up the phone. Now all I had to do was find an excuse why I needed to be alone with my brother tonight.

* * *

Getting time alone with Dave proved to be an easy task. Liz discovered the hotel offered free entertainment every Friday night. Hula addict Stan was delighted to watch the show with Brian and Liz. Mother, relieved that Dave was free, was exhausted from the strain of the last few days. She had no issue with her offspring spending some time together.

I grabbed the keys for Dave's car and headed down the barren lava-rock-lined highway toward Kailua town. I realized this was the first time I'd been by myself in eight days. I love my mother and my friends, but it was nice to have a few minutes of down time to reflect on the week's events.

I glanced out the car window at the proclamations of love spelled out on the Hawaiian version of graffiti—white coral set on black lava rocks. Did local couples replace the stones when they replaced their lovers? When my husband replaced me three years ago, I was a total wreck. I had no self-confidence or self-esteem. But I'd bounced back. My banking career had taken off and I'd even begun dating.

Okay, the dating thing hadn't gone all that well. And my self-image still needed a little work. But I felt good about myself finally, and what I had to offer someone in a future relationship. Keeping a marriage alive seemed to be difficult for everyone, my brother included. It's one thing to suspect your husband or wife is having an affair.

It's quite another to suspect your spouse is a killer.

I arrived at Steve's condominium just before sunset. He lived in an older project, but based on the number he supplied, his unit was only steps from the ocean. The elevator creaked its way to the fourth floor. I turned to the left and strolled down the concrete walkway until I reached Steve's unit.

Dave must have heard my sandals click-clacking because he swung the door open before I had time to knock. His eyes looked bleary and were almost redder than his beard. He held a bottle of beer in one hand while he hugged me with the other.

I noted a typical Hawaiian framed welcome on the wall requesting that all shoes be removed. That was fine with me. My bunions could use a break from their leather prison.

"Thanks for coming," Dave said. "Can I get you anything?"

"I'm driving so I'd better not have any alcohol. How about a soda?"

Dave grabbed a can of cola out of the refrigerator. I peeked inside, curious to know what a bachelor's refrigerator looked like. Steve had it stocked with fruits, veggies, yogurt, beer and soda. No wonder the ship captain was in such great shape.

I followed Dave out onto the lanai where we caught the last flickers of the setting sun. As the ball of fire plummeted into the watery depths, I thought I saw a lime-colored burst of light on the horizon.

"Wow, is that a green flash?"

"Yeah, as long as there aren't any low clouds on the horizon, you can see them frequently. Whenever I have the time to actually watch a sunset, I think how amazing it is that I live in paradise." Dave picked up his long-necked bottle, guzzled half of it then wiped his lips with his fist. "Although lately it's more like *Paradise Lost*."

I sat in a beige cushioned chair, and Dave flopped down in a matching chair on the other side of the glass-topped table.

"So what's going on?" I sipped on my soda then placed the can on the table.

Dave described his night in jail. Only one other guy had landed in there, and they'd placed him in another cell, so Dave hadn't been saddled with a cellmate. He knew he wasn't guilty, so even before his attorney showed up, he'd waived his rights and answered the detectives' questions as best he could. It turned out he was able to provide them with new information regarding some of Keiki's recent activities.

"What kind of activities?" I asked. "And why didn't you tell me, or the police, sooner?"

"Remember, when the detectives originally interviewed me, I was traumatized that Keiki died due to what I thought was my negligence. Then when they arrested Regan for murder, all I could think about was getting my wife out of jail."

"And hours after Regan was released yesterday, you were arrested."

Dave took another slug of beer. "Those metal cots in jail are perfect. Not for sleeping, but for pondering what you did wrong. Or in my case, wondering what information I might possess about the killer."

I waited for Dave to share at his own pace, although I had to restrain myself from kicking his ankle to hurry up.

"I was seeing Keiki," he said.

Damn, I said to myself, as I knocked my soda all over the table. Dave rushed inside and brought out a wet sponge and a few paper towels.

"You're just as clumsy as you were thirty-plus years ago." He shook his head as he wiped up my sticky mess.

Just as he'd cleaned up after me three decades earlier. The French would say, «Plus ça change, plus c'est la même chose.» This American would say, "Once a klutz, always a klutz."

"Remind me to remove any liquids the next time I reveal something important," he said. I started to respond, but he shushed me. "And I need to be more specific. I did meet with Keiki twice outside the restaurant, but I was not—let me repeat— not having sex with that woman."

Gee, where had I heard that phrase before?

But my brother continued to look directly at me. No flinching. No twitching. He had nothing to gain and far more to lose if he lied to me or to the police.

"You heard Keiki used to date a guy her own age named Joey?" he asked. When I nodded, he continued. "She told me she started seeing someone else, a man with more wealth and sophistication than her former boyfriend."

"Do you know who she started dating?" Finally, a clue to the guy's identity.

Dave shook his head. "Nope, she didn't share his name and I really didn't care."

I sighed. Typical man. No nose for news or for gossip.

"What she did share," he said, "was that Joey took it real hard when she dumped him. I guess he told a few friends he was devastated enough to kill himself. Then he had that fatal accident at Koffee Land."

"Several people think he jumped off that zip-line tower on purpose. That it wasn't an accident." I said. "I saw it today. It's pretty high."

"It could have been suicide or an accident. But Keiki thought it was something else." Dave sipped his beer and stared out at the horizon.

"What else could it have been other than suicide or an accident? That only leaves—" Dave's eyes locked on mine as I realized what the third alternative might be.

CHAPTER THIRTY-EIGHT

"Murder? Keiki thought someone murdered Joey?" My head was spinning and I hadn't even touched a drop of alcohol. "Why? And who?"

He shrugged. "Why and who are both big questions now that she's dead. Joey called Keiki the night before he fell off the tower. Said he wanted her advice on something. At first, she thought he might be looking for a way to get back together, but he convinced her he was worried about something going on at Koffee Land."

"Did they have a chance to talk?" I asked.

"No. Joey died before they got together. She originally thought his death was a tragic accident like everyone else. Then a couple of people like his brother, Timmy, claimed Joey killed himself because of her. After Joey's phone call, she knew he wouldn't have committed suicide before they talked."

"Did she tell the police about her concerns?"

"No, she was still thinking it through, trying to figure it all out. She never mentioned any names, but she said it could have a huge impact on someone important to her. After sleeping on it last night, or rather *not* sleeping on it, I mentioned our conversation to the police. It turns out Joey's accident is still an open case. Anytime someone dies in an unexplained incident, the police keep the file open until it's resolved to their satisfaction."

"So we could be looking at a double murder," I clarified.

"We?" He lifted an eyebrow at me.

"Hey, you're the one who invited me over. By the way, what is the deal with you and Regan? Why are you spending the night here at Steve's?"

"I honestly don't know what's going on with my wife. Three years ago, when we first put together plans for the restaurant, it was such an exciting adventure. It was risky putting all of our assets into a business with a ninety-percent failure rate, but Regan couldn't have been more supportive. And the restaurant did well. Not enough income for the two of us to live on, but not bad for a new venture. She enjoys her profession and never complained about working to keep us afloat."

"When did Regan start working at Koffee Land?"

"Their controller quit about six months ago. Walea told Regan about the opening after Victor mentioned it to his family. He said they were having a tough time recruiting someone. CPA's don't exactly grow on palm trees on this island. And it was a lot more money than she was making at her old accounting job."

"Regan seems devoted to her boss and her job."

"Yes, she is." He rubbed his reddish beard that seemed to have acquired some new white hairs in the past few days. "Shortly after she started working there, she began putting in long hours. I couldn't figure out if it was all work or if some play had crept into the equation. Have you met Ritz? He's very smooth, very—"

"Very Cary Grant," I acknowledged, "but just because she works for a handsome boss doesn't mean Regan is having an affair with him."

"I know, but in the last few months we've drifted apart. I was afraid to question her because I wasn't sure I wanted to know if something was going on between her and Ritz. When Keiki approached me about her problem, it felt good to be needed by someone."

"Especially someone as gorgeous as Keiki."

Dave lifted his arms, palms out, and threw me a sheepish grin. "Hey, middle-aged guys need an ego boost every now and then, especially when their forehead is expanding an inch a day. And I have to admit, I was fairly certain Regan and I were headed down the highway to divorce court."

I felt like whacking him on his ever-increasing forehead. Middle-aged men can be such putzes around beautiful young women. "Okay, so Keiki came to you regarding something going on at Koffee Land. Why wouldn't she share the name of the person she was troubled about? Was she worried about their reputation? Or concerned that revealing the problem could result in some backlash to her?"

He shrugged. "I don't know. It could be something involving her family. Or maybe she was working up the nerve to disclose something about my wife and Ritz."

"I wonder why she thought Joey could have been murdered." I nibbled on my lower lip. "He must have seen something while he was working on the zip-line."

Dave nodded. "So the killer could be anyone. I can't believe I'm saying this, but it could even be my wife."

Whether it was the breeze shifting from the north, or Dave's comment, I suddenly shivered.

"Do you think Steve owns a light jacket I could wear?"

"Sure. He won't mind if you help yourself."

I opened the slider that led from the lanai into the master bedroom. It felt weird being alone in Steve's room, which was exceptionally tidy. A dark forest-green quilt and oversized pillows covered his king-size bed. His three-drawer bureau was a beautiful piece of furniture, made out of teak wood and carved in an intricate pattern. Beautiful though it looked, the last place my fingers should be walking was through Steve's drawers. I needed the answer to some serious questions, and they did not include whether the *Sea Jinx* captain wore boxers or briefs.

I pushed the mirrored door aside, hoping I could reach in and grab a windbreaker or sweater from his closet. The door jammed, leaving only a four-inch opening, not sufficient for me to reach inside the closet. I glanced down and noticed a piece of paper stuck between the door and the runner.

I reached for the paper, but it refused to budge. I yanked one more time and discovered the paper was actually a small photo. I brought the photo up to my face. Huh!

Why was Keiki smiling at me and what was she doing in Steve's closet?

CHAPTER THIRTY-NINE

I raced back to the lanai.

"You didn't find anything to wear?" Dave asked.

The goose bumps on my arms seemed to be increasing exponentially. I threw the photo at my brother.

"What are you—?" Dave stopped mid-sentence as he grasped the photo. "Where did you find this picture of Keiki?"

"On the floor of Steve's closet."

Dave stared at it for a full minute before responding. "Gosh she was lovely. But why would Steve have a photo of her?"

"I have no idea. Could Steve be the older man she was seeing?"

Dave flipped the photo back and forth in his hand as he gazed out at the ocean. "Man, I never saw that one coming. I know Steve dated someone a while ago, but he said he broke up with her." Dave's eyes met mine. "I had the impression he was becoming interested in you."

I rested my chin on my palms. "I kind of thought so myself. Especially after that last boat ride."

And especially after that burning kiss.

I sure do know how to pick them.

"Hey, just because we found Keiki's photo here doesn't prove anything. It could be work related," Dave said. "You know, for promotional reasons. She performed on his boat occasionally."

"True." Then I remembered a conversation from earlier today. "Amanda from the *Sea Jinx* said she saw Steve and Keiki together away from the boat on several occasions. Although she said the meetings took place awhile ago."

Dave and I stared at each other.

"Do you still want to spend the night with Steve?" I asked.

Dave slumped in his chair. "I don't know where to turn right now. I'm too exhausted to spend another night arguing with Regan, and now I'm not sure about staying here."

"Why don't you come back to my hotel? I'm sure Stan would let you bunk with him."

"I don't know about that."

"C'mon, the worst that can happen is Stan will talk your ear off all night."

"Or lend me his clothes." Dave snickered as he stood and followed me back inside the condominium unit.

I was relieved Dave retained his sense of humor. I couldn't imagine the stress he'd been under since the discovery of Keiki's body less than six days ago. Dave gathered his things while I loaded our dirty dishes in Steve's dishwasher.

Even suspects deserve to come home to a tidy kitchen.

We stepped into the elevator, which chugged down the three floors to the lobby. I could have made better time walking down the stairs. And if we'd taken the stairwell, we also wouldn't have been so surprised when we reached the ground floor.

The doors opened with a clang, followed by an "oh shit" from my brother.

Steve looked as surprised as I felt. "Where are you two going? Dave, aren't you spending the night?"

Dave froze in place, eyes wide. Lips silent.

Great. He picked a heck of a time to relinquish his big brother "I'm in charge" status to his baby sister.

"My mother was anxious to see Dave," I explained. "She's been beside herself with worry so we're going back to the hotel."

Steve looked surprised. "Did you get a room there?"

"No, I'll stay with Stan," said Dave.

That comment made Steve's blond eyebrows merge into a bushy question mark. "Okay, buddy, whatever you want. It's too bad 'cause I invited some friends over for a poker game. I thought it might lift your spirits to hang with us. But I'm sure you'll have an interesting time hanging with, um, Stan."

"Maybe next time," Dave replied. "This week has been pretty tough on Mom."

"Sure, I get it. Hey, Laurel, can I have a word with you?"

Dave and I exchanged looks, but he waited while Steve and I walked out to the open-air lobby.

"I'm worried about your brother," Steve said. "He told me about some of the stuff he shared with the cops. I hope the information won't put him in any danger."

So did I. Especially danger from the friend he'd shared the information with.

"I don't know who Keiki's murderer is, but they aren't getting near my brother."

Steve put his arm around my shoulder and drew me close. I swear I am the worst detective in the world. Here I was ready to put the guy in jail and throw away the key, and he still made me tingle.

I drew away from Steve. He looked perplexed but let me go. "So how will you keep Dave occupied for the next couple of days?" he asked.

I nibbled on my lower lip. "I hadn't really thought that far ahead. Liz arranged an ATV tour of Waipi'o Valley tomorrow morning so we'll try to include Dave."

"That should be a great trip. I wish I could join you, but we have a morning snorkel sail."

Steve's comments and actions seemed so normal I decided my suspect meter must be broken. There was no way such a nice guy could kill anyone.

Dave called out. "Hey, Laurel, let's get going."

I said goodbye to Steve and joined my brother. As Dave and I walked to the parking lot, I looked back. Steve was talking on his cell, frowning, as the doors of the elevator closed.

Dave took over the driving detail, which was fine with me. I realized that I'd been up since five this morning. Dave must be equally exhausted since he'd only slept a few hours in his cell. I replayed my conversation with his friend in my head.

"I can't imagine Steve as our killer." Dave echoed my thoughts.

"Me either." At least, I preferred that someone who kissed me was *not* a killer.

"You know if the cops don't come up with any other suspects, they can arrest me again."

"What kind of evidence do they have?"

Dave shot a glance at me then returned to stare at the dark and almost empty road ahead.

"In my opinion, a lot of the evidence is circumstantial," he said. I rolled my eyes. "How about your lawyer's opinion?"

"I guess it depends if the Prosecuting Attorney thinks she has a sufficient case against me."

"So share. What do they have?"

He drummed his fingers against the steering wheel. "Well, like I said, some people—I don't know who—saw me in town with Keiki those couple of times. It's not like we were trying to hide our meetings."

"They must have more than that."

"There is. An opened bottle of beer with my fingerprints was sitting on the rock wall, but it probably got missed when we cleaned up. The police also ran tests on those pieces of broken glass they found on the lava rocks below the restaurant. They got the results back and it showed something."

I gasped. "Like drugs?"

"A type of drug, I guess. They tested it, and it turned out to be Ambien."

"The sleeping medication? Do any of your bartenders or servers use it?"

He shrugged. "I have no idea if any of my employees use it. Unfortunately, I do."

My head swirled with Dave's new revelation. "So Keiki was poisoned?"

"They weren't originally sure if her death was an accident, suicide or murder. But the toxicology results showed that Keiki had Ambien in her system. Enough to put a dance troupe to sleep."

"Lots of people take Ambien. That's very circumstantial evidence." I loved the sound of that word "circumstantial" rolling over my tongue. Made me feel like I almost knew what I was doing.

"I think that's one reason they didn't feel they had enough hard evidence to charge me with murder—yet. Although Detective Lee stated that Walea pointed an incriminating finger at me. She claimed Keiki had a rendezvous arranged with her boss."

"You didn't meet Keiki, did you?"

He shook his head. "No. But when I arrived home after the reception, Regan and I got into it once again. She accused me of sleeping with Keiki, and I denied it. Then she stormed into the bedroom, slammed the door and went to bed, I guess. I watched TV awhile then went for a walk. Thought the night air might clear my head."

"Heck of a time for a stroll," I muttered, shaking my head at my alibi-less brother. On the other hand, his eyelids remained twitch-free. It appeared he was telling the truth.

"Hey, it's Kailua, for Pete's sake. This is as safe a town you can live in as anywhere."

Unless you're a hula dancer caught up in some nefarious activity.

"I guess if you were gone, Regan could have met Keiki at the restaurant and slipped Ambien into something she ate or drank." I glanced out the window at the passing scenery wondering if I should ask Dave the question that kept nagging at me. "Do you honestly think your wife could be the killer?"

"I don't know what to think. Ever since Ritz wangled this deal with *The Bride and the Bachelor* show, Regan's been wound tighter than a championship yo-yo."

"Was she stressed enough to fight with Keiki over you?"

"My wife can accomplish anything she sets her mind to," he replied. "Even murder."

CHAPTER FORTY

Saturday morning arrived far too early. I stumbled into the bathroom and stared at my bleary eyes. Once I returned home to Placerville, I would need another vacation to recover from this one. It seemed wrong to go on the ATV outing when we should be detecting, but it was the excursion I'd most looked forward to since we'd first planned this trip. Plus I felt my brother could use a break after his horrendous week.

The island brochures described the Waipi'o Valley as beautiful, serene, and a sacred area in the Hawaiian culture. With vistas 2,000 feet above the valley floor, twin waterfalls and a black sand beach, it was a guaranteed once-in-a-lifetime experience. Unfortunately, the only way to experience the beauty was to drive a four-wheeled all-terrain vehicle, or ride a four-heeled all- terrain horse.

The guys chose the gas guzzler, of course.

I yawned and followed the scent of coffee brewing in the miniature coffeemaker. I poured a cup then joined my mother on the lanai. She put down her magazine and stared at me. My hair was so wild and frizzy I was surprised the tiny yellow songbirds that greeted us each morning hadn't moved in and turned my head into a vacation nest.

"You look like crap," she commented, but in her usual elegant manner.

"Mahalo, Mother."

"Honey, maybe you should stay behind and rest. We're only here until tomorrow. Don't you want some time relaxing on the beach?"

"I'd like to spend a month lying on a chaise lounge with a daiquiri by my side, but that's not going to happen either."

"Did you and Dave come up with any brilliant deductions last night?" Mother asked.

I dumped a packet of sugar in my cup, sipped some coffee then opened one more packet. "Nothing other than the realization he can't trust anyone outside of our family."

"I hate to fly home and leave him all alone to fend for himself," she said. "Even though he was released, he's on the front page of the morning newspaper. The police stated the case is still an open investigation. Do you think that means they could arrest him again?"

"According to Dave, yes, they could." I stared at the distant ocean view. "How would you feel about extending our stay a few days?"

"I was going to suggest it myself. Why don't I skip the ATV ride and stay behind to change our reservations? Will your children mind if we're here a few more days? What about the bank?"

"The kids will be fine. They dote on their grandfather and he's probably spoiling them to death. And work won't be an issue." After saving the president of Hangtown Bank's reputation last year, I had a feeling he could spare me for a few extra days.

Although I'd worried about taking the ATV excursion when we should be investigating, Dave was thrilled to take the tour. Especially after he stopped at the restaurant and discovered reporters hoping to get an interview with a recently released murder suspect. We all agreed the break would be good for him.

Winding our way through Waimea cowboy country, we passed cattle farms and horse ranches set against the backdrop of snow-topped Mauna Kea. If I squinted, I could even see the world's largest astronomical observatory perched atop the 13,796-foot summit.

The rolling hills at this high elevation reminded me of the California gold country, except this tropical terrain received far more rain, leaving the hills greener than the finest emeralds. On my next trip to Hawaii, I was packing my cowboy hat and boots for a little *Paniolo* riding on the range.

I only hoped that any return trips to this beautiful island would involve a relaxing vacation and not a visit to my brother in a Hawaiian prison.

At the ATV tour center, our small group along with some other patrons mounted our red four-wheelers. Les, our friendly guide, demonstrated the use of the hand brakes and throttle, which seemed easy enough. We lined up in a straight formation, behind our leader. Although I'd never driven an ATV before, the instructions appeared fairly simple. I'd recently piloted a snowmobile. How hard could it be?

I strapped on my helmet, grabbed the handlebars and got ready for the ride of a lifetime.

CHAPTER FORTY-ONE

My first thought: I'm going to die!

My second thought: I'm going to die without ever having sex again.

That realization woke me from the fog of sheer terror that engulfed me when I realized my ATV was only a few feet away from crunching into a massive eucalyptus tree. I swerved to squeeze in between two gigantic trees, and my back tire nipped a palm on the right.

Thud! The tree I'd whacked attempted to return the favor by clobbering me with one of its coconut projectiles. It missed by a couple of inches. How did I get this far behind the rest of the group? And why weren't they looking for their missing friend?

I weaved my vehicle between a few more trees and finally reached a grassy meadow and scenic viewpoint where the rest of the tour group waited.

"What happened to you?" Liz asked, as I rolled to a stop next to her.

"Me?" I said. "Which way did you guys go?"

Stan pointed to a wide trail rutted with tire marks.

Oh, so that was the trail.

"I took an alternate route," I responded.

The tour guide snorted and Liz rolled her eyes.

"You're supposed to stay with the group," Liz said. "We weren't sure what happened to you until we heard you playing bumper cars with the trees."

Everyone's a critic.

The guide motioned for our group to follow him. I attempted to do a U-turn and discovered ATV's aren't that maneuverable. By the time I circled back, I was stuck at the end of the line again with a bunch of strangers. This time I would remain close to the group. The last thing I wanted was to find myself alone on one of the many trails leading in and out of this immense valley.

The clouds that had threatened to drench us all morning finally let loose. The patter of rain sounded like elves tap-dancing on my helmet. My eyelashes were working overtime blinking away droplets of water. I wondered if anyone had thought of installing windshield wipers on the helmets.

The trail seemed mushier by the minute. Tiny puddles rapidly turned into small streams. I knew that the all-terrain vehicles would not have any difficulty maneuvering in the mud. I, on the other hand, was not an all-terrain woman. I gripped the handlebars as if my life depended on it. Ahead of me, the riders reduced their speed to a crawl. A misty fog hovered over us as we reached the higher elevation of the rim overlook. The next time I visited the Waipi'o Valley I was bringing my yellow slicker and carrying a thermos of hot chocolate in my backpack.

I pulled alongside the other riders. Stan lifted his visor and shook his head in bemusement. "Looking a little raggedy, darling. You do know the visor goes down to cover your face."

I knew it now.

"I bet this ride is beautiful when it's not raining." I peered into the mist and pointed to the left. "Is that the waterfall over there?"

Stan squinted. "I think so. What a shame about the weather. We'll have to come back another time."

Yesirree. We'd have to do that for sure. I parked the ATV and wandered over to listen to Les. He pointed to a few distant landmarks, including the waterfall and the black sand beach far below, but the falling rain made it difficult to see them clearly. On a normal day, we would ride down to a small pool where the group could frolic and swim. Since the weather wasn't in a frolicsome mood today, everyone agreed with his decision to return to the center.

We loaded up in single-file formation. I ended up in the rear again with a rider behind me who was smart enough to bring raingear. It was comforting to have someone following me. I wouldn't have to worry about being stuck by myself if something happened to me or my machine.

The sooner this expedition ended, the happier I'd be. We might even arrive back at our resort in time to get in some last minute beach time. I visualized the perfect afternoon—lying on a lounge next to the ocean with my Kindle in one hand and a daiquiri in the other. And since it was a daydream, I visualized a hunky guy next to me—a guy with... with...I was so deep in thought trying to decide if my dream date was a blond, blue-eyed sea captain or a police detective with Godiva-brown eyes, that I didn't notice the ATV on my preoccupied tail.

Wham! My tush lifted in the air from the jolt of a machine ramming my vehicle. With a drop of over a thousand feet on my right, this was no place for an overly anxious driver. The trail was so slick, I was afraid to speed up to try to get away. I also didn't want to risk any backward glances checking on the rider behind me. Maybe he would realize his mistake and drop back.

Bam. The vehicle slammed into my back right tire. The jolt sent me flying off my ATV. I landed on the slick grass and began sliding. Down, down, down.

Right over the rim.

CHAPTER FORTY-TWO

The beauty of the flora and fauna in Hawaii never ceases to amaze me. Another wonderful attribute is the hardiness of the foliage. As I tumbled down the side of the mountain, my flailing arms managed to latch on to a thick green vine. I sucked in huge gasps of air while I clung with both hands to the remarkably sturdy plant.

I breathed deeply, trying to calm my stomach, which had catapulted up to my throat the moment I was airborne.

I had no idea if the rider who crashed into me was still in the area. Did he do it on purpose? Talk about road rage. And where did my own machine run off to? Had it crashed into a tree or even worse—another rider?

I yelled and screamed to no avail. The group was probably miles away by now. Would anyone realize I was missing before it was too late? Did Les keep track of the riders? Tears rolled down my muddy cheeks as I realized I was hanging from a cliff.

Alone and on my own.

Where was a blue-eyed or a brown-eyed hunk when I needed one? Although at this point, I would take a cross-eyed, cross-dressing hunchback if he could haul me back up the mountain.

Get a grip, Laurel. Or, at least, maintain the one you have. Thank goodness for my broken corkscrew back home. If it wasn't for my weekly fight with the wine cork, the biceps in my right arm would never have been strong enough to hold on until help arrived.

If it ever arrived. I shifted so I could look around to get my bearings, but the movement caused my left knee to scrape against some jagged rocks. The vine I clung to dropped a few more inches. A couple of stones bounced down the hill, pummeling my arms and legs.

The stalk of the plant drooped lower and lower and so did I. My tenuous grip was loosening, and I had no idea if the plant could continue to support my weight.

If I'd only skipped that second macadamia nut muffin at breakfast.

My head ached as if someone was repeatedly punching my helmet. The pounding increased as rumbling sounded above. Was my attacker returning to finish the job? Then the ground above me started to shake.

This had better not be an earthquake. I was in no mood for a natural disaster. I was enough of a walking, talking disaster without any help from unseen geologic forces.

A line of bright headlights beamed above, almost blinding me.

"Yoo hoo, Laurel," shouted Liz. "Hang on, luv. We're here for you."

"Don't let go," Stan yelled.

Like I would?

I cautiously lifted my head and spotted our tour guide anchoring a rope around a large boulder near the rim overlook. I hoped it was strong enough to support both our weights. The rubber soles of his shoes bounced off the cliff face as he worked his way down to where I clung to my sagging lifeline. In no time at all, Les was by my side and tying another rope around my waist. I walked, crawled and occasionally slipped back a few feet as I climbed uphill. With the entire group working together to hoist me up, I eventually made it to the top.

Once I reached the overlook, I could have kissed the ground, but I'd had enough close and personal contact with the muddy soil. I decided to kiss Dave, Stan, Liz, Brian, and the tour guide instead.

"How did you fall over the rim?" Liz asked. She wrapped her arm around my bruised and aching body, giving me a gentle squeeze.

"I was rammed from behind." The minute I uttered those words, everyone stopped talking.

Les whirled around, his dark eyes startled. "What?"

My eyes scanned the group of people gathered around me. "Someone rammed me. He wore a helmet so I have no idea what he looks like."

"Would you recognize the driver's clothes?" Stan asked, morphing into Hawaii Five-O mode.

"He was wearing raingear." I scrutinized the other riders more carefully, none of whom was dressed in any type of protective clothing. Could my assailant have stripped off his raingear and be hiding in plain sight? That was a disquieting thought. I rubbed my palms over my cheeks then looked at them. My hands were raw, covered with mud and something that resembled the color my hair stylist used on my roots.

"Oh, luv, your hands and face are bloody well messed up," Liz said. "And I left my Aloe Vera packets in the hotel. They're so soothing in moments like this."

"Yes, there's nothing like some soothing Aloe Vera lotion to erase the memory of FALLING OVER A CLIFF!"

"Are you up to driving yourself back on your ATV?" Les asked. "If not, you can sit behind me."

The weight of making a decision about how to drive back to the ATV center suddenly seemed like the weight of the world, and I dropped to the ground. Dave immediately flopped down next to me. He put his arm around me and reminded me of all the numerous incidents in the past when I'd managed to return home after falling off my bicycle, out of a wagon, off my skateboard, and off the roof of the doghouse.

Yes, I was pretending to be Snoopy. Doesn't every five-year-old?

By the time he'd finished regaling me and the other riders with some of my childhood antics, Dave had me laughing so hard over previous incidents in my checkered youth that my ribs ached even more than before. Once again, just as he'd done many decades ago, my big brother came through for me.

Dave offered to have me ride behind him, and even though it was a tight fit for us siblings, I smiled in agreement.

Like they say, blood is thicker than water, and I had the blood dripping down my face to prove it!

CHAPTER FORTY-THREE

By the time we reached the tour office, I felt beat-up and beat. I practically fell out of the ATV, but Les, our guide, was by my side in seconds, prepared to escort me into the building. My friends and brother were right behind me. The minute the woman in the center laid sympathetic eyes on me, she reached under the counter and pulled out a full-size first-aid kit.

"Gal, you look like you been run over by an ATV. Did that machine give you some trouble?"

I nodded, which made my head feel like it was stuck between two cymbals performing a rendition of "The Stars and Stripes Forever."

"She had a run-in with a cliff," Stan said. "I think the cliff won."

"Well, you come with Naomi and I'll get you all fixed up like new."

Naomi led me into the backroom where she proceeded to smother my assorted body parts with fragrant oils. An assortment of BandAids soon dotted my arms and legs. Liz had followed us in and the two women compared notes on their favorite healing lotions and potions. My friend assured me that Naomi's *kukui* oil combined with Liz's special Aloe Vera salve would turn me into a new woman. No one would ever know I'd experienced a literal cliff-hanger.

On the car ride back to the hotel, I struggled to remain awake. Worried that I'd suffered a concussion, Dave insisted on nudging me every time my chin dropped to chest level. We finally stopped at a

Starbucks in Waimea. Dave decided if a double shot of espresso and one of their dark chocolate bars wasn't sufficient to keep me from dozing, then we would need to find an urgent care facility.

For years, Dave had claimed I needed to have my head examined.

The gasps from a few customers when I entered the store, warned me I must look like a complete disaster. There had been no mirrors in the ATV center so I almost suffered a heart attack when I entered the ladies' room and saw my image reflected over the sink. I looked like a cast member of *Survivor*.

And not one from the winning team.

After five minutes in the bathroom, I realized nothing outside of laser surgery or black magic would improve my appearance. I joined the gang seated at a table in the corner. Brian must have gone outside to make a call because he walked back in, stuffing his cell in his Bermuda shorts pocket.

"How do you feel, luv?" asked Liz.

"Like a convoy of ATVs ran over my body."

"You're lucky to be alive," Brian said. "Did you see how far down that drop was into the valley?"

Yes, indeed. I'd definitely noticed the two-thousand-foot drop into the valley below me. My hands trembled as I gripped my drink. Dark brown drops of hot espresso dotted the table.

Stan grabbed a napkin and cleaned up my mess. "So tell us why you think you were intentionally knocked off your ATV?"

I sipped the dark brew and let the coffee work its comforting warmth into my stomach before I replied.

"The driver rammed me twice. The first time I managed to hold on to the ATV, but just barely. I figured he was simply a tailgater and hit me accidentally. The next impact was more forceful. It had to be intentional."

"Do you think it was a case of road rage?" Liz tapped her stir stick on the table while she contemplated the possibilities. "Even if no one in the group admitted to it?"

I shook my head. "I suppose there are crazy drivers anywhere, but it felt like such a personal attack. I've mulled it over, and now I'm wondering if it had something to do with Keiki's murder. Maybe someone wanted me out of the way."

"They almost succeeded," Liz said dolefully.

"Who knew you were going to be on the ride this morning?" Brian asked.

Dave and I exchanged glances. At least one person knew about our excursion. But he should have been out riding the waves this morning. Not riding on an ATV.

CHAPTER FORTY-FOUR

Regan called Dave while we were en-route to the hotel. With the reality crew arriving at Koffee Land the next day to begin filming, Regan claimed that Pilar insisted she stay onsite overnight to assist them with any issues that might come up. Victor would be unavailable due to Keiki's memorial service the next day.

A range of emotions crossed Dave's face as they conversed. Anger that his wife was placing her career over her husband once again, seemed to be followed by relief that he didn't have to worry about said wife sleeping next to him that evening. At least one thing was certain. Regan wasn't anywhere near Waipi'o today.

We dropped Dave at his home so he could clean up. Since Brian had to be in court Monday morning, this was the newlyweds' last night on the island. Brian and Liz wanted to run errands and pick up souvenirs to take home. Her eyes twinkling, Liz declared she had a special surprise in store for me. Knowing my best friend's quest to discover the next anti-aging miracle cream, she probably planned on emolliating me with some slick new spa item she'd discovered on the island. With my arms throbbing from my cliff-side descent, I welcomed anything that would soothe my aching limbs.

Dave agreed to drive over to the hotel and dine with Mother, Stan and me later this evening. My watch showed three o'clock, and, concussion or not, I needed a nap. Maybe I could find a hammock near the beach. Once my mother saw my condition, I sincerely doubted she would let me rest without a lengthy grilling.

Fortunately, Mother was out when I entered our room. I flopped on the bed, a huge mistake, since the firm mattress was not designed to soothe a battered body. The walk into our marble bathroom entailed only five additional steps, but my limbs were so stiff and sore it felt like five miles. A hot toddy and a hot bath sounded wonderful.

And a *hot Tommy* to hug me and kiss my many boo boos sounded even better.

I shook my bedraggled curls. It was a good thing the detective wasn't on the island. There was no way I wanted Tom to see me in my current condition. Most women would worry their boyfriend wouldn't be interested in a body as bruised and battered as mine. My detective, on the other hand, would shift into investigative mode. The last thing I needed was another lecture.

The bath proved the perfect cure. My aches disappeared beneath the hot water and jasmine-scented bubble bath provided by the hotel. The bubbles not only soothed my physical aches and pains, they cleared the fog from my brain.

Did the driver of the ATV intend to kill me or just delay me from investigating any further? As far as anyone knew, I was supposed to fly home the next day. Did I possess some critical knowledge pertaining to the murders? Even if I still hadn't figured out what it was yet?

Much as I hated to admit it, the most likely suspect had to be Steve. I sank deeper into the bath, my sigh so robust a bevy of bubbles floated out of the tub. The ship captain had employed Keiki on several occasions. I found that photo of the dancer in his bedroom. Although he hadn't come right out and said he was interested in her, he admitted he'd found Keiki enticing. It would have been easy for Steve to frame Regan, or his best friend, Dave. Plus he'd invited me on board the *Sea Jinx* the night I almost drowned.

The final nail in the coffin I felt like shoving him into was that he knew I would be at Waipi'o Valley today.

I jumped out of the tub and grabbed one of the oversized fluffy white towels from the rack. The relaxing heat from the bath was nothing compared to the white-hot anger that surged through my body toward the person who'd tried to kill me.

I needed to stop him before he did any more harm to me. Or to anyone else.

CHAPTER FORTY-FIVE

Imagine my astonishment when I arrived at the hotel restaurant to dine with my mother, Dave, Stan, and a surprise guest.

Steve. The man I'd recently voted most likely to be our killer.

As I slid into the vacant chair between Steve and Stan, I sent a "what the heck were you thinking" look across the table to my brother. He threw his palms up indicating he was as clueless as I was.

My mother provided the answer to the question in our eyes. "I ran into Steve in the lobby and invited him to dine with us. I knew you wouldn't want to leave without spending some time together, Laurel."

Steve casually placed his arm along the back of my chair. I shot him an accusing look. He either didn't recognize an accusatory stare or he was an exceptional actor.

"Your mother's timing was perfect," Steve said. "I dropped by because I wanted to talk to both you and Dave."

How convenient, since I also wanted to talk to him. "How was your snorkel expedition today?" I hoped my question would catch him off guard and he would reveal his true whereabouts this morning.

"We had a decent turnout," he said. "We were a little short-handed, but I think everyone had a good time." His knee touched mine ever so slightly. "Of course, it would have been more fun if you were on board serving drinks."

Steve winked at me. "Wearing that attractive tablecloth."

I blushed at his distracting compliment. Focus, Laurel. I twisted in my seat and stared at him, trying to ascertain if he was lying. "So you weren't at Waipi'o Valley this morning?"

Steve looked at me as if I was suffering Alzheimer's symptoms. "No, remember, I told you last night we had an early morning sail. Your mother mentioned you had a slight accident. Those ATV's can be tricky when you're a beginner."

"They can be especially difficult if someone tries to kill you."

"What?" Steve and my mother gasped simultaneously. I forgot that Dave and I decided to inform my mother I'd had a minor accident, not that someone had forced me to learn rock climbing in one not-so-easy lesson.

"The driver of one of the ATVs intentionally rammed me," I apologized to my mother. "We didn't want to upset you."

"I don't understand." Her face turned whiter than the napkin resting on her lap. "Who would do such a thing?"

"Someone who knew we would be riding ATV's in Waipi'o today," Dave said. "That leaves one person we know of." He leaned forward, his expression fierce as he glowered at his best friend. "We told Steve where we were going last night."

Steve's expression quickly changed from confusion to a mix of disbelief and anger. "You thought I had something to do with it? That I attacked Laurel on her ATV? Are you kidding me, pal?"

Steve rose from his chair and threw his napkin on the table as he glared in my direction. "And here I thought you were beginning to have feelings for me. I sure do know how to pick them." He turned to my mother. "Barbara, thank you for your invitation, but I think it's time for me to leave. Good night, all."

Steve strode out of the restaurant and into the lobby without a backwards glance. Stan threw me a guilty look. "You might want to stop him. Don't forget we told Keiki's parents we were going on the ATV ride. I also told Tiffany. And a guy at the front desk I was kind of flirting with last night."

Hmmm. Now that I thought about it, I'd also told Ritz about our trip, and he could have shared it with anyone. Geez. Was there anyone on the island who *didn't* know our travel plans?

Dave shot out of his chair and zipped around the tables, chairs and servers to catch up with Steve. In the space of a week, Dave had lost an employee and possibly his wife. Now it looked like we'd chased away his best friend.

I followed in Dave's wake. I felt horrible that we'd accused Steve of attacking me when all our evidence consisted of was my suspicious nature and the crumpled photo of Keiki I'd found in his closet.

I was an even worse detective than Inspector Clouseau.

I hustled as fast as I could, but every inch of my thighs and calves ached. I finally caught up to Dave and Steve arguing in the lobby. I shoved myself between the two men. "Hey, guys, stop right there." Dave's face was almost as red as his receding hair and beard. Steve was tight-lipped and cool, but he didn't try to leave.

I ordered them to follow me to a grouping of chairs in the lobby. Dave collapsed into one of the soft cushioned seats while Steve remained upright and tense.

"Look, Steve, I can see why you're upset." I cringed as my bruised booty made contact with one of the smaller settees. "We thought there was a ton of evidence pointing in your direction."

Steve lifted a brow. "Anything you could have shared with me before I vaulted to the top of your suspect list?"

"Look, man," Dave said. "We found a photo of Keiki in your closet the other night."

"Why were you going through my things?" Steve's reply was cooler than a cup of Hawaiian shaved ice.

"Dave and I were sitting on your lanai talking," I explained, trying to mend the rift I'd created between the two men. "The breeze from the ocean picked up, and I felt chilled, so he suggested I borrow a jacket from your closet. When the sliding door jammed on a piece of paper, I grabbed it and saw it was a photo of Keiki."

"That's your evidence? Good thing you aren't applying for a job with the Hawaii police department," Steve said. "Keiki asked me to take some photos of her a while ago. I use a professional camera for the cruise passengers' pictures. She was submitting an application to be a contestant for that reality show they're taping at Koffee Land."

Dave chimed in with his own accusations. "We also told you about the ATV trip."

Steve ran his hand through his unruly blond hair. "I mentioned to the gang at poker last night that your group was going up there.

I've never taken the ATV ride and I was curious if anyone else had been on it. You didn't say it was a secret."

Dave and I exchanged glances.

"Who was at the poker game?" I asked.

"The usual suspects." Steve smiled slightly. "I didn't mean it that way. Or maybe I did. My crew was all there. Plus Rick, the guitar player, and a musician friend of his he brought along. That's one of the reasons I wanted Dave to participate. I knew you were concerned about your sister falling off the boat, and I thought this would be a great opportunity to discover if my crew saw anything suspicious that night. Or if someone would admit to pushing Laurel, either intentionally or accidentally. Beer is an excellent accelerant in getting a confession."

Dave shrugged. "That wasn't a half-bad idea. I wish you'd told me about it in advance."

Steve frowned. "You never gave me a chance. You insisted on returning to the hotel, remember."

I sure did remember. Boy, I sucked at detective work.

"Did you learn anything from the guys?" I asked.

Steve nodded. "That's why I drove down to the hotel to see you tonight. Timmy normally joins us for our Friday night game, but he didn't show last night. I figured with everyone well lubricated, I could bring up your concerns about being pushed and maybe lure them into revealing something."

"Did your plan work?" I asked.

"It was a very successful fishing expedition."

CHAPTER FORTY-SIX

"What did you use as bait?" I asked.

Steve's smile managed to be both sexy and sincere as he replied, "You."

I leaned back into the cushions. "What?"

He winked at me. "I told the guys how much I enjoyed your company. That I was trying to woo you back on the boat again but after your last life-threatening experience, you refused. I think the guys really felt my pain."

Hmmm. They should feel *my* pain!

"After a few beers Rick finally admitted he might have seen something."

"Why didn't he say anything before?" I asked.

"Rick had gone back up on the deck looking for his cell. He figured he must have left it behind when they were playing. The rain was coming down heavy and visibility was difficult, but he thought he saw you at the stern. Then less than a minute later when he located his phone, he looked up but only saw Timmy in the same area. He didn't think about it again until we realized you were the one who'd gone overboard. When you showed up okay—" Steve stopped as I glared at him. "Well, not entirely okay, but at least you were alive. Rick figured there was no need to say anything more, especially since he didn't see anything conclusive."

"Did Rick question Timmy about it?" Dave asked.

Steve shook his head. "Rick and Timmy aren't exactly buds. But he apologized to me for not mentioning anything earlier."

"Remember that night on the boat when I first encountered Timmy below deck, I saw him shove some packages in a small locker and put a padlock on it. Is there any chance he's selling drugs?"

Steve sighed and looked pained. "I didn't want to believe it when you first mentioned it, but you may be on to something. Timmy not only didn't show up for the poker game last night, he never showed up for the sail today. And he never called in. With Amanda off on that reality show gig, we ended up short-handed."

I pondered how easy it would have been for Timmy to learn about our ATV ride from one of the crew. Very easy, it seemed. I was about to question Steve further when Stan interrupted us. "Regan's on the phone for you, Dave. She said you weren't answering your cell so she called your mother."

Dave leaned over and shook hands with Steve before following Stan back to the restaurant.

I stood and smoothed my sundress, prepared to follow my brother.

"Please sit," Steve said. "I have something to say."

I plopped back on the loveseat half wishing I could hide beneath the overstuffed cushions. I was embarrassed we'd accused Steve of murder, although my theory seemed so plausible a few minutes earlier. Steve parked himself next to me, his muscular thigh pressed against mine. For a minute, we sat in silence. The lilting sound of Hawaiian music drifted up from the bar below. Steve leaned close. The tips of his fingers grazed my reddening cheeks as he tucked an errant curl behind my ear.

My eyes widened as I realized he was about to kiss me, and there was a strong possibility I would kiss him back.

The sound of someone clearing his throat behind us broke the spell. I shifted closer to the side of the small sofa, unsure if I was relieved at the interruption or not. What would Tom say if he could see me now?

Seconds later, I had the answer to that question.

CHAPTER FORTY-SEVEN

"Tom!" I squealed as I jumped up. "What are you doing here?"

"I might ask you the same question." The detective's angry eyes darted back and forth between Steve and me.

I was so eager to greet Tom that I almost climbed over the loveseat, but I'd already fallen over a cliff today. I didn't need to add to my collection of bruises by falling on top of Tom. I zipped around the sofa anxious to jump into his welcoming arms.

That's when I noticed *no* arms were reaching out to welcome me. Instead, Tom stood rigid, his arms folded, right foot tapping, and eyes sparking with outrage.

Steve also stood, arms folded, left foot tapping. They resembled a set of matching angry bookends. I had a feeling neither Dear Abby nor her sister, Ann Landers, ever encountered a situation like this.

For some reason it's either raining men or I'm in the midst of a three-year drought.

Fortunately, Stan arrived to save me.

"Tom, boy do we need you," Stan said. "Your girlfriend almost went home in a body bag today."

Trust Stan to find a way to stop everyone in the lobby.

His remark fortunately distracted Tom from the vision of me cuddled up next to the good-looking captain.

Within seconds, my toes dangled above the marble floor as Tom lifted me, enveloping me in his muscular arms. He smelled like a mixture of lime and musk, but with an exotic hint of plumeria added to the mix. Our lips fused together, and every ache and pain from the day's misadventures disappeared.

Heat coursed through my body, and we probably would have stood melded together all night if a few spectators hadn't started clapping. Tom gently set me down and I reluctantly untangled my arms from around his neck.

"Are congratulations in order?" yelled one woman, pointing at her left hand.

Tom's face colored and he shook his head. Despite my state of euphoria from that sizzling kiss, I was disappointed at how quickly he'd responded in the negative.

I glanced in Steve's direction. He leaned against a column, his expression quizzical. My own expression wasn't any less questioning. I turned to Tom. "How did you get here?"

He flapped his arms. "I flew."

Very funny. "No, what are you doing here?"

"The trial was delayed a week, and after talking to Brian yesterday, I decided to take a few days off. I thought you'd be pleased to see me. But..." Tom shot a look in Steve's direction. "Perhaps I'm interrupting something?"

"No, Steve and I were just discussing the murder. He's been very helpful."

Tom's eyebrows furred together. "I could see how accommodating he was trying to be."

Steve smirked and inched so close that his lips almost touched my ear lobe. "We're not done here," he whispered. Then he kissed my cheek and sauntered out of the lobby.

Tom still looked annoyed so I tucked my arm through his. "Now that you're here, what's on your agenda?" I asked.

He smiled the smile that made his crow's feet crinkle and my lady parts tingle.

"Knowing you, there will be plenty on my agenda." He leaned closer. Instead of the kiss I anticipated, he yawned in my face. "Sorry." He looked at his watch. "It's almost midnight California time. It's been a long week."

"It's been a long day for me, too." I winced as he embraced me and drew me in tight.

You can't get much past a homicide cop, even a weary jet-lagged detective. "How are you feeling? Brian and Liz told me about your accident when they picked me up from the airport."

"It wasn't an accident." I bristled at his assumption that the person who rammed me had not done it on purpose. "That ATV driver intentionally tried to send me over the cliff."

Tom ruffled my hair. "Hon, what are the odds someone knew you were taking the ATV tour, arranged to be on said tour, and managed to get you alone and knock you off the vehicle?"

Detectives are so darn logical. When he put it that way, I almost agreed with him. But every inch of my bruised body declared him to be wrong.

Although he did call me "hon." That was one heck of a distraction.

Liz and Brian hurried toward us, both beaming like Cheshire cats on a catnip drip.

"How do you like our little surprise?" Liz wiggled her eyebrows. "Or, rather, our big surprise."

I grinned back. "Tom is the perfect antidote for today's incident."

"We worried about you detecting on your own without us along to protect you," Brian said. "So we lured Tom over here for a few days."

My smile disappeared as I debated what they used for a lure. My sparkling personality? My penchant for getting into trouble?

Another dead body?

I glanced up at Tom and he quickly reassured me. "It didn't take much to convince me. Plus I was about to lose some of my vacation time if I didn't take it soon. After a good night's rest, I'll be ready for some sightseeing. And some relaxing beach time, of course."

"It's a beautiful island. And tomorrow there is something special on the agenda."

He leaned in and whispered in my ear. "Is it a quiet and romantic getaway? For just the two of us?"

I smiled. The two of us plus a few hundred mourners. What better place to discover the beauty of the island than Keiki's memorial service?

CHAPTER FORTY-EIGHT

Despite becoming involved in a murder investigation, this trip had provided a wonderful opportunity to learn more about the Hawaiian culture. Not only are the indigenous islanders the most gracious people in their attitude toward their *ohana*, their own family as well as any extended family, but they also bid farewell to their loved ones in a unique manner. This morning Keiki's family members and close friends would ride outrigger canoes out into Kailua Bay for a short ceremony. Then they would disperse her ashes into the ocean and pray for her spirit to depart in peace.

Although Victor and Kiana had invited us to their house for the memorial reception, we weren't close enough to their family to participate in the seaside ceremony. Not to mention that two of my own family members were suspects in the murder of their daughter.

Talk about awkward.

Since I had a murder to solve and anyone could watch the service from shore, I planned to be one of the onlookers.

Our group assembled in the lobby to bid tearful goodbyes as the newlyweds headed to the airport. Brian almost looked relieved as the bellman carted off their luggage. Preparing for his murder trial the following week would probably seem like a vacation compared to spending his honeymoon with my family.

Dave and Regan each planned on stopping by Victor and Kiana's house later in the day, along with the owners and staff of Koffee Land, who would take turns paying their respects to the family.

Tom and I wound up being the only ones watching the seaside ceremony from the shore. The sight of the six outrigger canoes arranged in a semi-circle beyond the reef was more moving than I'd anticipated. Even when someone is not personally acquainted with the deceased, there is nothing like the poignancy of a memorial service to make you reflect on your own life. Your achievements and what you hope to accomplish in the future. At this point in my life, my accomplishments comprised a very short list consisting of my two wonderful children. By the time I depart this earth, I hope that list will have grown exponentially.

My eyes teared up, and I swiped my fist at my cheek. Without a word, Tom reached into the pocket of his khaki slacks, pulled out a handkerchief and handed it to me. I dabbed my eyes then gave it back to him. He eyed the mascara-dotted cloth and stuck it back in his pocket.

"You okay?" he asked, with a sensitivity I found surprising.

"Yeah." Another sob almost erupted, so I took a couple of deep breaths before I replied. "This has been an emotional week. It's not often two family members are arrested for murder. And even if the police discover the real killer, I'm fairly certain Dave and Regan are headed for divorce court."

Tom put his arm around my shoulder. "Once the police wrap up the case, your brother and his wife may be able to save their marriage. Sometimes it just takes time to heal those rifts."

I nibbled on my lip, curious if Tom would discuss his previous marriage. "You sound like an expert on that subject."

"Even the happiest of couples have issues. Communication or lack thereof is the biggest source of marital breakups." Now it was Tom's turn to be pensive. My question probably brought back a ton of memories of his late wife who'd passed away a few years earlier.

I mentally kicked myself for bringing up this tragic subject, but Tom leaned in and kissed me on my surprised, but very receptive lips.

"Let's make sure we keep those communication channels open at all times, okay?" His eyes were soft, his tone tender.

"Always. I'll never keep anything from you."

"Good. So I don't have to worry about you getting into trouble trying to find a killer without me, right?"

Nope. With my detective by my side to protect me, I couldn't possibly get into trouble.

Could I?

* * *

After the seaside burial, I drove the rental car through downtown Kailua pointing out various places of interest such as Hulihee Palace, the former vacation home to Hawaiian royalty. I decided to continue on Alii Drive rather than head immediately for the highway. I pulled into the lot at Daiquiri Dave's and turned off the ignition.

"What are we doing here?" Tom asked.

"I thought if we stood in the exact spot where Keiki was murdered, you might get a better feel for the crime scene," I said. "The Hawaii police would be lucky to get your input."

"That's not a bad idea." He eased his six-foot-three inches out of the sedan. "I doubt the local officials want my feedback, but let's take a look."

The door to the restaurant was locked which I'd already anticipated so I led Tom around the left side of the building to the public viewing area.

A middle-aged woman sat on the lone concrete bench overlooking the ocean. A shrill howl echoed from below. As we approached, the woman peeked over her shoulder and smiled.

"Terrific view isn't it?"

I nodded and looked around for her pet. "I could have sworn I heard a dog."

She laughed. "That's Ruckus, my beagle. Aptly named, I might add. He's easily bored so I let him loose."

I peered over the edge and saw Ruckus barking his pea-sized vocal cords off. "Looks like he found some buried treasure."

"Unfortunately Ruckus isn't the most discerning treasure hunter around." She leaned over the wall and whistled. "C'mon, boy, back here."

Her beagle might be a little ADHD, but he knew to obey his mistress. His owner, Helen Morris, introduced herself as a retired history teacher who'd moved to the island six months earlier. In less than thirty seconds, Ruckus was running in circles around us.

He dropped his clump of seaweed booty on the ground then sat quietly with his tail swishing, waiting for applause from his mutual admiration society.

A small item glinted among the seaweed. I leaned over to pick it up but met with resistance from Ruckus. Since I preferred to keep all my digits intact, I withdrew my hand. Helen had better luck. She tossed him a liver treat and reached for it herself.

I peeked over her shoulder as she plucked the item, iridescent in the bright morning sun, from its seaweed nest.

"It's an earring. Pretty stuff," I said.

"It's abalone which is very popular in Hawaii. There are all types of variations, but most have a greenish or blue hue." She squinted at the earring. "There's something caught on the hook. I can't tell what it is without my glasses."

I put my hand out to grab it, but my professional cop beat me to it. He scrutinized the earring then looked up. When his eyes met mine, I felt as chilled as if a bucket of ice just dumped on me.

"It may look like leather," he said, "but I think it could be a piece of skin."

Helen and I leaned forward and gawked at the brilliant earring with the infinitesimal piece of skin attached to the wire.

"You don't suppose—that earring belonged to Keiki?" I asked.

Tom shrugged. "It could belong to anyone who's been in this area or even dined at the restaurant. Although it's odd the skin is still attached."

"Could Keiki have pulled it off her killer?"

"Killer?" Helen drew back and yelled for Ruckus to return. I quickly explained about Keiki's death the previous weekend, although I skipped a few details—such as my family members' arrests.

Tom looked frustrated as he stared at the shiny item in his hand. "Too bad I don't have any evidence bags with me."

I reached into my purse and grabbed a small clear baggie. I never leave home without them. Convenient for buffet leftovers as well as evidence. I dropped the earring into the bag and placed it in a side pocket of my purse.

Helen seemed as anxious to leave our company as Ruckus was to explore new territory. We said goodbye and got into our car.

"You need to turn that earring over to the police," Tom said. "It could contain the DNA of the victim, or the killer."

"Of course. I'll do it right after the memorial service."

Tom was right. The earring might be an important clue. Or it might not. For all we knew the item could have been buried for days or weeks before the murder. But before I turned it over, I would check with my sister-in-law to see if the earring belonged to her.

It's not like I was withholding evidence from the police. I was merely storing it for them.

All I had to do now was pray that the owner of said evidence wasn't married to my brother.

CHAPTER FORTY-NINE

Tom and I enjoyed the leisurely ride to Victor and Kiana's house. I drove so he could enjoy the lush south Kona scenery.

"I assume today's visit isn't just a sympathy call," Tom said. "Will we be searching for additional clues amid all the condolences?"

"Maybe." I kept my eyes glued to the curvy road. "My plan is to keep my eyes, ears, and lips open."

"Lips?"

I nodded and smacked my lips. "They have terrific pupus here."

Tom laughed and we spent the rest of the drive chatting about our "case." In the past, Tom and I had been on opposite sides of a murder investigation, and I'd been forced to morph into Nancy Drew to keep myself, and later my boss out of prison. Now I felt like we were part of a detecting duo. Nick and Nora to the rescue.

All we needed was a Schnauzer, matching fedoras and a very large bottle of gin.

We drove past the Yakamuras' house. Cars lined the street in all directions, including the rental my mother and Stan drove. We ended up parking a few blocks away. As we walked up the long gravel driveway, the lilting sound of a Hawaiian song floated toward us. Since the music seemed to come from the backyard, we headed that way. We arrived in time to see Walea and three other dancers pay tribute to Keiki.

My breath caught as I watched the dancers' eloquent movements to the words of a plaintive melody. Multiple spigots opened, and tears rained down my cheeks again. At the rate my tears were erupting, Tom needed a handkerchief as big as a bedspread. The thought of that beautiful and talented young woman's life cut short was heartbreaking. Until this moment, I'd been determined to prove the innocence of my family members. Now I was even more committed to finding the murderer for Keiki's sake.

The musicians put down their instruments, and the dancers dispersed to visit with friends and family members. Eighty plus people milled about the backyard, but I had yet to see any of my own family wandering about. A man standing in front of me taking photos with his phone completely blocked my view. I accidentally bumped into him and his phone crashed to the ground.

"I'm so sorry, let me get that." I bent over, but he was faster and grabbed it first. We barely missed a forehead collision. I wobbled on my wedge sandals, on the verge of falling, but Tom grabbed my hand and kept me upright.

"I'm sorry," I apologized to the man's back.

He turned around and surprised both of us. "Ms. McKay, what an odd coincidence. I didn't expect to see you here." Detective Lee's eyes narrowed when he met Tom's cool gaze. Lee must have recognized a kindred spirit because he put his hand out and introduced himself.

Tom shook Lee's hand and said, "Detective Tom Hunter with the El Dorado County Sheriff's Department."

A half-smile formed on Lee's thin lips. "So you've brought in reinforcements from California? Your brother doesn't have faith in the Hawaii Police?"

"Of course we do. Tom is my…." I hesitated. What was Tom's official title in my life other than investigating detective?

"I'm Laurel's boyfriend joining her for a few days," Tom said. "Completely off-duty. I'm looking forward to exploring your island. I've never been to Hawaii before."

I grinned. I could get used to that word—boyfriend.

Lee tapped his phone against his palm. "There are many wonderful attractions to explore on our island although some are more dangerous than others. Such as the ATV ride in the Waipi'o Valley. One hears rumors that occasionally a tourist gets rammed and almost killed."

My mouth opened wide enough to stick a foot-long Subway sandwich inside. "How did you hear about that?"

"We've been watching everyone involved in this investigation." Lee's unblinking eyes locked on Tom's face. "I'd advise you to keep an eye on your girlfriend. Someone is not happy with her. And I don't need another murder on my island."

"Don't worry," Tom replied coldly. "It's under control."

Lee strolled off, undoubtedly to terrorize someone else. It actually made me feel better knowing the detective was on site assessing the crowd. If he was checking out Keiki's friends and family then he was less likely to be arresting my friends and family.

I had some investigating of my own to do, but couldn't figure how to go about it with Tom by my side. Despite his earlier remarks that he planned to assist me, I doubted he would interfere with an official investigation. Especially now that he'd met Detective Lee.

I led Tom over to a bougainvillea-covered arbor where Keiki's parents greeted their guests. Maybe he would come up with some pertinent question I'd overlooked so far. Kiana stood placidly next to her husband and stepdaughter, as elegant and graceful as ever. Her dark hair flowed down her black linen sheath. I couldn't tell whether it was her natural demeanor, or if her doctor had prescribed some "tranquility" drugs.

Victor didn't seem to be holding up as well as his wife. His eyes looked bloodshot and his face blotchy. Even though Keiki was his stepdaughter, the young woman had lived under his roof for over eight years. As a parent, I would imagine if something this devastating happened to one of your children, it would leave an emotional scar that would last forever.

I introduced Tom to Keiki's parents.

"I'm so sorry for your loss." Tom reached out to take Kiana's hand. "I'm a widower and I know how painful it is to lose someone, although one should never lose a child."

Kiana held his large palm in her tiny one. "*Mahalo* for your kind wishes, but my daughter is at peace at last."

Walea, who stood next to her stepmother, rolled her eyes. I worried she would go off on another "slut of a stepsister" tangent so I jumped in before she could mouth off. "I heard Keiki tried out for *The Bride and the Bachelor* reality show."

Walea nodded. "She was excited when she found out she was a contestant. I was happy for her. I hoped her dreams might finally come true."

"Such a sad situation," I said. "The bachelor could have been her Mr. Right."

Walea frowned and shook her wavy mane. "Keiki could have cared less about a proposal from Jacques Cointreau, although he had looks, money and fame. All she really wanted was the notoriety and glamour of participating on the show."

"It could have been a big break for her if she wanted an acting career. We stopped at Koffee Land after we saw you on Friday," I said. "The reality show was holding a reception for the participants. Did you know Amanda is a contestant?"

"I didn't realize she'd made it, too." Walea said. "Amanda's the one who told Keiki about the show to begin with. They've known each other since they were both cheerleaders in high school."

A ha. Did I know a former cheerleader when I met one or not!

"She seems like a sweet kid," I said. "I hope the show works out for her."

Walea nodded. "I do too. The two of them were friends, but it seemed like they were always competing with one another. Whether it was for boys or beauty pageants, my little sister always had to be number one."

A woman whose long gray braid trailed down the back of her flowered *muumuu* walked up to Kiana and whispered in her ear.

"I'm sorry, I guess we're out of coffee," Kiana said. "Will you excuse me? I need to make some more for our guests."

"Can I help?" I offered. Making coffee seemed the least a member of my family could do to assist Keiki's parents.

"Mahalo, you are so kind. There are two coffeemakers on the counter, and you'll find the coffee beans in the pantry."

Tom and I walked away, and I pointed to my mother and Stan across the lawn. "Why don't you join them while I get the coffee started for Kiana. Just watch out for anyone with a suspicious look on his or her face."

"I'm a homicide cop. Everyone looks suspicious to me," Tom said. When I frowned, he kissed my forehead. "Don't worry, you're currently exempt from that description."

For a change.

I opened a screen door that led directly into the kitchen. The beautiful Koa wood cabinets gleamed, but I didn't see anything that resembled a pantry door. Maybe the pantry was located outside of the kitchen.

I wandered down a hallway, past a laundry room, and opened a door. Nope, that was the garage. I went in the opposite direction, but the only door I found led to a linen closet.

I walked back down the hallway and opened the door leading into the garage again. Maybe in Hawaii they built pantries in the garage for better storage in the humid climate. The Yakamuras' garage contained a car and a truck, a tool bench and the assortment of stuff that tends to accumulate in garages. Although their accumulation of "stuff" appeared far less messy than mine did. One more item to add to my spring-cleaning to-do list when I returned home.

Off to my right was a white-paneled door. As I drew closer, the smell of fresh coffee assaulted my senses. Finally. Then I realized a small brass padlock hung on the doorknob. I shook the padlock and it came loose. It seemed somewhat odd for Victor and Kiana to padlock their pantry. They must have unlocked it so they'd have access to the storage area during the party. With an extra push of my hip, I shoved the door wide open.

Talk about the mother lode. This door didn't open to a pantry. It opened to a huge room running the length of the two-car garage. Inside the room sat piles of one-hundred pound burlap bags of coffee beans. All labeled with a familiar logo in lime green and purple.

KL for Koffee Land.

CHAPTER FIFTY

The potency of a ten-by-twenty square foot room stuffed full of coffee beans was enough to bring on a caffeine migraine. I started counting the bags then gave up. There were at least a hundred of the huge sacks containing what looked like pulped green coffee beans stored in the room. A table near the entrance was bare except for a stack of unmarked brown bags.

I shut the door to the private room and re-entered the garage. My head reeled with questions and a coffee hangover. I knew Victor managed the coffee operation, but would that also entail distribution? Even with my limited knowledge of the business, it didn't make sense for so many bags of Koffee Land beans to be stored off-site. I kept trying to think of a reason for the secret stash, but nothing came to mind.

I entered the house, retracing my steps down the long hallway to the kitchen. Walea stood by the counter, waiting for some fresh coffee to brew.

"We wondered what happened to you." Her eyes narrowed and I wondered if I smelled as if I'd been bathing in coffee beans.

"I needed to use the powder room. Sorry I didn't get the coffee started. Is there anything else I can help you with?"

She gave me a funny look and shook her head. I went back outside, my brain creating and abandoning a variety of scenarios regarding the coffee stash.

I noticed my family and friends congregated under a huge banyan tree. Regan was just the expert I needed. I barreled across the green lawn and reached the group in seconds.

"We were about to send a search party for you." Tom's tone sounded light, but his eyes indicated he'd been anxious about my absence.

"Sorry. Something distracted me." I turned to Regan. "Just out of curiosity, how is your coffee distribution handled?"

Her expression suggested I'd drunk one too many cups of coffee, or alcohol, if I had a burning desire to learn the answer to that question right now. "You mean how do we sell our coffee?"

"Yes, sort of. Do you also sell your beans to other coffee farms?"

She shook her head. "No, some of the smaller farms sell what we refer to as parchment—that would be the dried green beans—to some of the larger more established processors. Then they handle the milling, roasting and distribution of the product. We process only our own beans at Koffee Land and sell directly from there, either to customers who come into the store or to people who order over the internet. Knowing Ritz and Pilar, eventually they'll expand and start selling to grocery stores and other outlets."

"Why do you want to know?" Mother asked.

"Oh, just idle curiosity."

Stan and Tom snorted simultaneously at my response.

Honestly!

I took Regan aside. "So you don't store Koffee Land beans any place outside the farm?"

She shook her head. "No. What's going on?"

I looked in the direction of Keiki's parents. I couldn't accuse them of theft during this reception honoring their deceased daughter. That would be too cruel. But did those bags in the storeroom have something to do with Keiki's murder?

"I've been talking to people and heard bits of conversation here and there," I replied. "When we took that tour with you the other day, you discussed the value of green coffee beans. The bagged coffee you sell ranges from thirty-five to forty-five dollars. Aren't the beans themselves worth significantly less?"

"It depends whether it's a good crop year or not. A bag of green beans is usually worth from $9 to $10 per pound. With the borer beetle destroying crops like they have at Koffee Land and other farms, the price has gone up in the last few years."

My analytical brain kicked into gear. A hundred-pound bag of green coffee beans could be worth close to a thousand dollars. And there had to be at least one hundred bags in that storeroom if not more. We weren't talking pennies.

We were talking a hundred thousand dollars. And that was just for the beans stored in the room at this moment. How many coffee beans had made their way in and out of Victor's garage in the past few months? Or years?

CHAPTER FIFTY-ONE

I glanced at Victor who stood alone by the patio. It appeared that he, in turn, was watching me. I worried that Walea had mentioned my wandering around their house without supervision.

My lips felt dry so I reached into my purse for my pink lip gloss, which was tucked into the side pocket, right next to the evidence baggie containing the earring we, or rather Ruckus, had discovered. This would be the perfect opportunity to hand it over to Detective Lee. But, first, I needed to show it to Regan.

I pulled Regan away from the group once again and led her to a shaded corner where we could be alone.

Her lips curved into a half-smile. "More urgent coffee questions?"

"Maybe, later. I found a piece of jewelry and wondered if it belongs to you." I grabbed the clear bag and held it in front of her face. She looked curious but not concerned.

"Can you take it out of the baggie?" she asked.

Probably, but I couldn't chance adding any more of Regan's DNA to the evidence file for this case. I also didn't want to tell her where I'd found it.

"I need to keep it secure for now," I replied, evading the question. "It's an abalone earring. Is it yours? Or have you seen it on anyone else?"

She shook the bag, trying to get a clear view of the earring, but even I could see it was difficult in the shade. Regan moved away from the tree and into the sunlight. She brought the bag closer to her face.

"I have a couple pairs of abalone earrings. I love the bluish green hues, but I don't remember losing one. I can check when I get home tonight."

"Do you know anyone else who owns a pair?"

"I don't know of anyone who *doesn't* own a pair. They sell them everywhere. They're pretty, fairly inexpensive, and durable." She scrutinized contents of the baggie. "It looks like something is stuck on the wire. I wonder what it could be."

"Yes, it is most curious, isn't it?" said an annoying familiar voice.

"Detective Lee, I was looking for you." I threw a friendly smile in his direction, but it bounced off his grim façade.

"Of course you were. Would you care to share anything with me, or do you normally keep abalone earrings in sealed bags?"

No wonder the man made detective. He must be part dolphin because his hearing was sonar quality.

Regan watched as I plunked the bag into his open palm. "Where did you find the earring?" she asked.

"At the outlook next to Daiquiri Dave's."

Regan gasped. "Where Keiki went over the wall?"

I nodded. "Tom and I stopped to take a look this morning. While we were there, a woman's dog dug it up. I planned to hand it over to you, Detective. This was my first opportunity."

Sort of.

He sniffed. "If you see any more dogs digging up jewelry, I would appreciate a phone call. Immediately." He reached in his pocket and pulled out his card. Then he led me away from Regan.

"Ms. McKay, despite your lack of knowledge regarding the chain of evidence, you seem like an intelligent woman. And an empathetic person as well. Please do not let your feelings for your family lead you to destroy any evidence you come across. It could result in harm to others. And possibly to you."

"I appreciate your concern, but Detective Hunter is here to protect me."

"Yes, I recognized his name from your official file."

I stepped back. "You have a file on me?"

"Every potential suspect in this case has a file. Let's make sure yours doesn't turn into another murder book."

Detective Lee strolled across the lawn leaving me with my mouth open. Not an unusual state. The sound of a soft Hawaiian melody snapped me back to the present. I recognized Rick, the young musician who played at Liz's reception and on Steve's boat the other night, strumming chords on a guitar. As his bare arm moved up and down, the tail of his dragon tattoo flashed then disappeared again.

Henry stood next to him playing his ukulele. The guests had moved aside to make room for the dancers whose timing was impeccable as their arms and hips moved simultaneously, sharing the story told through the music.

The music suddenly stopped, and the dancers halted. Several guests swiveled their heads in the direction of the gate. I followed their gaze to see my brother walk into the yard.

When Dave realized he was the center of attention his face turned redder than the bougainvillea bushes lining his path. Now that I thought about it, he probably hadn't spoken to either of Keiki's parents since her death. I could understand why he felt he should attend. Keiki was not only an employee, she had also confided in him. Would her parents be pleased or upset that he stopped by?

One person indicated his displeasure immediately. Henry dropped his ukulele on the ground and marched up to my brother. I was too far away to hear their conversation, but since Henry began to poke Dave in the chest, it didn't look like he was welcoming my brother with open arms.

Someone needed to clue Henry into the aloha spirit. My mother circled the two men, prepared to jump in and rescue her offspring if need be. I noticed Lee creeping closer as well, although his intent was most likely to catch someone incriminating himself.

Tom appeared behind me. He wrapped his muscular arms around my waist. "What's going on? Do I need to break anything up?" It felt so good to have someone to lean on for a change.

"I'm not sure. The guy yelling at Dave is Henry, Walea's husband."

"So I'm guessing the guy who looks like you except for the balding hair and..." Tom's voice trailed off as his palm lightly brushed the curved part of my body that bore no resemblance to my brother.

PING!

I slapped myself mentally. There would be plenty of time for pinging later.

I grabbed Tom's hand and hauled him into the melee. "Tom, meet my brother Dave. And this is Henry. He's the excellent ukulele musician we heard earlier."

"I enjoyed your playing, Henry. And Dave, it's a pleasure to finally meet you."

"Same here. I appreciate you jumping in and saving my little sis from that killer."

Henry's eyes widened. "Killer? What are you talking about?"

Tom and I exchanged glances. "Let's just say murder has brought the two of us together on more than one occasion," I said.

"We can sure use your help investigating Keiki's murder," Dave said to Tom before he turned back to Henry. "I've said it over and over, but I'll repeat it once again. I did not kill Keiki. She came to me for advice and I tried to help her."

"Keiki came to you for advice?" I jumped when I realized Victor had joined us.

Dave stuck his hands in his pockets and rocked back and forth. His eyes flicked from Henry to Victor then back to me. "Keiki said Joey was concerned about something going on at Koffee Land."

"Joey wasn't involved in the coffee operation," Henry said. "He worked for me putting in the zip-line." A worried expression crossed his face. "What did he tell Keiki?"

Victor put a reassuring hand on Henry's shoulder as he addressed my brother. "I doubt my daughter knew anything about Koffee Land worth discussing. Dave, I appreciate your gesture coming to our house today, but your presence is making my wife uncomfortable. I think it would be better if you left now."

Dave looked embarrassed as he glanced at me. Detective Lee joined us and drew Dave aside from our group. They conversed briefly then Dave spoke to me. "I guess I better leave. Laurel, I'll see you and Tom later on."

Tom and I watched along with everyone else as Dave left with the detective. Victor and Henry walked off and rejoined their wives.

Regan raced up to join us. "Where are Dave and Detective Lee going? Is he under arrest again?"

I shook my head. "No, Victor thought it best for Dave to leave. He claimed Dave's presence was making Kiana uncomfortable."

Regan stomped her foot as I looked on in astonishment. "Well, that's just wrong." Then she ran out the gate after the two men.

"What was that all about?" Tom asked.

"I don't know. My brother and his wife are the perfect candidates for Dr. Phil's show. Or maybe Jerry Springer."

We waited to see if Regan would re-appear, but she and Dave both must have left. Detective Lee also did not return and I hoped his lack of an appearance did not signify that one of my relatives was back in custody.

We said brief farewells to Keiki's family, all of whom seemed anxious for us to depart. As I went into the house to make a pit stop before the long drive, I noticed the woman with the long gray braid and dressed in the green muumuu, brewing a pot of coffee.

I walked up to her. "That sure smells good. Do you know which brand it is?"

"It's Victor's own coffee. He grows beans here, roasts them himself and then sells them to some of the locals."

Interesting. I had many more questions about the nature of the garage storage room, but I would save them for the next day when I took Tom to Koffee Land. As we walked back to our rental cars, we discussed Victor's enormous coffee stash. Mother and Stan agreed it was odd, but they also thought there could be an easy explanation. Perhaps Victor liked to recycle the cast-off Koffee Land bags. Or Ritz needed beans stored off-site.

I shoved the mysterious coffee cache to the back of my mind. As Tom and I drove back to the hotel, I concentrated on a burning question that had nagged at me since Tom's arrival yesterday. A question that caused my body to create its own version of a Kilauea eruption.

Tom flashed one of those melt-in-your-arms smiles at me. Be still my heart and all those girly parts that were celebrating in advance. Geez, you'd think it had been years since we'd partied with anyone.

Oh yeah, it had been. Shoot. Would I even remember how?

I pondered if it truly was dead bodies keeping Tom and me apart. Was I the one who was afraid of our relationship escalating? How could I expect to take the place of Tom's deceased wife in his heart, or in his life? Was he looking for a replacement, or just someone to do the horizontal hula with?

And why was it whenever Tom and I were together, I had far more questions than answers?

CHAPTER FIFTY-TWO

Tom and I managed to sneak away from Stan and the others for an intimate evening at the hotel's best oceanfront restaurant. After consuming an excellent seafood dinner and finishing off an equally excellent bottle of wine, we strolled down to the surf, hand in hand. I almost forgot to worry about where our relationship was going. Standing barefoot on the beach, our arms entwined around one another, seemed a wonderful way for it to begin.

The smell of Tom's cologne and the taste of his soft lips against mine made me forget about everything except the need to be with him. Our bodies surged together as the waves crashed around us. The noise of the waves made it almost impossible to hear him crying out my name.

Wait a minute. As far as I knew, Tom wasn't a ventriloquist. If his lips were locked on mine, who was yelling for me?

Actually, more to the point, who wasn't calling my name? When I pulled away from Tom's embrace, I discovered Regan, Dave, Stan and my mother staring at us. The next time Tom and I walked down to the beach, I was attaching a "do not disturb" sign to the back of my head.

My family can find more ways to ruin a romantic evening. With my fists clenched on my hips, I shouted over the boisterous waves. "What's the matter?"

Stan bounded up to us, his entire body pulsating with excitement. "Dave and Regan had a heart to heart talk," he said. I muttered, "Finally," and glared at my brother and sister-in-law in the distance.

Stan went on, "When they started discussing what each of them knew individually, they put two and two together, and came up with the killer."

Okay, that was probably a good enough reason to interrupt us, although it didn't mean I had to like it.

Tom and I grabbed the shoes we'd tossed on the sand. We walked back to the grassy area, so we could carry on a conversation without the din of the monstrous waves crashing around us.

"What did you two discover?" I asked Dave and Regan. Despite having our kissing interrupted, I couldn't help but smile to see them with their arms wrapped around each other's waists.

Nothing like detecting to bring a couple together, I always say.

Dave looked sheepish. "Once Regan and I realized we'd both jumped to conclusions suspecting each other of having an affair, we started comparing notes."

"Yes." I impatiently tapped my sandaled foot anxious to return to Tom's embrace.

"I didn't know Joey had shared his concerns regarding Koffee Land with Keiki," Regan said, "until Dave told me that was the reason he'd met with her away from the restaurant." She leaned over and kissed him on the cheek. "And Dave wasn't aware I'd heard a conversation between Joey and Henry regarding the safety of the zip-line platforms. Joey was concerned the pilings weren't deep enough to support the forty-foot towers."

"That could be serious," Tom interjected.

"The original structures weren't supposed to be that high, but they decided to raise them when they added the tandem line," Regan explained. "I overheard that conversation a few weeks before Joey's fall but assumed Henry and his crew corrected the problem. I know they did some repair work after Joey fell off the platform."

"Or jumped," Stan added.

"Or was pushed," Dave said. "I don't know if we'll ever discover the truth regarding his fall."

"The murderer could have killed Keiki if he thought she knew too much," I threw in.

"Henry must be the killer." Dave punched his right fist in the air to punctuate his announcement. "That's why he kept threatening me. To throw us off his scent."

"Your theory's plausible," Tom said. "But not conclusive. I'm sure Detective Lee has considered all of Keiki's family members as potential suspects, including her brother-in-law."

"Yeah, but does Lee know about the conversation between Joey and Henry?" I asked Regan. "Did you tell them when you were arrested?"

She shook her head. "I never thought of it until a few minutes ago when Dave and I began comparing notes."

I reached into my purse and grabbed my cell. Interesting how two detectives in two different states were on my speed dial.

Definitely not something to tweet about.

My call landed in Lee's voicemail, giving me only twenty seconds to state my message. Shoot. I couldn't even order a meal from McDonald's in that amount of time. I told him to meet us at Koffee Land at ten in the morning.

And to bring his handcuffs.

CHAPTER FIFTY-THREE

Homicide definitely trumps hot hotel sex. Not that Tom and I had made any plans to roll around the 800-thread-count sheets in his room. For some reason, confronting a murderer in the morning seemed easier than confronting a man in my bed the morning after. I was beginning to think I needed some couch time.

What I couldn't figure out was if I needed it with Tom or with a therapist!

By the time my alarm sounded, I'd thrashed around so much my sheets looked like I'd hosted a busload of tourists under the covers. At least one problem was resolved the previous evening—Dave and Regan's relationship. They were making out like teenagers when they headed home to their condo.

Tom had politely escorted Mother and me back to our room so my night ended with one chaste kiss and the promise of more to come tonight. All we had to do was ensure the police arrested Henry this morning. Then we could relax and enjoy the remaining two days of our vacation.

Since all the zip-line work had been completed, Regan wasn't positive if Henry intended to stop by Koffee Land, even though today was its inaugural run. Once she reached the office, she would call and notify him his final check was ready for pick up. It was a substantial sum, and she was confident he would pick it up in person rather than wait for the mail.

Detective Lee hadn't returned my message so I didn't know if he was busy with another matter, or just ignoring the musings of an amateur sleuth. Tom possessed zero authority on the island. He was coming along solely to ensure I didn't attempt anything I'd regret later.

I'd gone on my laptop the night before and Googled zip-line construction. I discovered a previous accident on the island that had occurred because the pilings hadn't been driven deep enough into the shifting volcanic soil to support the height of the zip-line tower. Did Joey threaten to share his concerns with Ritz? Or the authorities?

Unfortunately, everything we'd learned so far was hearsay, and we'd based our deduction solely on statements made by Joey and Keiki. Statements that could not be corroborated by anyone still living—other than our suspected killer— Henry. I tried to find a flaw in our logic, but our suppositions made sense to me. Regan had overheard a conversation between Henry and Joey regarding the safety of the zip-line tower. Joey had confided in Keiki about a concern regarding Koffee Land. Henry had threatened both Dave and me on different occasions, and he'd been on the *Sea Jinx* the night I fell overboard.

I was also comfortable with our plan. We'd devised an excellent strategy to lure the suspected killer to Koffee Land and we'd notified the police. We even had a backup detective although he was more moral support than official backup.

We arrived at Koffee Land and found a temporary barrier blocking the entrance. A sign indicated the coffee plantation was closed to the public this week. How did I forget the reality show began filming today? Should I warn Lee to be discreet? No blue lights flashing or sirens blaring?

Tom and Stan moved the barrier so it only partially blocked the driveway. That way Henry could get in as well as the police, assuming they were interested in my nocturnal musings. When we drove up to the parking lot, we found it filled with vans, trucks, cars, and people.

"Do you think we can watch them tape the show?" Stan asked me, eyes hopeful. Reality TV trumped detecting as far as my pal was concerned.

"I don't have a clue," I replied as we walked up the sidewalk to the entrance. The door to the center bore a "closed" sign, but when

I pushed on the door, it opened. My sister-in-law knew we were coming, so they must have posted the notice for any tourists who ignored the driveway blockade.

I walked through the deserted center calling out Regan's name. Victor's and Regan's offices were vacant, as was what I assumed was Ritz's office, far grander than the other two. Plus a bigger clue: the walls were loaded with plaques and trophies engraved with his name.

"Maybe everyone is out on the set," Tom said.

That's why he's the top guy in the sheriff's department. And in my heart.

"Sounds like the perfect excuse to visit the pavilion. Stan will be thrilled. I just hope he doesn't try to win the bachelor for himself."

We bumped into Ritz on our way out of the center. He informed us that the building was supposed to be closed since all of the staff was out on the set.

"Do you think we can watch them shoot the show?" I asked Ritz as he locked up the center.

"This is a closed set so we're not supposed to have any visitors, but I guess you're family of sorts. Just keep quiet once we get over that rise."

Running into Ritz was a convenient coincidence since my coffee questions had been percolating in my mind all night. Along with thoughts of the killer.

"Ritz," I said, "your operation is so amazing. I don't know how you've managed to maintain the quantity and quality of your coffee production on top of your other expansion plans."

Ritz puffed out his chest, clad today in a silky taupe aloha shirt and paired with taupe trousers. I wondered if the man even owned a pair of jeans. My gaze drifted to Tom's cute denim-clad tush, as he and my mother walked ahead of us.

That man was born to wear jeans. And some day I wanted to be the one to take them off him.

Back to my burning coffee questions. "Do you store all of your beans on the property? Ever use other temporary storage facilities?"

He shook his head. "No, we have plenty of space for our current crop. In fact, we have enough capacity to double production. That insidious borer beetle finally hit us this year so Victor has had his hands full ensuring only a small percentage of our acreage has been affected. Thank goodness for his expertise managing our crops."

If Ritz only knew that Victor's expertise may have diverted coffee beans away from Koffee Land and into his own hands. I wondered what drove the long-term employee to cheat his boss. Did it have anything to do with his family? Perhaps it was expensive supporting Kiana? And what about Keiki? Did she factor into Victor's theft?

Or did Victor factor into her murder? I couldn't imagine Victor killing his stepdaughter. The grief in his eyes appeared to be real.

But so was Keiki's murder. Very very real.

CHAPTER FIFTY-FOUR

The pavilion area looked exactly how I expected a reality TV show set to look.

Pandemonium in paradise.

Cameras, computers and people everywhere. In the pavilion itself, a dozen young women in colorful outfits chatted with one another. It didn't look like anyone, much less the four of us, would be noticed in the melee.

I finally spotted Regan and Tiffany, both recognizable by their lime green Koffee Land shirts.

I turned to Ritz. "I see Regan but I don't want to interrupt her. Do you know who that woman is?" I pointed to an elegant Chinese woman dressed in a summery silk suit who conversed with one of the camera crew.

"You don't know Stacey Leung-Crawford?" Ritz's tone indicated his admiration for the woman.

No, that was a name I would definitely remember.

"She used to be the evening news reporter for KXXA news in Honolulu."

"I haven't had time to watch the local news." Except for the terrible evening when the police arrested my brother, which miraculously did not make the late night news.

"Stacey is a big deal on the island, and one of the producers of *The Bride and the Bachelor*. She hopes it will be hugely successful and make national prime time. I think Stacey is determined to make national prime time herself. Follow me. I'll introduce you."

I was more than happy to follow Ritz, and my detective trio trailed behind us. The female contestants and Jacques Cointreau, the male star, stood near what appeared to be a refreshments tent. He looked hot which wasn't surprising given the above normal temperatures today. The Bachelor chugged half a bottle of water then dumped the rest on his head. The water did nothing to mar Jacques's striking good looks and bronzed, muscled body.

Quite the contender. If I were twenty years, twenty pounds and two kids lighter, I'd have auditioned for the show myself.

Not really, I thought, stealing a glance at Tom. Our last two days together had given me renewed hope for our relationship. Maybe one of these days the two of us would star in our own bride and bachelor reality show. But without millions of viewers looking on.

A couple of men wearing Koffee Land polo shirts stood under the zip-line tower. "Are the contestants taking a zip-line ride today?" I asked Ritz.

"Yes, that is one of the reasons we had to rush construction," he replied. "The final inspection was completed Friday so the inaugural ride will be today. Jacques will zip with five of the women." Ritz pointed to the sky where a helicopter was flying in from the south. "They can film the ride from above. Isn't it amazing?"

He was right. It truly was remarkable. These girls were lucky. Even if they didn't land a husband, they would still have the adventure of a lifetime.

Ritz tapped the famous island newscaster on her pink silk shoulder. She whirled, a look of annoyance crossing her delicate features. Seeing Ritz, her expression changed from irritation to delight. She leaned forward to let the elegant plantation owner air kiss each of her perfectly made-up cheeks.

"Ritz, you wonderful man, what a breathtaking spot you have here. I'm so glad you suggested it for our show."

"But of course. Koffee Land has everything one could desire."

Stacey's gaze drifted over to Tom Hunter, who was eying her with his usual cool composure.

"And who is *this* handsome man?" Stacey widened heavily mascaraed eyes as she questioned Tom. "Are you interested in auditioning for our next *Bride and the Bachelor* show?

Tom smiled and crossed his hands in front of each other in a "no way" gesture. "Nope. I'm not an actor. Just a tourist."

She smiled a brilliant smile of her own and reached into an off-white lizard handbag that screamed Prada. "Here's my card in case you change your mind. You have a natural attractiveness. The women will eat you up."

Hey. The only woman who got to eat Tom up was me, and I wasn't sharing my dinner. I introduced myself to Stacey, who merely nodded. She didn't hand over a business card so she evidently didn't anticipate any male contenders noshing on me.

When Ritz and Stacey left to find the reality show's director, Regan and Tiffany joined our group. My sister-in-law looked tired, but happier than I'd seen her since our arrival.

I nudged her arm. "How's Dave?"

"He's fine. We were up late last night, um, talking." Regan giggled. "I told him to sleep in. He should be here any time though. He wanted to participate in catching..." she stopped when she realized Tiffany was absorbing every word. "Tif, honey, why don't you check out the food tent and see if they need refills on coffee or anything."

Tiffany smiled and bounded off toward the tent.

Regan shook her head. "Ah, youth. Dave wanted to be here when the police arrested Henry." She spun around, her expression puzzled. "I haven't seen Detective Lee yet. Didn't you call him?"

"I left three messages. I don't know whether something more important came up or if he decided Henry isn't a viable suspect. Did Henry pick up his pay check yet?"

"It's tucked away so he can't grab it and run. Ritz said Henry was coming by to make sure everything was okay for the initial run." She chewed on her thumb. "It's still difficult for me to believe Henry would kill Joey and Keiki because he was worried about his reputation. Tom, do you think we could be wrong about Henry?"

"Hey, you know my position. I think you should all stay out of the detective's way and let him solve this case," Tom said. "I'm just here to make sure Laurel doesn't do anything stu..." he stumbled then finished, "stupendous."

"Nice save," Stan remarked.

"Weeks of practice," Tom shot back.

Men. Gay or straight. They were all annoying at times. I turned my back on both of them and glanced around to see what the contestants were up to now. The women, all equally adorable ranged from petite to tall and sported hairdos that ran the gamut from short blonde bobs to long ebony manes. The pavilion looked like a mini-United Nations with a myriad of ethnicities represented.

Amanda caught my eye and waved. The vivacious marine expert appeared to be in her element. I grabbed Tom's hand and led him over. Between the beautiful contestants and Ms. Leung-Chandler, I wasn't leaving Tom alone for a second. Otherwise, before I knew it, he'd be signed up as the poster boy for the *The Bride and the Bachelor, Cougar Edition*.

"Hi, Laurel, isn't this exciting?" Amanda eyed Tom curiously and I introduced him as my boyfriend from California.

She furrowed her brow. "Does Steve know you have a boyfriend back home?"

My face colored and I diverted the conversation to something safer than my love life. "Did Steve find someone to help out while you're shooting the show?"

"Timmy finally showed up for last night's sunset sail so Steve said he could fill in for me temporarily. Steve was really ticked off about his disappearance. But Timmy has listened to my lectures for months now so he should be okay. I feel kind of bad about taking off for the show."

"Where did Timmy go?"

Amanda's eyes opened wide. She looked left then right as if she were about to disclose a state secret. "I asked him about it, but he said it would be better if I didn't know. He had things to take care of. Something about his family's honor, whatever that means."

"So he's been gone since Friday?" I mulled over Timmy's disappearance for the last three days. Where had the young man gone, and what had he been up to? Too bad he hadn't shared anything with Amanda.

"Do you get to ride on the zip-line today?" I asked.

"No, I was a last-minute substitution and the girls were already selected for the zip-lining. Jacques and I are going to picnic at the beach instead." Her green eyes grew misty. "I think a picnic will be so much more romantic."

She stared at the bachelor, her gaze intent. "Once he and I are alone, we can really make progress in our relationship. I'm sure none of these other girls have researched him like I have. We're a perfect match."

Amanda noticed Stacey Leung-Crawford beckoning to her. "Oops, gotta run." She raced off to join the bevy of beauties heading to the viewing deck. We wished her luck then walked back to join Stan, Mother and Regan.

"Henry's here," Regan said. "He and Victor walked by a few minutes ago. I swear Victor looks like he's aged a decade. Keiki's death has really shaken him. I hope he doesn't fall apart if Henry is arrested."

"Does Victor need to be here today?" I asked.

"He wants to ensure the camera crew doesn't go into any areas where our current crops are planted. We don't need any more crop infestation. I was reviewing the numbers Victor provided from last week's cherry picking, and they totally suck."

I had a feeling the sucky numbers had more to do with the excess coffee in Victor's garage than a beetle colony residing at Koffee Land.

"Has anyone ever stolen beans from Koffee Land?" I asked Regan.

She frowned. "Are you worried some of the film crew or contestants might try to break into our warehouse and steal beans? The building is locked and no one has access other than Ritz, Victor and me."

"Why would anyone want to steal coffee beans?" Stan asked. "It's not like you can hide them in your underwear or anything."

Regan nodded. "Yeah, all the beans are stored in hundred-pound bags. I suppose someone could break in and steal the bags from the warehouse at night. But why?"

Financial gain for one thing. And I'd just discovered the person I suspected of stealing the beans had access to the warehouse.

Was it time to get the Kona coffee crook to 'fess up?

CHAPTER FIFTY-FIVE

I decided to discuss my suspicions with Regan before confronting Victor. I told her about the enormous coffee cache in his garage. She was understandably stunned. "That's impossible. Victor would never steal from Koffee Land. This farm is his life."

Being the pragmatic detective who dealt with criminals on a daily basis, Tom jumped into the conversation. "Circumstances can change people and turn honest men into thieves. Maybe he's suffered some financial losses recently."

Regan mulled over Tom's comment. "Victor has been acting oddly the last month or so, but I thought it was due to the beetle infestation he was dealing with here. Or Joey's death. Keiki had dated Joey on and off for several years and I knew Victor was fond of him."

"What should we do?" asked my practical mother. "Do you want to discuss it with Ritz first?"

I looked around for Ritz. Stacey Leung-Crawford was formally interviewing the Koffee Land owner. No point ruining this wonderful publicity-filled moment for Ritz. Even if one of his employees was a caffeine crook.

I spun around looking for Victor. He stood by the zip-line, talking to Henry.

"Regan, why don't you and I speak with Victor," I said. "Give him an opportunity to explain himself. Maybe there's a logical explanation for what he's done. Tom, could you keep Henry occupied until Detective Lee gets here?"

Tom frowned. "I'm not obstructing an official investigation."

"I'm not asking you to interfere with the investigation, although they haven't done such a great job so far." I pulled my cell out of my purse. "See, there's nothing from, oh…crap," I said, noticing Lee had indeed called. I'd forgotten to turn the mute off this morning. I listened to Lee's voice mail. He and a couple of officers were en route and should arrive around eleven. I checked my watch. Ten minutes to eleven.

"Detective Lee should be here any minute," I told Tom. "I'm sure he'd be grateful if you could detain Henry until he arrives."

"I'll come with you," my mother said to Tom.

"You're not going anywhere near Henry," Tom said. "Your husband, my former partner, would have my badge if I put you in any danger. Why don't you and Stan go back to the visitor center and wait for Lee and his men. You can direct them so they don't waste time trying to locate us."

Isn't it amazing what a rational plan you can come up with when a real detective is involved?

Tom, Regan and I left the pavilion, passing by an array of cameras, computers, and other equipment, none of which I could name, but all of which required long thick black cords extending to the electrical outlets in the pavilion. Five contestants were sequestered in one area along with two of the Koffee Land guys who'd worked on the zip-line. Those girls must be zip-lining with Jacques today. As we walked up the hill, the scenery once again blew me away. The view from above would be jaw-dropping. In my case, since I'm afraid of heights, it would also be stomach-dropping.

Deep in conversation, Henry and Victor didn't notice us approaching until we were almost on top of them. Henry looked up first. He held up his hand, signaling to Victor to be quiet.

"Can we help you?" Henry wore his perpetual frown. At least he wasn't yelling for a change. If Henry was Keiki's murderer, he was certainly the crabbiest killer I'd ever encountered.

"Tom was curious about the zip-line operation," Regan said. "He wondered if you could show it to him before the contestants begin their rides." When Henry looked annoyed, she elaborated. "Ritz would be grateful if you would take the time to assist his guests."

Throwing Ritz's name into the equation worked its desired magic. Henry could hardly refuse a request from his employer. He told Victor he'd catch up with him later, then motioned Tom to follow him up the four flights of stairs to the platform above.

"I guess I'll return to my office," Victor said, "I've got some paperwork to do."

"How's Kiana doing?" I asked.

He shrugged. "How do you think she is doing? She buried her daughter at sea yesterday."

"That must have been so rough on you, especially after Joey's fall from the tower." I shifted my gaze to the zip-line tower where Henry and Tom chatted. Tom pointed to something on the other side of the wide canyon.

Victor reached into his shirt pocket then realized it was empty. "I left my cigarettes in my car. I'll see you later, Regan."

I stepped in front of Victor before he could disappear. "Have you been stealing coffee beans from Koffee Land?"

He started. "Did Keiki tell you that?"

"No, I barely knew her, but I was in your garage yesterday."

He flinched and took a step back. "What were you doing there?"

"I offered to make some fresh coffee for your guests at the reception. Kiana told me the beans were in the pantry, but when I couldn't locate the pantry in the house, I went into the garage and discovered your secret room."

"Dammit," he grumbled, "that room was supposed to be locked."

"Laurel told me there were at least a hundred bags of beans," Regan said, "all in Koffee Land bags. How did they get there and why are you storing them?"

Victor looked like a deer caught in the headlights of a very big truck. Off in the distance I heard the sound of a siren. So much for Detective Lee's discreet arrival.

Victor glanced toward Henry and Tom who were climbing down from the tower. They had almost reached the bottom of the stairs.

I tilted my head and stared at the tower platform high above us. It was a long way to fall. Joey would have been cautious working so high, especially if he was by himself. But what if he wasn't alone? What if someone he trusted stood next to him?

Not his boss. But what about the father of the girl he'd dated for several years. A man who'd been like a father figure to him. Someone he trusted and admired.

Someone he'd discovered stealing from his employer.

What would Joey have done?

And what did Victor do?

CHAPTER FIFTY-SIX

Victor's eyes met mine. I froze as he grew stone-faced, his eyes as hard and bleak as lava rock. As multiple sirens blared, I relaxed my tense shoulders. Regan and I had Victor cornered. There was nothing he could do now.

Except grab my wrist with his left hand and twist it behind my back. His right hand was also busy.

Aiming a gun at my head.

"Victor," Regan screamed. Without a second's hesitation, Victor performed some elaborate move with his leg, knocking her to the ground. She lay motionless.

"Regan," I yelled and tried to reach her. My movement prompted a whack on the side of my head.

"Ow." A tiny rivulet of blood seeped into my copper strands, ruining my first good hair day since we'd arrived in Hawaii.

When Tom saw the commotion, he bypassed the last six stairs and leapt to my rescue. Once on the ground, he realized nobody was messing with Victor. Not when he had a gun pressed to my perspiring forehead.

"Victor, what are you doing?" Henry yelled, as he went to help Regan up off the ground.

I wanted to ask the same question, but the gun-in-my-skull approach turned out to be the one surefire method of shutting me up.

Victor pushed me in front of him but kept his weapon glued to the back of my head. Once we were a reasonable distance from Tom and Henry, he shoved me around to face the distant pavilion. That's when I realized we were also facing the troops.

Detective Lee, dressed in his usual Tommy Bahama apparel, strode up the hill with at least a dozen uniformed officers. There would be no escape for Victor in that direction without a shootout.

No one had asked for my opinion, but I wasn't big on the shootout option.

Behind what looked like the entire Hawaii Police Department, a contingent of television cameras filmed all the action, including Victor and me. The bevy of contestant beauties giggled and strutted, not fully clued in to the fact that this reality show had turned into *Law and Order*, the hostage version.

With all exits blocked, there was only one direction for Victor to go.

Up!

CHAPTER FIFTY-SEVEN

Victor kneed me in the back and I lurched up the stairs. My red sneaker slipped off my left foot and landed on the ground. Darn. That was my comfiest shoe. He'd better let me pick it up later.

On second thought, would there be a later? What was Victor's plan or did he even have one? As I stumbled up the stairs, with a gun inches from my back, a myriad of possibilities whirled through my brain. None of them featured a good ending.

By the time we reached the tower platform, Victor was breathing hard—either from stress, or the forty-five steps we'd just climbed. Trust me. I'd counted each one. It might be time for Victor to lay off the nicotine.

As he wheezed to catch his breath, I inched a few feet away. The gun remained leveled at my head. I could sense Victor's brain churning in an attempt to formulate an escape plan. I decided to distract him.

"Victor," I said, "I know you killed Joey. But I don't believe you meant to."

His eyes filled with sorrow. "No, I only climbed up here to talk to him alone. Keiki had called me the night before and said Joey was concerned about me. She didn't elaborate so I didn't know how much Joey had confided in her. I knew he saw me taking bags of coffee out of the warehouse when he worked late one night."

"You wanted to explain to him your reasons for the theft?"

He nodded and the gun bobbled slightly. "Joey was like a son to me. His father died when he was a young kid. I thought he would be sympathetic once he realized I had no choice but to take the beans since the beetle destroyed my own crops. I did it for my family." Victor swung his free hand out, demonstrating the size and magnificence of Koffee Land. "It's not like Ritz would notice the loss. Or even care about the quality of the beans. All he and Pilar care about is fame."

A voice blaring out of a megaphone filtered its way to the top of the tower.

"Come down now. Before anyone is hurt."

Victor shook his head.

"We have sharpshooters posted across the grounds. Release your hostage now."

Sharpshooters? I didn't like the sound of that. Neither did Victor as he shoved me in front of him. Despite his heavy panting, the distance between the gun and my head had not widened.

Victor stared at the crowd far below then yelled at Henry who stood off to the side. Henry pointed a finger at himself and mouthed something. He walked over to Detective Lee and grabbed the megaphone.

"Victor, come down, please," Henry said. "Don't do this to your family."

With his left hand, Victor motioned for Henry to climb the tower. Detective Lee, Henry, and my own personal detective consulted. Then Henry started the long climb up.

"Are you letting me go?"

"In a manner of speaking."

This was a heck of a time for Victor to go all inscrutable. Henry reached the top of the platform and threw his arms out as if to hug Victor. His father-in-law responded in a less familial manner by leveling the gun at him.

"Victor, what's going on? That detective said you killed Joey and Keiki? That's crazy."

"I could never kill my daughter," Victor said, "and that's how I always thought of Keiki. As my daughter. Joey's fall was an accident, but the detective is right. It was my fault. I came up here to discuss a personal matter with him. When Joey wouldn't listen, I grew frustrated and shoved him."

His eyes clouded over. "I'll never forget the sound of his scream. I raced down the stairs. When I reached the bottom of the tower, I could tell he was dead. It was too late to help him. So I left. Left Joey there to be discovered the next morning."

"It's not too late to confess to the police," I said. "They'll understand it was an accident. As for Keiki..."

"I didn't kill Keiki," Victor screamed. His eyes bulged, and for a minute, I thought they would pop out of their sockets. Lee shouted via the megaphone once again.

"Enough of this," Victor said. "Henry, strap her into that harness and attach her to the line at the far right. Once she's clamped in, you can climb back down. Then it will be my turn. For now, I need her as my hostage."

"But..." I started before Victor shushed me.

"Do all hostages talk this much?" he muttered, watching as Henry attempted to get me into the zip-line harness, not the easiest task when dealing with a full-figured woman.

Henry finally succeeded in buckling me in. He reached into his pocket, pulled out a pair of tan gloves and handed them to me.

I stared at them in confusion.

"Put them on," he said. "You'll need them."

"Stop talking to her," commanded Victor. "You can go back down."

"Please," Henry pleaded. "Let us help you."

Victor shook his head. "It's too late for me now. Just tell...," he hesitated and blinked his eyes rapidly. "Tell my daughter and Kiana I love them."

Henry sighed and disappeared down the stairs. With his exit, any hope that Victor might release me, disappeared.

CHAPTER FIFTY-EIGHT

Trapped in my harness, I was a tiny—okay not that tiny—pawn in this entire drama.

I swiveled my head left. "Victor, please don't do anything you might regret." Which by my definition would include anything involving his gun and me.

He glared. "No wonder you're still single. Do you ever stop talking?"

Geez. Someone woke up on the wrong side of his bed. But where would Victor wake up tomorrow? Did he have an exit strategy? And if so, how did I fit into his plan?

He began strapping himself into the harness on the zip-line running parallel to mine. The two lines were about six feet apart. With my torso hooked to the line, I couldn't get out of the contraption without help, so I wasn't a menace to Victor. That didn't mean he wouldn't shoot me if I provoked him. Apparently, his concept of provocation included my chatter.

Footsteps pounded up the stairs. The troops must have thought Victor was harmless now.

Crack! The sharp retort of Victor's gun told them otherwise. I twisted to the right and peered down the steps. Uniformed officers crouched at the first and second landings. A brown-haired man, dressed in jeans and a white polo shirt lay on the stairs.

Victor shot Tom?

I screamed. Victor raced over to my side and shoved me. With my legs dangling in the air, I gasped as I began zipping above the valley WAY below. I shrieked loud enough for them to hear me in Sacramento.

My family and Tom's faces flashed before my eyes as I soared through the air. My contacts watered as the treetops whizzed past in one giant green fuzzy blur. I vaguely remembered reading that the rider can control the speed of descent, but Henry hadn't shown me how.

I zoomed above the canyon, afraid if I looked down I'd pass out. Eventually I would smack into the next tower's platform, but no guide would be there to assist me. At the rate I sped toward the tower, it would be mere seconds before I crashed.

CHAPTER FIFTY-NINE

I finally recalled seeing something attached to the cable above my head. I pulled it with all my might. My head whiplashed back and forth but I immediately slowed. I was grateful Henry had lent me his gloves. Otherwise, my palms would have been rawer than steak tartare. I sailed into the platform at a mere five miles an hour, landing with a thud on the platform.

I bent over, gasping for air. My knees wobbled as I turned and looked back across the canyon. After my speedy ride, my ears felt so clogged, I couldn't be certain if more shots had been fired. Was Tom the man I'd seen lying on the stairs?

I was stuck in zip-line hell unable to go to my boyfriend's rescue.

Or even my own since I had no idea how to unclamp myself from the zip-line. Where oh where was Victor?

The answer appeared a thousand feet away from me. Someone dressed in a brown shirt barreled toward the platform. What were the odds Victor was coming to rescue me? I didn't need my mathematician daughter to tell me they were pretty low. If I wanted to leave this tower alive, it was up to me. Victor's hands clasped his harness, but he could have tucked his small gun anywhere.

I swiveled my head right and left searching for something on the platform I could utilize to give Victor a proper greeting.

Thank goodness, Henry's crew hadn't finished their clean-up. I saw a loose fragment of wood a couple of feet long leaning against the side of the platform. I frantically tried to release the clasps that

DYING FOR A DAIQUIRI

were binding me. It was even harder getting the contraption off than it had been getting it on. I worried I would be too late.

I looked up. Victor was slowing down, seconds away from greeting me. My fingers felt like I was wearing thimbles on all ten digits.

Finally. I was free. I bent over and with board in hand, prepared to meet a murderer.

CHAPTER SIXTY

Bam!

Victor's head drooped forward, and a trail of blood trickled down his right cheek.

I must be either stronger or angrier than I'd realized. I only wanted to stop Victor, not kill him

I struggled with his harness so I could perform first aid on the man. He surprised me by suddenly reaching into his pocket.

"Stay back," Victor ordered, the gun wavering in his shaky hand.

Okay. Enough of this nonsense. I kicked my remaining shoe as high as a Rockette. The gun tumbled out of his hands, bouncing into the canyon. As Victor watched its descent, I whacked his skull once more with the hunk of wood.

He slumped over, unmoving. Voices calling from the other side thrilled me to no end.

Minutes later, Henry landed on my platform. Shortly after his arrival, one uniformed officer arrived. Detective Lee zipped over last. His eyebrows lifted as he saw Victor strapped in the harness, head lolling to one side.

"Is he dead?" Lee asked, in the same tone of voice he might have used if I had squashed a bug.

"I don't think so."

Lee grunted and mumbled something that sounded vaguely like "too bad." I grabbed the detective's forearm and shook him hard. "Is Tom okay?"

"The bullet went through his thigh. An ambulance is on the way to take him to the hospital."

"Will he be okay?" I asked again, needing confirmation.

The roar of the helicopter drowned out his reply but he nodded.

"Are they filming this?" I asked, reflexively wishing I'd stuck a comb in my short's pocket.

He shrugged. "It's difficult to stop a news crew from doing its job, but they've agreed to help us out. We've asked them to load up Mr. Yakamura here and take him in for processing at the police station. We'll get his full confession then."

"What about me?" I looked in all four directions but couldn't detect any means of transportation that didn't involve my body hanging from a cable.

Detective Lee's smile widened. "You get to ride the entire zip-line course for free. Heck of a deal."

CHAPTER SIXTY-ONE

The next hour was a blur. A treetop zip-lining blur, since the only way to get back to the center was to ride all eight runs. With Henry by my side providing me with zip tips, I felt like a pro by the time I reached our final stop. A jeep identified with the KL logo waited for Henry and me at the last platform and transported us to the visitor's center. Lee and the other officer accompanied Victor in the helicopter.

Tom was my primary concern and his health was all I could concentrate on as I flew over all five hundred acres of Koffee Land. My goal was to get to the hospital fast. But, first, I had to hug every member of my family. Stan got two hugs because he'd recovered my missing shoe.

Ritz was beside himself with the discovery of Victor's theft and subsequent murders. Regan decided she should stay at Koffee Land and try to do some damage control. I visualized the director, producer and Stacey Leung-Crawford huddled together, trying to assess whether a murder and kidnapping would help market the show. What was it PR people always said? There's no such thing as bad publicity. Ritz would soon discover if that statement was true.

My personal mission was to check on my wounded detective. We all jumped in the rental car and Stan drove, following the police to the hospital where the ambulance had taken Tom. When we arrived, the nurse informed us he was still in surgery. She escorted us to the waiting room where I paced back and forth, my legs still rubbery from flying through the air.

"Laurel, you're going to wear out the carpet," said Mother.

"I feel so horrible. Here Tom came over for a few days of R&R and he ends up getting shot because of me."

"Well, you wondered how he felt about you," Stan said, "Guess you have your answer."

I mulled this over. "Tom would have done the same for any hostage."

Stan shrugged. "Probably. But how often can you say a fella took a bullet for you."

Hopefully never again.

In mid-afternoon, they moved Tom from the recovery room to his own room. After the staff got him settled, the nurse announced a family member could visit him. The three of us exchanged looks. None of us qualified for that role.

"I'm his fiancée," I finally said. The nurse's dark eyes zeroed in on my bare and ring-less left hand.

"Tom just proposed last night and the ring didn't fit," I replied. Stan grinned and gave me a thumbs-up behind the nurse's back.

She threw me a suspicious look and I smiled sweetly. "I just want to say hi. I promise I won't tire him out."

"The man took a bullet for her." Stan dramatically placed his hands on his heart demonstrating he should stick to loan underwriting, not acting.

"Exactly," she said, "which is why you get five minutes and that's it. And just you, the fiancée or whatever."

I took an elevator up two floors then went in search of room 417. I thought the occupant of the first bed was a cadaver until I realized the body wasn't cold yet. The man just looked old enough to be Methuselah's grandfather.

I pushed a blue curtain aside and found Tom asleep, his face pale and his right arm connected to an assortment of tubes. I sat in the orange plastic visitor chair next to his bed and carefully lifted his left hand. The poor guy didn't need to be disturbed. I just wanted to hold onto him and thank him, even if he was sedated and unable to hear me.

Tom's hand was large, strong and remarkably mobile for a guy recovering from anesthesia. His thumb rubbed mine in a circular fashion in an area on my hand that was evidently a long-lost erogenous zone. I scooted my chair back, and his eyes flashed open.

"You're awake?" I asked, ever the brilliant detective.

He sighed. "Thank God, you're alive. Before they loaded me in the ambulance, someone said Victor had been captured. But no one knew where you were."

"I was playing Tarzan and Jane zip-lining through the jungle. Unfortunately my Tarzan was on his way to the hospital instead of by my side."

His tired eyes apologized. "I'm sorry I wasn't there for you."

"Are you kidding? You got shot trying to stop Victor. How can I ever thank you?"

Tom tried to prop himself up on the pillow but his IV lines tangled. I leaned over to unscramble them. Tom was in a weakened state and needed those fluids.

But evidently he wasn't so weak that he couldn't grab me with his good arm and draw me close. "Having you in my arms, or at least one of them, is thanks enough."

His lips met mine. The heat of his lips coursed through my body. I felt faint and put my hand out to steady myself. Then I realized I was about to press down on his thigh, exactly where he'd been shot. I shifted my left hand and it landed in a more central location. His quick response was more than I'd anticipated.

Wow. It was good to know it takes more than a bullet to deactivate my detective!

CHAPTER SIXTY-TWO

The Nazi nurse arrived to discover us mid-embrace. I was ushered out of the hospital with a stern warning not to return until the next day if I wanted my "fiancé" to heal properly. After a day of zip-line bonding with nature, I would have loved to drop into one of the hospital's empty beds for an hour or two, or twelve. Stan drove Mother and me back to the hotel where dinner and a soft duvet awaited. We were out for the count before ten o'clock.

Mother and I might have slept until noon if Regan hadn't called my cell at nine.

"How are you feeling?" she asked.

I shifted under the covers. Ugh. "I'll survive."

"Excellent. We have a surprise for you at Koffee Land."

"Gee, thanks, but I think I've encountered enough surprises at Koffee Land to last me for this vacation." Or a lifetime.

"Please, Laurel," she pleaded with me. "Ritz is so grateful you discovered Victor's coffee-stealing scheme and solved the murders that he wants to honor you at a banquet tonight."

My senses were starting to awaken even without my morning coffee. "How do you define 'honoring' me? Is he going to present me with a gold-plated coffee bean?"

"They're going to film our dinner for the news tonight. And Ritz has some type of award for you."

"Regan, tell Ritz thanks. I'm not really into that kind of publicity. He can ship a bag of Donkey balls and a thank you note to Placerville. That's reward enough."

"Please. It would mean so much to your brother and me. And I'm sure your mother would be thrilled."

Hmm. I'd never won anything before. Unless you counted my "Catawba melon" trophy for the highest gross in a golf tournament. I was fairly certain that didn't count. If it made my family happy, I could sacrifice myself and accept whatever Ritz offered.

I agreed that Stan, Mother and I would arrive at Koffee Land by four that afternoon. Mother was thrilled at the invitation and even more excited that Regan and Dave's marriage seemed on the mend. It was hard to believe it took a murder investigation for them to resolve their differences. But when communication flounders and imaginations go wild, it sometimes takes adversity to bring a couple together.

I wondered how successful the winner of *The Bride and the Bachelor* would be in keeping their televised relationship alive and well. Based on the *People* magazine covers I peruse at the supermarket, the life span of a televised marriage proposal is shorter than the life span of a fruit fly. Was the reason for the short-lived engagements due to the contenders' desire for fame and notoriety, not for a real relationship? Amanda seemed sincere in her efforts to win the heart of Jacques Cointreau. But according to Walea, fame and fortune were the sole reasons her stepsister had entered the competition.

Oddly, we'd never learned the name of Keiki's older boyfriend. Could it have been Ritz? With Koffee Land as the venue for the reality show, he possessed enough influence to get her on the show. But why would he want to kill Keiki? Did she threaten to tell his wife about his infidelity?

Maybe Pilar had discovered the affair herself and decided to remove Keiki from the show and out of Ritz's life.

My head spun with an endless pool of suspects. Detective Lee had informed us he was certain Victor would eventually confess to both murders. Lee might be comfortable with his suspect, but I was far from positive that we'd discovered Keiki's killer. Victor's protestations that he had nothing to do with his stepdaughter's demise had seemed heartfelt to me.

Mother and I spent a few hours picking up souvenirs for my kids and her husband. I found a cute sundress for Jenna and figured there was a fifty percent chance she might not hate it. It's so difficult to buy for teens.

I'd spoken with Ben earlier in the day, and he'd asked if I would bring home one of the giant sea turtles for him. Instead, I chose a stuffed turtle and a children's book on marine life from the well-stocked Kona Stories bookstore. One of us might as well learn something about ocean inhabitants. Someday Ben might grow up to become a marine biologist like Amanda.

I leafed through the book while I waited for my mother to finish shopping. Contrary to what I'd previously thought, humpback whales do not mate for life. Instead, they come to Hawaii every year in late winter and early spring so the males can chase after the females, frequently wooing them with their singing. The males head butt and tail slap other males who chase after the same hottie female.

When it comes to spring break, boys will be boys. The similarities in wooing behavior were interesting although I'll take a two-legged suitor any day of the week. Or even a one-and-a-half-legged guy like Tom.

I felt bad that I hadn't seen Steve since Tom's surprise arrival. What an idiot I was to be suspicious of him and the dead dancer. I'd feel better if I could make amends before we flew home the next day.

I called Regan back and asked if Steve could be included in tonight's celebratory dinner. Since it was a Tuesday, he wouldn't have a sunset sail on his schedule. And I wouldn't have to worry about the guys duking it out with Tom still stuck in the hospital. I called Tom before we left for Koffee Land. He sounded bored and anxious to leave, but the doctor insisted on keeping him one more night for observation. If our dinner didn't drag on too long, I hoped to stop by for a short visit on our way back to the hotel.

Shortly after four, Mother, Stan and I pulled into the long drive to the center. We'd spent so much time at Koffee Land this past week, it was beginning to feel like my second home. A big sign informed visitors the center was closed for a private event. Another sign directed invited guests to head to the pavilion.

Soothing Hawaiian music poured out of the first-rate speaker system. The camera crew followed Stacey Leung-Crawford around the property as she pointed in various directions, extolling the virtues of the destination coffee plantation. The commentator was dressed to perfection in an elegant ivory sheath and matching high-heeled sandals. That dress would remain stain-free for less than five minutes if I wore it. I guess on-camera newscasters are more graceful than yours truly.

The three of us stopped at the bar and ordered drinks. My lillikoi daiquiri arrived in a coconut shell with the requisite orchid, pineapple slice and maraschino cherry on a swizzle stick. I sipped the refreshing concoction and smiled. Talk about the nectar of the Gods. I'd bet Pele, the fire goddess, would have been a lot less vengeful if she'd drunk these on a daily basis.

I waved at Regan who stood between my brother and Steve. They chatted with Ritz and a tiny dark-haired woman with piercing black eyes and a beak-like nose. Regan motioned to us so we walked over to join them.

Before I could embrace my brother and sister-in-law, Ritz engulfed me in a hug that threatened to bruise the few remaining body parts not injured during the course of this vacation.

"Here she is," he shouted, holding up my right arm in his left, making me feel like the winner of the World Wide Wrestling championship. The men all cheered. The guests, some of whom looked as confused as I did, applauded as well.

The tiny woman introduced herself as Pilar. "So you are the magnificent Laurel," she said, her gaze running from the top of my desperately-need-a trim curls to my slightly scuffed turquoise wedges.

"Um, yes, I am the magni...–I'm Laurel. It's so nice to meet you. Ritz has told us..." My voice trailed off when I realized Ritz had told us zilch about his wife. "So how is the reality show coming?"

"They're behind schedule due to yesterday's little hiccup." Pilar appeared miffed by the scene with Victor the previous day. I was a tad miffed myself when she described my hostage situation as a little "hiccup."

"My husband needs to be more cautious when selecting employees," she muttered.

"I still can't believe Victor stole from me and killed young Joey." Ritz shook his head ruefully. "And his beautiful stepdaughter. Unbelievable."

"Keiki seemed like such a sweetheart," Stan interjected.

Pilar sniffed. "That young woman was no sweetheart. When she discovered something she wanted, she went after it."

My mother and I exchanged glances. Who or what was Pilar referring to?

As I attempted to think of a way to question Pilar without accusing Ritz of any hanky-panky, she answered my question. "That Keiki wheedled her way into Edward's heart. Or more specifically, into Edward's pants."

I almost dropped my cocktail when Stan and Mother both shouted in unison. "Who's Edward?"

"Edward Maples is the director of *The Bride and the Bachelor*. He's also the father of one of Keiki's dancer friends. As soon as Keiki discovered he was responsible for choosing the contestants, she went after him like a heat-seeking missile."

"Now, dear." Ritz attempted to soothe his wife. "Keiki would have made an excellent candidate for the show."

She rolled her eyes. "We have a nice line-up of girls now. And hopefully there won't be any more hiccups." Pilar lasered a frown in my direction. I merely smiled. My goal was to remain in a hiccup-free zone all night.

Stacey Leung-Crawford joined us. "Laurel, how nice to see you have recovered from yesterday's dreadful affair."

Now here was a woman who took a hostage situation seriously.

"Thank you," I said. "I'm just relieved the police have Victor in custody."

"We'd like to interview you on camera now." Stacey pursed her lips and looked me over. "Do you want to put on some make-up?"

I thought I already had. "No, I'm good." My goal was to get the interview over without looking like a complete idiot.

Stacey and I left the others and headed toward the bank of cameras. We passed the *Bride and the Bachelor* contestants who glimmered and shimmered in the bright sunlight. Their slinky dresses were far removed from your basic Hawaiian *muumuu*. Amanda had tucked her signature flower into her long blonde hair. Today she chose a coral hibiscus, pinned over her left ear, which perfectly matched the flowers on her strapless dress. I gave her a thumbs-up as I walked by.

When we reached the area below the pavilion, I came face to face with an array of cameras.

Great. Nothing I love more than the opportunity to embarrass myself on TV. Was I a lucky *wahine* or what?

Stacey motioned to the closest camera guy. "Ted, I want you to pan the contestants. Try to get a close-up of each one. Then zoom in on Laurel and me."

Stacey smiled and patted my knee, which was shaking more than a hula dancer's hips. "You'll be fine," she assured me.

As she observed the camera crew filming the contestants, her expression morphed from Ms. Congeniality to Ms. Executive Producer. "That stupid girl. I keep telling her if she's going to wear a flower in her hair, it has to be over the right ear."

"Huh?" I responded.

"That blonde girl, Amanda, she insists on wearing a flower over her left ear. Hawaiian tradition maintains that wearing it over her left ear signifies she is already taken. That she has a boyfriend, a lover. I've told her over and over, but that girl just can't seem to get it right."

Geez. What a perfectionist, I thought, as Stacey mumbled under her breath about dumb blondes. She yelled at Amanda, pointing to her ear, but Amanda just shook her head no. In my opinion, if Amanda wanted to wear her trademark flower over the wrong ear, that was her decision. She must have a perfectly good reason for her floral faux pas.

I ogled the beautiful women who were dressed to the elevens in sequined or beaded cocktail dresses. Some of the women wore rhinestone earrings so long they brushed against their shoulders. I personally thought Amanda looked terrific in her floral floor-length dress, its simplicity set off by the tropical flower over the "wrong" ear. She'd left her other ear unadorned.

And Amanda was definitely not a dumb blonde. Not with a degree in marine biology. No one appeared more driven to win the bachelor than her. I'd assumed her daily floral adornment was due to her love for Hawaiian traditions. But if that was the case, why did she flout custom and insist on wearing a flower over the wrong ear?

Or did she have to cover that ear for a specific reason?

CHAPTER SIXTY-THREE

"Amanda mentioned she was a last-minute substitute," I said to Stacey. "What did she mean by that?"

"When we were notified of Keiki's death, we had to find a replacement and fast. Amanda was on the list and available to jump in." Stacey sighed and looked at her watch. "We're behind schedule so there's nothing I can do about her now. Are you ready for your interview?"

When I didn't respond, she repeated herself. "Laurel, are you listening?"

I was listening. But I was also adding two and two together and not liking the result.

Stacey poked my arm and greeted her viewers.

"Tonight I'm joined by a woman who survived a true crime episode that occurred here at Koffee Land yesterday. Laurel McKay was taken hostage by a vicious murderer who killed not once, but twice on this island." Stacey shoved the microphone in my face. "What did it feel like to have a gun pointed at you?"

Not so good. Kind of like the last time a gun was pointed at me. And why was it every time a gun was pressed to my forehead, I needed to pee? What was up with that?

"I was worried, of course, but deep down I didn't think Victor would hurt me."

Stacey stepped back and splayed her palm across her chest, as if stunned by my comment. "But the man threw one of his workers off the zip-line platform. And he murdered his stepdaughter!"

"I still don't believe that Victor killed Keiki—" I protested. I stared at the contestants once again. How far would someone go to marry her Mr. Right? What measures would she take when she discovered that her friend had made it as a contestant on the show instead of herself? The "friend" who always won, whether the prize was boys or beauty pageants. Once again, Keiki had ruined her chance of winning, but this time she'd also destroyed her opportunity to meet the man of her dreams. My gaze settled on Amanda as her defiant green eyes met mine.

Stacey flashed me a confused look. "If Victor didn't kill Keiki then who did?"

I pointed to Amanda and yelled. "That girl!"

Multiple cameras wheeled to follow my accusing finger. Amanda froze in place then turned and ran toward the parking lot, stumbling on her four-inch heels.

A sea of stunned faces surrounded me, but no one made a move to stop Amanda who'd recovered from her misstep. Was there a way to slow the fleeing suspect? We had to do something. I looked down at my drink.

Darn. I hated to waste the delicious daiquiri, but someone had to stop her. I dumped the liquid, bent my right arm back and hoped four years of playing outfield for my high school softball team would come in handy.

The coconut projectile missed Amanda's head but caught her squarely in the back. She fell forward, tripping over the hem of her long dress. I slipped out of my wedges and raced to grab her before she could run off again. With my brother close behind, we cornered Amanda in less than a minute.

Dave held her thrashing arms, and I pinned her down by sitting on her. Sometimes an extra *malasada* or two *does* come in handy.

During the struggle, Amanda's coral hibiscus fell off. I could now see the large crusty scab on the bottom of her left ear lobe.

"Let me go," Amanda screamed. "I have a show to do."

"Amanda, we know you killed Keiki." I pushed my weight down on her struggling legs.

"She slept with the director and stole my spot," Amanda hissed. "She knew how important this show was to me. I begged her to drop out. To give me an opportunity just once. But she made fun of me. Said I'd never beaten her in anything before, and I wouldn't now. She told me I didn't stand a chance with Jacques. She laughed at me. Said I was a nobody and I'd always be a nobody." Amanda's bitter laugh sent chills down my spine. "I showed her."

Stacey and the camera crew arrived to capture our capture. Stacey huffed and puffed from her short jog. Her shortness of breath didn't stop her from shoving the mike in Amanda's flushed face. "Do you have anything to say to our viewers?"

Amanda leaned in to the microphone. "Remember to call 889-328-0012 and vote for me." She smiled at the camera while Dave and I exchanged glances. This girl was officially a tropical fruitcake. Liz once joked that just because someone is a murder suspect, it doesn't mean they aren't entitled to meet the man of their dreams.

I doubt that killing off your competition is what Liz had in mind.

My mother had already called Detective Lee who wasn't far from Koffee Land. In the interim, Dave and Steve tied Amanda to a tree using some of the TV cables. Steve, a master of nautical knots, guaranteed she couldn't get away.

Amanda seemed to be reveling in all the attention. No one would ever refer to her as a nobody again. When the Bachelor stopped to gaze at the crazy woman who could have ended up as his bride, Amanda beamed as if she'd received Jacques's marriage proposal. Between the live cameras and the flashing iPhones, this incident was certain to go viral in no time.

By the time Detective Lee arrived, Amanda had shared all with an audience of millions. She even explained how she'd committed the murder. Keiki thought she was meeting Edward the director for a midnight rendezvous. Instead, Amanda showed up, apologizing for their earlier argument and offered to celebrate Keiki's success. The dancer could hardly refuse such a gracious request.

Keiki filled two glasses with daiquiri slushies. When she went to the ladies' room, Amanda dumped some fast-acting sleeping pills in her friend's daiquiri, put the drink back in the blender, and voila! A daiquiri guaranteed to send you to dreamland. Or in Keiki's situation, to her death.

When Keiki became sleepy, Amanda guided her over to the rock wall. Keiki tried to hold on to Amanda for support but only succeeded in ripping off her killer's earring before she tumbled to her death on the rocks below.

Steve's eyes almost popped out of their sockets as he listened to Amanda's true confession.

"Geez, I can't believe I hired that ding-a-ling," he said.

"A deadly ding-a-ling for sure," I commented. "I see a temporary insanity plea in her future."

Stan chimed in. "I see a new reality show in her future—Amanda does time."

Mother shook her head. "I never would have guessed that girl's desire to win the bachelor would lead to murder."

"People do the craziest things in the name of love. Or what they think is love." I gazed at my brother and sister-in-law holding each other tight. "It's a shame it took Keiki's murder investigation to bring Dave and Regan back together, but at least there is one positive result of this whole affair."

"I can go home with a light heart after seeing the two of them together," Mother said. "I'm sorry this trip didn't turn out to be much of a vacation for you."

"You mean getting pushed out of a boat, thrown from an ATV, and involuntarily going zip-lining isn't your idea of a vacation?" I asked my mother. We both chuckled. I would have stories to share when I returned to the bank.

During a commercial break, Amanda confessed to ramming me off my ATV. After we told her on Friday we had new evidence regarding the killer and needed to solve the case before we left town, she'd become worried. Steve had included her in his Friday night poker party and that's when she learned we were going on the ATV ride the next day. I never even considered that Amanda was one of the players.

Since Amanda didn't have to be at Koffee Land on Saturday, she devised a plan to incapacitate me until my flight home, leaving her free to pursue her marital dreams. Her parents lived in the Waipi'o Valley so she was familiar with all of the trails and the tour excursion times. All she had to do was take one of their ATV's and catch up with our group. Her intent was just to hurt me, not send me to my death. While I was happy to discover Amanda didn't intend to kill me, that didn't make her any less of a looney tune.

Detective Lee joined Mother and me. "Ms. McKay, thank you for, um, subduing the suspect."

"Anytime." I smiled. "As you can see, Amanda provided you with a full confession."

He frowned. "I'm not sure how the Prosecuting Attorney will feel about her babbling on the air. We'll worry about that later." He tossed a hopeful glance my way. "You're going home tomorrow?"

I nodded. "Yes, I hate to leave the island though."

"And we'll be sorry to see you go." Lee managed to keep a straight face. "Let me know if you're ever on the island again."

"Do you want to get together?" I asked, surprised by his invitation.

"No, I want to know when to plan my own vacation."

CHAPTER SIXTY-FOUR

We spent another hour with Lee and his men, but after Amanda's televised true confession I had little to add. I was ready to take off when Steve appeared by my side.

"I don't suppose you'd like a permanent job working on a boat?" He grinned. "We provide great benefits."

I smiled. I had no doubt working for Steve would be beneficial for any single woman. "That's a great offer, but it's time for me to get back home to my kids and my..."

"Boyfriend," Steve interjected. "He's a lucky guy."

Well, technically, Tom had yet to get lucky, but one of these days—

I blushed. "I hope you didn't think I was leading you on. As you may have gathered, Tom and I still have many issues to resolve."

"Love is complicated," he replied. "Just let me know if you ever want to sail away into the sunset."

"I will, although next time I'm going to require that your crew complete personality profiles in advance."

He shook his head back and forth. "What are the odds someone that cute could be such a nut? I had a sit down with Timmy yesterday and told him he needed to confess what he'd been up to before I let him back on the boat."

"Was it drugs?" I asked.

"Let's just say he was taking care of a "financial" transaction for his older brother. Timmy's father passed away two years ago.

After losing Joey, Timmy couldn't bear the thought of something also happening to his brother, Mike, his only remaining relative. Mike had been hanging out with a bad crowd. Timmy swore he and his brother will never get involved in illegal deliveries again. It's not easy for these young guys, but I'll be there if he needs someone to talk to."

"He's lucky to have someone like you," I said. "By the way, did Timmy ever confess to pushing me overboard?"

Steve looked sheepish. "He came clean but I'm still not certain how to handle his confession. He saw you struggling with the life vests and went to help. A gust of wind knocked him into you, and then you went over the railing. He was completely freaked out, but before he could say anything, Rafe noticed you in the water. Between Timmy's previous threats to Keiki and his other illicit activities, he was afraid you as well as the authorities would assume he'd pushed you on purpose. Since you were rescued so quickly, he decided to keep mum. He asked you to please forgive him."

"I knew it was Timmy," I cried, feeling vindicated in my assumption. But with so much tragedy occurring in the young man's life recently, I couldn't bear to be responsible for him going to jail for an inadvertent push.

"Tell him I'll forgive him if he promises the next time he knocks a passenger overboard, he'll confess a lot earlier." I hugged Steve good-bye and was pleased that nary a body part tingled at his touch. My hormones had finally gotten their act together.

It was getting late and I wanted to see Tom before visiting hours ended. I didn't know if he would be well enough to travel home the next day with the rest of us.

When Stan, Mother, and I arrived at the hospital, a nurse informed us Tom had already checked out and returned to the hotel.

"Such a shame he left so soon," she confided. "His George Clooney eyes were so distracting I almost forgot to unplug his IV before he left. Do you know if he's on the market?"

I informed her Tom was not on the market. He had a girlfriend, one who couldn't wait to be in his arms. I just hoped he felt well enough to put his arms around said girlfriend.

Stan played chauffeur which played havoc with my nerves. He insisted on driving under the speed limit so we could savor our last night on the island. I had mixed emotions about returning home. I couldn't wait to see my children. But much as I enjoy working at Hangtown Bank, experiencing life on the island and meeting people who'd had the courage to pursue new careers had me thinking.

And where did Tom and I stand? Who would decide when and if we would take our romance to the next level?

"You seem fidgety, honey," Mother called from the back seat. "I sense it has something to do with Tom."

Is she perceptive or what? Or are all mothers of adult children intuitive about their grown-up kid's needs?

I twisted in my seat and peered into the back of the car. "I guess all the marital melodrama of the last few days has me wondering if I'm ready to be in a relationship. It obviously takes a ton of work to keep a marriage on solid ground. Maybe I should stick to reading about romance instead of trying to maintain one."

"Reading is fine," Stan interjected, "but it's no substitute for the real thing."

My mother leaned forward and patted me on the shoulder. "When it's right, you'll know. Trust me."

Trusting my mother was easy. Trusting my own instincts was the real issue.

CHAPTER SIXTY-FIVE

My phone beeped as I inserted our room key into the door. I pulled my cell out of my purse and checked my three new text messages, all from Tom.

Message 1: You made the news once again.

Message 2: Are you okay?

Message 3: I'm lonely.

I grinned at the last message. Did Tom truly miss me or was he missing the excitement of his normal life, juggling Kristy and his career? And an occasional date with me. I dialed his cell.

"So now you're catching a killer a day?" He laughed. "What are you going to do when you return home? Join the Sheriff's department?"

"I think I'll enjoy the peace and quiet of underwriting loan files. At least no one ever wants to kill me at the bank." I stopped then amended my statement. "Unless I reject their loans. So what happened with you? I thought your doctor insisted you remain in the hospital another night."

"Lee called to check on me. I think it bothered him that a Hawaiian hostage situation resulted in the shooting of an out-of-state police officer. He offered to spring me from the hospital and sent someone to bring me back here. Of course, that was before you and Dave tackled Amanda and screwed up Lee's day. Nice throw, by the way."

I giggled, relieved Tom sounded so chipper. I was also relieved all the island drama that had tormented us was over.

"Did Amanda's confession make the local evening news?"

"Not just the local news. They've been re-playing your tackle and her confession during commercial breaks all afternoon. Not to mention national news. Jimmy Kimmel thinks you're a hoot!"

I plopped on the bed and slipped out of my shoes. "Jimmy Kimmel? Must be a dull news day."

"Maybe. Is Amanda as cuckoo as she sounds?"

"More than you can imagine. I think she's still hoping the callers will vote for her despite her arrest. If Detective Lee hadn't commandeered her phone, she'd be tweeting from the cellblock."

"Enough about that wacko. Right now, I'm imagining that I'm holding you in my arms." His low baritone warmed my heart and every nerve in my body.

"Do you feel well enough for me to come up for a few minutes?" I asked. My heart was pounding louder than the music playing in the poolside bar down below.

"Please."

CHAPTER SIXTY-SIX

I spent an hour making myself presentable for Tom. My skirmish with Amanda had added bruises to the tie-dyed collection left over from my ATV incident. Although considering Tom's somewhat precarious medical condition, it wasn't likely he would be privy to any of my battle scars.

Would he? I mulled over his comments and wondered how perky he felt. Was the island working its magic on the homicide detective or was I working my own magic on him? Did my crazy escapades turn him on? Or off?

I knocked on Tom's hotel room door then realized he'd left it propped open. I didn't want to be responsible for his medical condition worsening, so I planned to stay a few minutes then return to my own room.

"Tom," I called out softly. I pushed the heavy door open before closing it behind me. Tom sat in bed, leaning against the headboard, his leg propped up on two overstuffed hotel pillows.

For a guy who'd been shot less than thirty-six hours earlier, he looked darn good. He'd even managed to get some sun. Lying on the stairs of the zip-line tower with noontime rays beating down on your bloodied body is one way to get a tan.

I raced to Tom's side then stopped, afraid any sudden movement would result in a 911 call. I kissed his forehead and perched on the side of his bed.

Tom grabbed my hand and held it, neither of us talking for a rare minute.

"Did you know it sometimes takes a near-death experience to open a person's eyes?" he asked me.

"This entire vacation has been an eye-opener for me," I said. "Wondering and worrying about the difficulties of maintaining a relationship."

His eyes narrowed and his grip tightened. "So after what you've encountered this week, you've decided the difficulties aren't worth the reward?"

I looked away as I contemplated his question. "No. What I've learned is that a couple has to keep the channels of communication open at all times."

Tom rubbed my thumb and my nerve endings jumped around like a game of Tiddlywinks.

"Do you think you and I are ready to make that channel a two-way street?" he asked.

I hesitated then nodded. He bent his head down. As our lips met, the connection felt like more than just the heat of lust or passion. It felt right.

Tom drew me close and draped his left leg over mine. I pulled back for an instant afraid I might hurt him.

"Are you okay?" I asked, breathing hard, my head nestled against his chest.

He stroked my hair lightly. "I have never felt better."

"I don't want to do anything to make your injury worse."

His deep laugh and response was all I needed to hear.

"Haven't you ever heard that old expression—no pain, no gain?"

THE END

LAUREL'S FAVORITE
TROPICAL COCKTAILS

Laurel decided to hold a blog contest for daiquiri recipes and other tropical concoctions. A committee of cocktail connoisseurs sampled the recipes and proclaimed these very tasty winners.

THE CHRISTOPHER ROBIN
(Christine Hyde and Robin Ylitalo)

Fill a champagne flute halfway with your favorite champagne
Add one shot Malibu Rum
Add orange juice to below rim
Top with Grenadine

PAMA-TIKI (Sherry Joyce)

½ oz. PAMA Pomegranate Liquer (Pomegranate juice works too)
1 oz. white Rum
2 oz. pineapple juice (Fruit for the day)
1 ½ oz. sweetened coconut milk or cream of coconut (good for your
    bones, not your waistline)
Pour mixture in a tall glass filled with crushed ice. Add pineapple
    wedge for garnish. Turn on beach music, close your eyes
    and lay on the floor. You'll end up there anyway!

PEACH FUZZ (by Linda Lohman)

Into a blender add:
1 6oz can frozen lemonade
a cup or two of ice
sliced ripe peaches (to the top of the blender)
1 6oz can Captain Morgan's Spicy Run

LAUREL'S FAVORITE DAIQUIRI RECIPES

HEMINGWAY DAIQUIRI (as modified by Heather Haven)

1 1/2 oz light rum
1/2 oz maraschino liqueur
1/2 oz grapefruit juice
3/4 oz fresh lime juice
1/2 oz simple syrup*
2 dashes grapefruit bitters*
*optional

I admire Ernest Hemingway for many reasons, and second to none is his love for the cocktail. Add to ice in a shaker and shake that kitten until it purrs. Pour into a martini glass and add a toothpick with a grapefruit section and a maraschino cherry on it. Yummy!

THE DAIQUIRI TO DIE FOR (Peggy Partington)

One bottle of Rum (light or dark)
One lime
Two shot glasses or just a straw
One tropical beach
One handsome young man with six-pack abs
Put them all together and enjoy!

ACKNOWLEDGEMENTS

Many thanks and hugs to my critique group for their astute observations, unfailing support and willingness to answer hundreds of emails from me: Kathy Asay, Pat Foulk, Rae James, and Terri Judd. Thanks to friends who were willing to read the early drafts and provide excellent suggestions: Bonnie, C.J., Carole, Donna, Ed, Jana, Jonathan, Kristin, Liana, Linda, Lisa, Lynne, Mary Beth, Michele D. and Michelle K.

A special *mahalo* to everyone on the Big Island of Hawaii. A big thank you goes to Lt. Gerald Wike, Criminal Investigations, and Chris Loos, Media Relations for the Hawaii Police Department. I appreciate the advice I received from the staff at Kona Zip-line, Les at Ride the Rim ATV, Brenda and Joy at Kona Stories, and Lili Alba for her hula and tour assistance.

The support and encouragement I receive from my fellow Sisters in Crime (Sacramento and Northern California) and the authors who belong to Sacramento Valley Rose, California Writer's Club and NCPA keeps me motivated when my spirits flag.

I am extremely grateful to Ritz Naygrew and Stacey Leung-Crawford for their generous donations to the Sacramento Library Foundation, and to Steve Bohannon and Glenn Hakanson for their donations to the Sacramento Opera. I enjoyed creating all of your characters.

Thanks to my editors, Kristen Weber and Kathy Asay. Also to my wonderful cover artist, Karen Phillips, who created so many great choices for my Daiquiri cover contest. We never imagined we would receive advice from over 350 participants.

And last, but certainly not least, thanks to those fans from around the world whose emails make this journey so much fun. Keep them coming!

ABOUT THE AUTHOR

Although Cindy Sample's initial dream was to be a mystery writer, she put aside her literary longings for a weekly paycheck, landing a job as a receptionist. Her career eventually led to the position of CEO of a nationwide mortgage banking company.

After one too many corporate mergers, Cindy found herself plotting murder instead of plodding through paperwork. Her experiences with on-line dating sites fueled the concept for her first mystery, *Dying for a Date*. The sequel, *Dying for a Dance*, a finalist for the 2012 LEFTY award for best humorous mystery, and winner of the 2012 NCPA best fiction award, is based on her adventures in the glamorous world of ballroom dancing. Cindy thought her protagonist, Laurel McKay, needed a vacation in Hawaii, which resulted in *Dying for a Daiquiri*. Never has research been so much fun. Laurel will return to Placerville in *Dying for a Dude* (Fall 2014).

Cindy is past president of the Sacramento chapter of Sisters in Crime. She has served on the boards of the Sacramento Opera and YWCA. She is a member of Mystery Writers of America and Romance Writers of America.

Cindy has two wonderful adult children who live too far away. She loves chatting with readers so feel free to contact her on any forum.

Check out www.cindysamplebooks.com for contests and other events.

Connect with Cindy on Facebook and Twitter
http://facebook.com/cindysampleauthor
http://twitter.com/cindysample1
Email Cindy at cindy@cindysamplebooks.com